THE GREEN
Wizard

JOEL RIOJAS

Edited By: Alex Rada

Fulton Books
Meadville, PA

Published by Fulton Books 2022

ISBN 979-8-88731-157-9 (paperback)
ISBN 979-8-88731-158-6 (digital)

Printed in the United States of America

Acknowledgments

Thank you to my cousin Antonio Santiago for believing in the creative process that brought forth long nights and fun moments.

And a great thank you to my editor, Alexander Rada. Your work and guidance have not only helped this story grow but you helped me grow too.

Chapter 1

It was cold, dark, and windy, and the snow did not make things any easier by hitting me directly square in the face. I had been walking for so many days that I was exhausted, hungry, and scared. I had no clue where I was going, but I kept walking in the deep, harsh snow. I did not know how to survive in this kind of weather. I had realized my limits too late, and I was underprepared. I began to cry in defeat as I put my back against an enormous tree covered in snow. It was hard for me to admit I had no idea what I was doing. Fear began to creep up my cold body. I began to think of my family, wondering if I would ever see them again. Things were happening so fast that my depression would not allow my mind to keep up. I was lost, and for the first time in my life, I had to be honest with myself right then and there: I was in a bad situation. I looked up in the sky, but there was still nothing but heavy snowfall. Even with gloves and socks, my hands and feet were frozen. I wore a green beanie with a blue scarf, a brown jacket, and an orange hoodie. They didn't help much, and worse yet, my blue jeans were soaked through.

In the middle of the night, I was awoken by some rustling in the distance. I carefully looked around and eventually spotted a giant moose. I squatted down, half frozen and half scared, as the moose made its way past me. As the moose walked past me, I was amazed. Never had I seen such a magnificent animal so up close and personal. I also quickly became jealous at how confidently the moose moved through this snowstorm. I could see this moose moved with a purpose, and it angered me like no other. I despised the moose for its carefree nature. My hate for this moose, within a matter of minutes, had grown so high that I had decided I was going to kill it. I slowly followed behind as my mind battled my consciousness. I began to question who I was becoming. I had gotten so caught up in my mind that I failed to keep my eyes focused on the moose that I found myself face-to-face with. For a second, goose bumps ran through my entire body. I saw its massive dewlap first as I made my way up to its face and, finally, its benevolent antlers. I did not know what to do as something warm began to run down my leg. The next thing I knew, the moose kicked me in the chest, and I passed out.

A few mornings later, I found a stream of water that I began to drink out of like a madman. I was so thirsty that I felt bloated by the time I was done. I filled up a plastic bottle I had with me, but I quickly found that one was not enough. As I looked right across from me, I noticed a giant porcupine walking with its family. It was an inspiring image that had me thinking of my siblings and my extended family. That quickly fizzled away as I began to cough up black vomit. After I cleaned myself up, I was full of so much anger, hate, and frustration that I went after one of the porcupettes. If I was separated from my family by forces greater than me, then I would separate this family as well to ease my pain. I had mustard so much anger into my fist that I was going to punch the porcupettes to death until I got a reality check from the mom. The moment I saw her giant body raise her quills, my brain quickly processed danger, and I took multiple steps backward. I yelled at the top of my lungs, wanting to know what kind of monster I was becoming. Was there nobody that could come to my rescue? My heart ached in sorrow.

I continued walking until I was surrounded by nothing but heavily snow-covered mountains. As the winds picked up, I swear I could hear something else in the wind, almost as if a voice was calling out to me. As I looked around, I noticed that I was surrounded by mountain goats singing a tune that I was unfamiliar with. If anything, it felt like they were warning me to turn around and return home, that I was on a path that would end with my demise. The fire within me began to rise as I yelled loudly into the nothingness, "What else should I do?" I have failed in the big city. I have nothing. I am nothing. I just began to cry, pouring out heavy tears that ran down my brown cheeks, wishing I would just freeze to death. It felt like the mountain goats were letting the entire land know that a lost loser was dumb enough to come here. I yelled out in anger, tired of being labeled something. I did not care about who I was anymore, or about what others thought I was supposed to be. Yet again, I threw up black vomit. My throat burned with acid, and the aftertaste was fouler than spoiled meat and sour milk.

I fell to my knees, embarrassed, lonely, and afraid of what I was doing, let alone where I would end up. There were many days that my depression began to take its toll on me. I felt that if I just died out here, maybe I would find some kind of peace in a land I knew nothing about. As I went on, my mind began to play tricks on me. It wanted me to believe that I was seeing my dead father in the darkness, a man who was obsessed with killing others, including his family. For that very reason, he was shadow-banned into another dimension, out of sight, out of mind. I never realized in my life that I would wander into an area where the darkness was so strong, somehow giving power to my father by giving him access to me. I had to be even more careful now that my father was aware that I had ventured away from the light and that I did not have the protection of the family. At this point, what real protection did I even have anymore?

One family had come to rule over all the others, the Wiohez family. They were willing, at any cost, to do what needed to be done to eliminate any form of threat, whether that meant secret executions or using fear as their ally. For generations, they bought out more land, owned hordes of animals, and controlled many buildings in town. Their wealth only accumulated, while others either became poorer or lost everything, forcing them to rely on the Wiohezes' financial support. Cystone Wiohez, the father of my cousin Moy Wiohez, came from a huge family of twenty brothers and twenty sisters. Eventually, Cystone Wiohez began to buy out all the other families, and he even had many of his brothers and sisters marry into the ones that could not be bought out. My family had become weak over the generations, and when my father was shadow-banned for trying to murder me, it left the door open for the wolves. My family was torn apart. Some of my siblings went to one family to work for them as slaves, while others were assimilated into the family for the namesake. My family, the Kickfingers, had been known as both governors and business owners. However, over the generations, we were cursed to be consumed by the black vomit. I saw what the black vomit did over time to my father's brother, Ruben Kickfinger. It turned him against his own blood. Ruben looked like some sort of dark shadow. That day, I remember I was sleeping until I heard some screaming and yelling. I woke up, got out of my bed, and when I came out into the kitchen, I saw this horrific dark shadow rise over me, leading me to storm out of the house through the back door. I was so terrified that I could not dare look back until I was outside, at which point I remember hearing a loud bang followed by a wave of green light. The only thing we do know is that it will either claim your life at a young age, like my paternal grandfather, Andrew Kickfinger, or it will turn you into a dark monster like my father.

The last day I saw my mother, I was being hunted down to be murdered as the firstborn to the Kickfinger Family. I held a power that the Wiohez family and their allies had longed to silence. My mother, Lina Kickfinger, could only take me so far. She told me it was up to me to continue the journey. She gave me a heavy kiss on the forehead. As I stuttered trying to find words, my mother told me, "This will be the last time you will ever see me."

I asked, "Why?"

My mother wiped the tears off my face, and with her sad, burdened brown eyes, my mother embraced me and quietly whispered into my ear, "Because I am not who you think I am." I did not know how to process her final words as she began to walk away. I reached my hand toward her as I began to run, but she began to quickly move out of sight. My father, Lumusi Kickfinger, had been an abusive man toward my mother. He had taken her at the age of thirteen from my grandparents. When I got older, I noticed, firsthand, the marks he would leave on her body. I remember I would always hear my father yelling that it was not him who was in control of his actions. It was his dark shadow. Yet when I would look on the floor, I would see his bottles of tequila and beer everywhere. When he would get drunk, he claimed he had dark powers that would force him to do terrible things.

In the darkness, my eyes began to play tricks on me, show-ing me dark shadows pursuing me. I would shut my eyes so tight it would hurt. I did not want to see those dark shadows that began to multiply, getting closer and closer. The dark shadows began to get so close that I felt their presence running up my neck. I think, at some point, I became delusional as I came across herds of caribou spread out for miles passing by me. I got the vibe they felt they were better than me, so, in my anger, I began to slap, kick, and punch as many of them as I could. The more I hurt them, the louder they got in mak-ing fun of me, calling me names until I got worn out from knocking out cold as many caribou my anger allowed. I lay there in the snow next to multiple motionless caribou as the others kept walking by me, mocking me. In my final effort, I gave them the middle finger. I felt like everything around me had been judging me and was able to see right through my wounded heart. These animals around me were brutal, and I did not know how much more of it I could take. I was on the verge of having a mental breakdown. My heart began to pound, and my brain felt like it was going to pop open like a bag of popcorn. I was shaking as my mind began to space out, and I started hyperventilating.

One of the days when the light from the sun was only out for about an hour, I felt something uncomfortable coming for me. I turned around and saw my father's shadow chasing after me with a knife. That look of rage was still in his face. I began to run as fast as I could to catch up to the dimming light in front of me. I could hear my father screaming like a madman at the top of his voice, yelling out at me every curse word in the book. In his rage, he called me a coward for not confronting him. I must had run for what felt like a good mile, terrified, until I had covered a good distance into the remaining light. His shadow had stopped at the line of the light, and I could see my father's cold, dark eyes looking at me with a mur-derous intent. In his hand, he held a dark blade, ready to take my life. When you are shadow-banned, you cannot communicate with words, but I could read everything I needed to through his eyes. It was hard for me to see all this alone, but somewhere in my broken, beat-up heart, I knew I could manage as a green glow lurked in the distance.

One night, I had made a fire to keep my father away and whatever else lurked in the darkness. I had not been feeling well, so I lay down in the snow for a while with a blanket I took out of my green book bag. When I opened my eyes again, hours had passed, and I noticed the fire was nearly out. From across the flickering of the dying fire, my father stared at me, squatting in his black robes. As the light burned out, he reached out his hand across the firepit, getting closer and closer, to grab me when another hand snatched his. The fire was restored to its full brightness, and as the figure turned around, my grandfather, my mother's father, looked at me.

"You must take better care of yourself, dear boy," he said in his gruff and wise voice.

My grandfather, Remo, had been missing for ten years. No one knew what happened, but everyone just imagined that one night, he took off on his walk and never came back. A search team was sent out, but no body or trace of him was ever found. My grandfather touched my forehead, and his warm hand rejuvenated me. He also touched my heart, and that helped bring me some peace since it brought back warm memories of me eating ice cream with him.

"I-I-I missed you so much!" I screamed. I remembered all the years he had spent with me, raising me and taking me places while my father would spend his entire time getting drunk at the bars with other women. My grandfather smiled and told me, "Stay strong, and remember that you will never be alone." As my grandfather slowly faded out of sight, I looked to my right and saw bananas and other various fruits had been left for me. I gave my first smile in a while, but as I ate one of the bananas, I saw a green shadow in the distance. It caught my curiosity, so I went to look to make sure I was not imagining things, and nothing was visible save for few tracks in the snow that led nowhere.

The next day was not any easier. I had just crossed a frozen river, and now I was making my way through arduous mountain ranges. I had no idea where they were leading to. As I continued walking, I found myself face-to-face with a wild cougar. I was unsure what to do since the cougar was blocking the only path forward: a beat-up old bridge. The cougar began to speak to me! "In order to pass, you have to offer up something."

I told the cougar, "I have nothing to offer."

The cougar smiled as it licked its lips, telling me, "You are not getting creative enough is the problem."

I said, "Fine. I will give you a piece of my spirit as flesh for you to eat." My spirit had already been through all kinds of pain and torture due to my rough upbringing. How much would it hurt to have a cougar tear away something that had already been ripped apart? I quickly found it to be one of the most painful experiences you can have. The cougar threw me to the ground, got on top of me, and tore into my spirit, leaving me feeling violated. I had felt like this once before when my father had beat me up when I was younger. That same week, my friends had publicly humiliated me by throwing paint at me in class, and I got beaten up by the school bully. The cougar stepped aside, full and satisfied, telling me I could now pass. I hardly cared anymore at this point. I just wanted the hurting to stop. I grabbed the side of my ribs and limped along, wondering how much further I was going to manage.

I took a knee to rest for a bit, and I could hear nothing but absolute silence for miles. I closed my eyes and allowed myself to breathe to try and ground myself. When I opened my eyes, a bald eagle was chomping away on some dinner. I just stood there and watched in silence as I finally had some company. In the morning, I had finally managed to make my way down the mountain. I don't know why, but I was pretty proud of myself. I could see the sun slowly rising as I looked into the fresh body of water in front of me. Suddenly, a colossal whale rose out of the water with a thunderous splash. I have never seen whales up close in their natural environment. They were amazing creatures in my eyes. The whales were speaking to one another in their language, but then the whale yelled out something I could understand: "Run!" A wolverine and a hungry black bear were after me. I was so terrified that I was stuck in place. My brain was telling my body to move, but I was going nowhere fast. You could hear the whale shoot something out of its blowhole as a miniature silver orb lay in front of me. I grabbed the orb, and I felt I had been flung violently somewhere else. The wolverine and the bear were nowhere to be seen, but it felt as if I had never left. I put the silver orb in my pocket and continued on my journey. After many hours of walking, I came across a cabin in the woods. My stomach was growling so loud I wouldn't be surprised if the owner heard me from a mile away. As I got closer, it looked like someone had been butchering animals as I saw parts in dug-up pits, including salmon that had been hanging to dry. As I got closer, a middle-aged woman came out and looked surprised to see me. I asked her if I could have some food to eat because I was absolutely starving.

The woman said, "Sure, and from the looks of it, you need a bath and a change of clothes." I took a few steps forward and began to throw up black vomit everywhere. I passed out from pain and sheer exhaustion.

When I awoke, the woman had me sitting in a hot tub with bandages around my head and needles throughout my body. The woman looked at me with sad eyes, and I asked, "What is wrong?"

She informed me, "It has been a long time since I have seen someone in such bad condition."

I asked her, "What do you mean?"

She said, "First, I am healing all your spiritual wounds by stitching them up with my special needles. The spirit is nothing to play with. If you tear into it enough, you can die." As she said that, all the water around me turned black.

I asked the woman, "What is going on?"

"I'm detoxing your body from the dark poison that is inside of you."

I asked, "Like, literal poisoning?"

The woman explained, "It would appear someone who looked to harm you and your family slipped what I call the Black Blood into one of your ancestors' genes using dark powers. What happens over the generations is that the Black Blood begins to become stronger and stronger within your blood line that, eventually, the genes cannot get passed, and your bloodline dies out." I began crying heavily, and she asked me, "What is wrong?" I told her about my father being shadow-banned, and her eyes widened. The woman, this time, looked at me very closely and asked, "Where are you from?"

I told her, "From the great nation of Yehuda." Her brown eyes widened even more now to the point that she scared me. I asked her, "What is wrong?"

"There has not been someone from that land present here in quite some time. How did you get here?"

I told her, "I have no idea I had even left anywhere. One moment I was looking at the whales, the next thing I was being attacked by a bear and wolverine until I grabbed a mini silver orb."

The woman asked, "Where is the silver orb now?"

I told her, "It is in my pocket."

The woman gave a sigh of relief as she informed me, "I would have preferred that orb stayed where it belonged. It's the only one in existence."

I decided to ask the woman, "What is your name, and where the heck am I?"

"My name is Lata, and you are in the country called Devansh, the biggest continent on the planet. What is your name?" I told her that my name was useless and powerless, not worth mentioning. She looked at me in surprise and said, "It's Brownie Kickfinger, isn't it?"

"How did you know?" I asked, astonished.

She smiled while shaking her head. "You have your name tag on your book bag."

After taking a few days to heal, I came outside one morning to see Lata cutting up some fresh bear meat. I told her, "Thank you for all her help."

Lata looked at me and smiled. She told me, "Come over and help me finish cutting up this bear meat." As we worked together, she informed me, "There are many dangerous parts to Devansh, and if you are okay with it, I would like for you to stay for a while so that I can teach you the ways of this land. Also, you need to heal some more, but it will take years before your wounds fully heal." I was uncertain at first, but what other options did I really have?

I looked at Lata and said, "Sure!"

Lata said, "Good. You will go with me tonight to hunt for some wild turkeys."

I told Lata, "I have no idea how to hunt or shoot."

Lata chuckled. "I'm pretty aware of the mediocre skills and abilities that you currently have. I can fix that."

The night arrived, and we were in full winter hunting gear. The important thing was that I was fully layered, ready for any kind of winter now. Lata had given me a sharp knife as she held onto the rifle. Earlier in the day, she had shown me how to shoot, but she felt it was sometime away before she would actually let me hold any kind of firearm. We were quietly making our way through the brush. It was pitch-black out tonight without the marvelous moon. Lata ordered me to stay put for a minute because she had spotted something ahead. I stood in place for several minutes until I heard footsteps in the snow. I thought it was Lata until I turned around and saw my father. He began choking me, quickly holding me up against one of the trees. I pulled out the knife to stab him repeatedly, and nothing happened as I began to fade out. The next thing I knew, I could hear a rifle shot, and my father dropped me, taking a step back. As I looked on, I could see he was bleeding out black blood from his stomach. Lata shot my father again in the chest, and, for the first time, I could see fear in his eyes. As she was going to fire a third shot, he ran off quickly into the darkness. Lata asked, "Are you hurt?"

I said, "No. Just my ego."

Lata said, "It will be a while again before he decides to mess with you."

"Why do you say that?"

"Because I shot him with specially powered bullets made for people like him that have been shadow-banned. So not only did he feel those but it will take him time to recover."

I looked at Lata and said, "We didn't come out here to hunt any turkeys, did we?"

Lata said, "No, we came out here so I can buy you some time by sending a message to your father."

I told Lata, "My blade must be dull, because I stabbed him, but nothing happened."

Lata looked directly into my eyes and told me, "It is because, currently, you are no stronger than a butterfly." I looked away in disappointment, and I swear I saw a green shadow speeding through the woods. I told Lata to look, and by the time she did, it was gone. Lata asked me what it was that I wanted her to see.

I grumbled "never mind" as I wondered if I had imagined it myself.

One night, Lata summoned me into the living room of her cabin home and told me to take a seat. She wanted to let me know more about the country I ventured into. I was excited and always enjoyed learning something new. "Devansh started as a peaceful country, but over the years, things have changed with the rise of the Enlightened One. His subordinates, known as the Sharm, devoted generations to protecting him during his enlightenment. It is said by the Sharm that it took the Enlightened One two thousand years to achieve his current form. The Sharm say that he started by lying down on his back, meditating. Throughout the millennium, his body shifted positions, and after a while, those positions began to make symbols on the ground. Eventually, those symbols gave birth to six different silver orbs. While he was still in his enlightenment, word had gotten out about these silver orbs, and the people of Devansh began to go to war over them. Over time, the silver orbs were either destroyed or lost. At that time, Devansh questioned why we should use our natural resources when we could start to trade with other nations of the world. When our people met for the first time, it was magical. We all came to find out there were more continents on this giant world than we were aware of. Well, over time, Devansh felt we had superior technology, so it was decided by the powers that be that we would conquer all lands. My grandfather, Row, stole the last two remaining silver orbs from the Devansh government. They were after him, and he managed to destroy one of the silver orbs along the way. The army of Devansh had caught up to him and had him cornered. As they were going to lay fire down on him, he disappeared, and our connection with the outside world was lost. Not too long after, the Enlightened One awoke, terribly disappointed with the people of Devansh, so he went on a killing spree with his subordinates, the Sharm. Now he was infuriated and went all over the country, conquering every piece of land. The Enlightened One has been looking for the final silver orb for some time now, and you brought it back to him."

I was annoyed that I had been running from one situation back home to just run right into another here, and Lata could see that in my eyes. Lata made it clear "it was only a matter of time before the orb made its way back to Devansh. So we are going to have to make sure you do not misplace that thing." Lata looked at me and, in a serious tone now, directly looked into my eyes and said, "In no way can you allow the Enlightened One to regain that final silver orb."

I was lost. "Why not?" I asked.

"Because it's evil!" she snapped. "Because he is evil! He will use that final orb to conquer the rest of the world."

"Well, why can't I just give it to you?"

"I want nothing to do with it, and it came to you."

I asked Lata, "Well, how in the world do I destroy this thing?"

Lata looked at me and said, "That is a darn good question." Lata then got up to go make some fresh tea.

We went fishing one peaceful morning. Lata had been teaching me the local language, as well as showing me kung fu. It was very interesting to me that I had only known Lata for such a short time, yet it felt like I had known her forever. From what she has told me, she is the last of her entire family. I had been fishing when something enormous began to rise out of the water. It was a giant fish on legs. I panicked and began to scream when a rifle shot rang in the air, and Lata came over, telling me she forgot to mention they have some big fish that come out the river every now and then.

"They make for good eating, but be mindful of your surroundings. There are some big things in this country. One thing that I want you to be alert for when you are by yourself are the Rillers. They are savages that lurk at night that were transformed by the Enlightened One—monsters to do his bidding. They are primarily composed of people who went against the Enlightened One. The Rillers are reminders to everyone in this country of what can happen to you if you decide to not follow the laws of the land or worship and obey the Enlightened One. Unfortunately, the Enlightened One nor the government want to take responsibility for the Rillers' actions."

I really enjoyed showering in Devansh. The water felt fresh on my brown skin, and it became my place for meditation. Lata was always busy doing something, and when she would leave the cabin, she would always put on brown robes and grab a staff from out of the kitchen. When Lata left, I made sure to cook myself a nice breakfast with some coffee. I would clean the cabin and make my bed. I found it odd that she only had one picture in the entire cabin. It was a picture of multiple people wearing different-colored robes with pointy hats and staves. I really enjoyed the chocolate candy Lata would leave out for me. It was weird because at times it felt like she had been waiting for me. When I would go to bed, I would find myself tossing and turning in the middle of the night. On several nights, I remember seeing a bright green light appear to get closer and closer to my window.

I really got the hang of shooting a rifle, and I would go out in the morning to shoot rabbits so Lata could make stew. I got so good at subsistence living that I wondered why in the world I didn't live like this before. I now knew how to skin any wild animal, from rabbits to moose. Lata really surprised me when she cooked some moose tongue. It was by far one of the most delicious things I had in a taco.

It was always something with Lata. She never really let me rest. She had me paint the cabin green and put up the antenna. When the warmer months kicked in, she had me mow the grass and help her with the garden. I became pretty familiar with corn and potatoes. I enjoyed doing these activities with her. Lata was in shape, and her beautiful, natural white hair was mesmerizing. I came to enjoy her smile. It was always full of energy, and it motivated me to continue learning all I could from her. My favorite time of the day became when we would walk through the woods together, and Lata would point at the scattered statues of her prior family members. I asked Lata why they all seemed to be wearing a wizard hat. Lata joked, "For good looks." I laughed.

Lata enjoyed painting, so she set up two white canvases set on easels in the living room. Lata brought out the oil paint. I picked up the oval wooden palette, and, with my brush in hand, it was time to get messy. I had never done such a thing with my family, and boy was it fun painting and watching Lata. At one point, she flicked her brush toward me, getting paint all over me. I felt an inner joy like none other, so I flicked my brush full of paint at Lata, and we were locked in a paint battle. We both looked ridiculous covered in paint. At the end of the night, we looked at each other's work. I had painted a house that had the roof collapsed in. It was kind of depressing. Lata had drawn a valley. In this valley stood a green wizard. It really caught my attention as something inside of me felt a connection. That night, when I went to sleep, I thought of all fifteen of my siblings and wondered if my mother was okay as tears ran down my face. As hard as Lata worked, I was surprised to see she also knew how to have fun. She turned on her Bluetooth vinyl player, and we began dancing to what came across to me as house music. That day, Lata told me what she sees is that I don't know how to just be "in the moment."

"You got to smile more! Let yourself come out. Shine like the sun…or like the moon if you're a night owl."

That night, Lata had me wearing a blue robe that felt like something I had worn before. There were days that I found it weird that Lata did not ask any questions about where I grew up, my family, nor anything of that nature. It felt like she was just glad to have me in her company.

Chapter 2

I wanted to go hiking one day. The urge to get out just overwhelmed me. It had been a year, and I had been dying to explore more of Devansh. I had become familiar with the area around Lata's cabin. Mind you, her property is a good ten miles wide, but I wanted to go further now. I had been wanting to hike a trail called the Long Trail that led up to the Brady Mountains. Lata had mentioned how scenic the area was. I took a backpack with me that included snacks, a knife, a hunting rifle, and a cell phone that Lata made me take. I had my water-resistant hiking boots on nice and tight. This was it! I was going to make the best of today. I had decided to put some gel to spike my hair up so that when I would take pictures, I would look as handsome as any twenty-one-year-old could. At 170 pounds, and with all the training Lata had me doing, I was starting to admire my body for the first time with all my new little muscles.

The weather was not so bad those days when the winter had died down. The snow was melting, and all sorts of things could be seen, like butterflies, worms, and light bugs. I still made sure to layer up with my beaver gloves, balaclava mask, and wool socks. The temperature was somewhere in the low sixties.

I had finally arrived at the Long Trail, and everything was soaking wet with mud spots and puddles throughout the area. I saw wild birds flying through a valley teeming with amazing wildlife. I hopped on the trail and began making my way closer to the Brady Mountains to get a higher view of the area. As I got closer and closer to the mountains, I came across turtles and giant boulders that looked misplaced. I had even spotted a fox in the distance with my binoculars. It felt as though my soul was at home in this place. This place was abundant with natural wildlife, and for the first time, it warmed my heart to have had such an experience. I eventually came across a totem pole that had a bear, an eagle, a wolverine, a rabbit, a moose, a wolf, and a whale carved into it. I thought it was pretty cool, so I placed my hand on it for a moment and continued on. When I got to the base of the Brady Mountains, I decided to take a break. I pulled out my roll-out mat from my backpack and put up my poncho next to a few trees, tying it down with some cord I brought along. I lay down on the mat and began to snack on some protein bars, and I began to make up words while singing to my own tune, rejoicing in this moment of bliss.

I really took the time to soak it all in. I took several deep breaths, and boy was I high on life. I had never spent time with myself like this. In the big city, I was constantly living in the fast lane, caught up in all the drama. It brought a smile to my face seeing a rabbit family hopping along. This was such a treat for me. I wish one day to share these moments with my siblings. I am sure it will also make them smile. I figured that whenever the time came to be reunited with my family, I would have a few stories to tell. I must have lost track of time because I hadn't noticed that it began to get dark, let alone how quickly it was happening.

I looked up in the sky and saw a black moon. It sent goose bumps throughout my entire body. *Now what the heck could that mean?* I wondered. Something did not feel right about this, so I began to quickly pack all my belongings. As I started to walk away, I found myself jogging down the trail. I felt fear taking over me, and I was not sure why, but then I remembered the phone in my backpack, and I speed-dialed Lata. Nothing happened. The phone was dead, so I began running. I began to hear things around me. I could hear horrifying screams getting louder and louder until before me stood what looked like three dark shadows that I had never seen before. They looked at me, and one of them gave out a horrible screech. I brought out the knife Lata had specially created for me in case I ever came across any more dark shadows. As the three dark shadows approached me, I grabbed one and rammed my knife into its forehead. The other grabbed me from behind, but I was too quick, and I stabbed it multiple times in the stomach and one good plunge in the chest. The final dark shadow paused, standing still. I made sure to be careful of anything sneaky. I slowly began to walk away as I had my knife pointed directly at the dark shadow. I gathered it was either waiting for reinforcements, or it did not want to wind up like the other two.

I continued running as I could hear many more coming after me now. I had gotten tired of running. I felt a little bit of bravery arise within me. I looked for a spot that would give me some high ground with cover, got into the kneeling position, and started picking off as many of them as I could with the rifle I had in my backpack. I eventually ran out of ammo, so I made a run for it until I was eventually surrounded by twelve of them. From out of the darkness, my father appeared within the inner circle. For the first time in my life, I was not afraid to confront him. My father, Lumusi, directed the other dark shadows. "He's mine." Those words, deep down, kind of intimidated me. I thought he was not supposed to be able to talk, and here my father was directing the dark shadows with words. I started to wonder if my father was somehow getting stronger, which chipped a bit of my confidence away.

I decided I was not going to back down from my father, so I ran at him, full of anger, and before I knew it, he had dropped me to the floor with a quick punch. I had no idea what had just happened, but that hurt. My father grabbed me by the hair and headbutted me several times, breaking my nose. My blood had splattered everywhere, and I was annoyed at how much he seemed to be enjoying himself. I quickly began to lose my confidence, wondering what the heck I was thinking. I clearly made a mistake. My father grabbed me again and rammed my face into a tree. I hit the ground hard on my back, dazed. I was still semiconscious, so I pulled out my knife to try and stab him, but he grabbed my arm. I was powerless as he forced my hand into my stomach, digging the knife into my gut. As I fell to the ground, my mind was blank. All I could think was *this is the end*. I could hear all the dark shadows screaming at the top of their lungs, chanting for the death blow.

In those final seconds, I began to regret that I did not find a way to get even stronger in the time I had been with Lata. As my father picked me up and cranked his fist backward, a fireball hit him square in the face. He burst into flames and ran off, his painful screams carrying into the trees and through the valley. When I fell to the ground, I could see someone with a fire beard using a flamethrower, lighting up as many dark shadows as he could spot. I could feel the warmth from the heat of his fire beard as he approached me. He whistled, and a giant dog approached. The fire-bearded man put my body on the giant dog, strapped me on the dog's back, and told the dog, "Kake, take him to Lata while I take care of things here. Go!" As the giant dog ran off, I could see the crazy old man pushing back the dark shadows. I was losing so much blood that I lost consciousness.

I woke up to Lata's smile and saw myself once again bandaged up. Lata said, "You're lucky I know a lot about medicine. That wound in your stomach wasn't easy, but there's a couple ancient tricks that most healers don't remember anymore."

I told Lata, "Thank you!"

"What happened?" I asked.

Lata said, "There are many unnatural things that occur in Devansh, but I had only heard of the black moon from my grandfather, Row, who took the last orb with him into your country." Lata shook her head and told me, "Your father must have truly been a bad man to have this kind of power over the Shadow Dimension."

I asked Lata, "Who was the old man with the fiery beard?"

Lata told me as she touched my forehead to calm me down, "He is called the Engineer, but his name is Varun. For as long as I've known, Varun has lived in the Brady Mountains. He's been in this area even longer than my grandfather, Row. He and I, over time, became pretty good neighbors as we came to find out that we shared the same values and beliefs. We both would like to see Devansh be a world leader, a place of freedom from the Enlightened One, and a place of idealism."

I was pretty intrigued by this Varun, so I asked, "What is it that this Engineer does in the mountains?"

Lata looked at me and said, "Work to try and make Devansh a better place."

I asked, "What kind of work?"

Lata looked at me and smiled. "Rest for now."

I woke up ready to stretch out and eat some pancakes, scrambled eggs, and some toast with orange juice. I made my way into the kitchen and did not see Lata. I walked into the living room and saw she was glued to the television. I asked her, "What is going on?"

Lata worriedly mentioned, "There were riots going on all over Devansh, and the capital, Anika, has been hit the hardest."

"Why are people rioting?"

"It is because the Enlightened One has been sending out his followers, the Sharm, to kidnap people throughout the land. They're looking for information. They're looking for you!"

Lata looked at me and said, "He has sensed the silver orb, and it will eventually lead him to you." Lata noticed my confusion. "Anika is about seven hours from here by car." Lata turned off the television and went into the kitchen. "Relax, and let's eat."

After we ate an amazing breakfast, Lata brought out a box of chocolate candies that were so irresistible I must have eaten twenty pieces. I looked at Lata and told her, "Thank you for everything."

Lata smiled. "As long as you are enjoying yourself, that is all that matters."

Over the course of another six months, I helped Lata reinforce the cabin for the next winter. Her cabin, at first glance, does not look that big, but it is actually four thousand square feet in all. I became Lata's handyman, doing everything from plumbing and patching to installing cabinets. I was so happy learning all these things with Lata. It would have been wonderful doing things like this with my family growing up. Lata called me over to a barn that I never realized she had, and she showed me something marvelous inside: a Cessna 172 Skyhawk four-seat, single-engine aircraft. It was painted a vibrant green. Lata asked, "Do you know how to fly?"

I looked at her and said, "Nope!"

She chuckled. "From this day forward, I am going to show you everything about flying." The months with Lata just continued to fly by. I wasn't sure if it was because I had so much to do and learn or if it was because I was having so much fun. One day, I walked into my room, and I noticed something flickering red. It was the silver orb. I yelled out for Lata, and she came right away.

I asked her, "What is going on?"

She looked concerned. "They must be nearby." Lata put the orb into a small black book bag and went all around the cabin, turning off all the lights. Lata had me follow her to the panic room that she had built years ago in her free time. From there, we began looking at all the monitors to see if the cameras had spotted anything. Then she saw them: two drones flying nice and slow. They were taking pictures of the surrounding area. At that moment, Lata knew it was no longer going to be safe for us to remain at the cabin.

It was five in the morning, and Lata had us fully packed. She had decided we would go to one of her friends in a little village near the Brady Mountains called Varmington. Varmington was such a small village. No more than two thousand people lived there. On foot, it was going to take the whole day to get there, so we made off as soon as we were ready. We quietly walked off the path, not saying a word to one another. Lata led, and I followed with my mouth shut. Today was the first time I ever saw fog in this area. I had no idea how Lata knew where she was going in these conditions, but I figured she knew the region better than anybody. However, I would soon find out there was much more to Lata than her pathfinding skills.

The fog was so heavy that we had nearly missed the two Sharm directly in front of us. We came up from behind them, so they couldn't see us. Lata took off her gloves and touched both of them, freezing them still with her touch. I took a good look at the Sharm, and they tripped me out. They had purple skin with black eyes. I noticed they had long pointed ears. They had hands like mine, but teeth that resembled that of a hyena. One of the biggest things that stood out to me was the gold dot on their foreheads. I was curious to know if that was a birthmark or something else. Lata commanded the Sharm to tell her everything. The first one shouted, "I swore an oath to the Enlightened One!" took out a pistol, put it in his mouth, and pulled the trigger.

The other one quivered and spoke, "There are about twenty of us. We had been tracking the beacon emitting from the silver orb, but we were not sure exactly from where in this area. The Third is amongst us. He must not be taken lightly, for his abilities and power are vast.

"Where are the other two? The first and the second?" Lata asked, squeezing his arm.

The Sharm answered, "They are not with us." Lata gave a sigh of relief and touched the Sharm on the shoulder and gave him a suggestion. He pulled out his knife and plunged it into his heart, dropping dead over his comrade.

I asked Lata, "What is it that you're doing?"

She told me, "I have a power referred to as the Touch. Anything I put my hands on, I can give commands to. If I touch a tree and ask for some of its water, it will pour some into my hands. If I touch anything that is full of life, I can command it to decay or die." I was amazed, and I opened my mouth to ask another question. She waved her hand in my face and quickly shut me up.

"Get down, for now is not the time for questions."

We continued to go through the fog. I began to have a feeling that Lata created it. Everything was going perfect until I could hear screaming that made my heart sink. Lata knew right away it was Rillers. She got angry, realizing the Sharm must have led a pack of them here. I looked over the giant log that we were hiding behind, and I saw my first Riller. They looked like mindless kangaroos with a human face. This one's chest was soaked with blood. Another Riller came up from behind and started attacking the other. They were savages. As more came and started tearing each other apart, Lata had me slowly follow her out of there.

We eventually found a trench that we hid in to take a break for a bit. My hands were freezing until Lata touched them and said, "Warmth." I felt some of her heat transfer to my hands that spread throughout my body. Lata told me, "No matter what, whatever I tell you to do, you do it. No matter what! Okay?"

I told Lata, "I understand, but I want to know why you are getting so serious with me all of a sudden."

Lata told me, "Between the Sharm, Rillers and the Third, I am concerned if we would both make it alive." I did not like the sound of that, so I figured I would just have to hope for the best. We continued our journey on our bellies, crawling away from the feast that the Rillers had made of themselves.

Eventually, we were able to walk normally again. We came across an old bridge, and as I looked below, I saw a giant canyon. Halfway through, I really started to shake because I was afraid of heights, and this thing was wobbling in all kinds of ways. It took time, but thankfully, Lata relaxed me enough to get me across. When we finally got to the other side, a voice shouted behind us, "Traitors!" We both turned around, and a hooded figure bearing horns told Lata, "Hand over the silver orb."

Lata told the Third, "I do not have it."

"I am aware you do not have it, because I could hear its voice coming from him." As he pointed at me, the Third began to speak directly to me. "Hand it over, and perhaps the Enlightened One might show you a hint of mercy as he is tearing your heart out of your body." I was so frightened that I had nothing to say.

Lata told the Third, "He has nothing to do with any of this! He was just caught in the middle. Let him go."

The Third shook his head. "It does not work that way. His life will be taken for being in possession of that which belongs to the Enlightened One." The Third began to walk across the bridge as Lata grabbed both sides of the rope holding the bridge and ordered it to decay. The Third hopped off the bridge before the ropes snapped. As he pointed behind us, multiple Rillers had found us and began rushing our way.

We ran as fast as we possibly could until Lata touched me on my back and said, "Run faster." I felt like I was running forty miles an hour.

I yelled at Lata, asking, "How in the heck are the Rillers keeping up?"

"Because they are some fast sons of guns." One of them caught up to me and tried biting me and clawing at me as Lata touched it and yelled out, "Die!" The Riller just dropped dead. My legs began to give way, and we finally came to a halt as we could both hear the Rillers coming. I realized on this day that those things are relentless.

Lata looked at me and told me, "This may be that point where you will need to go ahead and get as far as you can without me."

I looked at Lata and told her, "I cannot do that!" Lata smiled and waved me off. Lata was tired herself as her legs had gotten wobbly. She was becoming worn down. I grabbed Lata and began helping her walk. As we turned around, five Rillers had finally caught up to us. One of the bigger Rillers came forward, and it scared the heck out of me when it's disfigured face was trying to talk. It was such an eerie, chilling sound that it gave me the creeps, sending goose bumps across my body.

It almost didn't sound like words, but it gurgled out, "Tear, tear, rip, and tear! Feast, feast on man flesh!"

I told the Riller, "Not a chance!" It came at me, and I stabbed it in the side. The Riller got angry and kicked me with both its feet, knocking the wind out of me. It was fine. I had felt something like this before.

I got up with my knife in hand and stood in front of Lata as her protector. The Riller came at me again, trying to claw at my face, as I tried stabbing it in the neck. I was being as careful as possible not to get too far from Lata. I felt the other Rillers were just waiting for me to get far enough from her to attack. I did the best I could, and in the end, the Riller kicked my left arm with both legs with such force, dislocating my arm and sending me face-first to the ground in agony. For whatever reason, I was determined to die a hero, at the very least. I managed to get myself up with the remaining strength I had to stand in front of Lata. The Rillers charged at me right as the Engineer with the fire beard came out the woods with a shotgun, killing all the Rillers with his fancy shooting.

The old man looked and me, then looked at Lata. "What the heck are you doing traveling alone with the silver orb?"

Lata looked at Varun and said, "You knew?"

The Engineer smiled as he lit a cigar using his beard. "I'm a lot older than you are, and I have a unique sense of smell. This boy right there is not from here. I smelled him the day he came over to this country. Heck, the day his daddy was trying to do him in during the Dark Moon, I was already ready for those damn shadow-banned bastards. Because that boy right there has been marked for death by his father."

"Enough for now!" Lata snapped.

The Engineer frowned. "You're right, Lata. Let me get us out of here and to a safer location." The Engineer gave each of us a gold chain to put on, and when he yelled out "Varmington," we found ourselves inside someone's living room.

A woman came into the room, and both Lata and Varun shouted out, "Vanya!" They swarmed one another, hugging and shaking hands. All the sudden, all eyes were on me.

To take off some of the tension I felt being directed at me, I asked Varun, "How is it possible to have a fire beard?"

Varun lit another cigar with his beard and cackled, being careful not to dampen his cigar with his saliva. "It is because I'm a genius and can build anything." Varun touched the side of his neck, and the fire beard extinguished with a sizzle. I felt like a little kid that had just been shown a magic trick.

"I implanted a chip in my neck that uses energy some of my body's energy to emit a fire beard. I'll tell you what, it takes up enough energy that I can eat whatever I want!" He laughed as he slapped his belly. "Oh, watch this! Fire beard!" As he bellowed, the beard reappeared with a flash. "It's even voice-activated!"

I was giddy and shouted, "That was the coolest thing I have ever seen!"

"Wait, wait, wait, watch this!" he said as he started rummaging through his vest.

"Enough!"

Vanya screamed so loud we all stood at attention like good little soldiers, and I saw (and felt) her sharp green eyes lock onto mine. In that moment, I felt a cold ice feeling run up my spine. Vanya yelled out to the others as she pointed to my eyes turning black as my veins began to pop out. I bent over and started projecting black vomit all over her wood floor. I collapsed beside the puddle, shaking. In those moments, I saw something that felt along the lines of a vision as a dark figure came out of the shadows. He walked into a circle of dark shadows, kneeling before him like a god. The figure began placing its hands on each shadow person's forehead that was kneeling, and each one began turning into dark fruit. The hooded figure took its time consuming all the dark fruit and then, with its staff, it shot a dark energy blast, ripping open what looked like a portal. The hooded figure slowly took its hoodie off to reveal its burnt face, shooting a black burst of energy in my direction, kicking me out of the vision.

Chapter 3

Vanya came up to me, scanned me head to toe, then turned around and looked directly at Lata and Varun. "You should have never brought him to my home."

Lata told Vanya, "We did not know who else to turn to."

"You knew that by coming here you were dragging me into your problems!" Vanya looked at Varun and started yelling at him. "Of all the broken people you have brought to my attention, you bring me, perhaps, the worst case." Vanya looked at me and asked to see the silver orb. I pulled it out of the black book bag and handed it to her. The moment the orb touched her hands, it began to flicker red. Vanya was amazed that no one, until now, had laid their eyes on the magnificence of the silver orb. Vanya looked at me and told me, "It will never stop calling to be heard. Its location will never remain a secret unless you find a way to destroy it!"

Lata interrupted Vanya, "You must know how to destroy it, right?"

Vanya began pacing the room until she sat down and told Varun, "Bring me a drink." Lata grabbed her pipe and began smoking, taking some deep puffs as she adjusted her glasses. She rolled up her brown sleeves.

Vanya looked at me again and told me, "I'm only going to tell you once. My father, Erya, was part of the Sharm when the Enlightened One awoke from his enlightenment. His real name was exposed by my father at the moment of his death. Erya was a loyal servant to the Sharm, but when the Enlightened One went around murdering and butchering the people of Devansh, he could not stand by and do nothing. Lata's grandfather, Row, was part of the original Nomek Traders that would go throughout the country, including into the east, now named the Land of the Gods. It is such a mesmerizing place filled with thousands of marvelous monuments, and at the center is the temple devoted to the Enlightened One. The Nomek were known for selling furs, but they specialized in rare metals like gold, silver, and platinum. The Nomek were ahead of their time. One in particular was a scientist known as Fami, the wife that made Row feel like a young man again. Erya was one of the first few Sharm to have seen the creation and appearance of all six orbs. As one after the other began to pop up, he began to see the treachery in the eyes of his own brothers who began to kill one another to lay claim to one of the orbs. When the first orb hit the black market, it went for billions. By the time word got out that one remained, a huge caravan began making its way toward the temple of the Enlightened One."

Vanya asked for a cigarette, and, after using Varun's beard as a lighter, she took a few deep drags and blew out some heavy smoke rings. "Well, the day before the caravan arrived, Erya handed the silver orb to Row to deliver to his wife. Erya was counting on Row's praise that she was the best scientist in the country, and he hoped that if anyone could dispose of the orb, it was her. The other five had already been destroyed. Row took the orb back to his wife, Fami, who, right away, was mesmerized by the orb. She wanted to find out everything about it as they made their way back home. The next day arrived, and the Enlightened One awoke from his enlightenment, demanding the six orbs. The remaining Sharm stood quiet as he learned of their fate, and they witnessed his rage grow. Not a second later, a huge caravan arrived at his temple, demanding the sixth orb. When the Enlightened One found out the orbs had all been taken by the people of Devansh, he, at that moment, snapped his fingers and turned them all to stone."

She paused and took a deep drag on her cigarette. "The next thing the Enlightened One did was summon all his Sharm legions to go across the country and butcher everyone for their treachery. That was also when the Enlightened One called forward his true enforcers, the First, the Second, and the Third, who quickly became feared throughout Devansh. Erya had been assigned to the First, who led the Sharm throughout the northern region of the country. So much blood had been spilt that the rivers flowed red. Erya just could not do it anymore. It was too much for him, and he cracked. He knew he had to do something before there would be nothing left of Devansh. So one night, he gave the slip and made his way south, looking for the Nomek Fami. After years of traveling, he finally found Fami and Row, who took Erya back to the cabin."

Vanya asked for another cigarette as she gripped her forehead with her hand, taking some time to remember the details. Vanya took one big drag from her cigarette, let out the smoke, and continued, "I am not exactly sure how things played out, but at some point, Erya asked if Fami had managed to destroy the orb. Fami pulled it out of her pocket, and it immediately started calling out to the Enlightened One. Erya knew it was now only a matter of minutes, or even less, before the Sharm showed up looking for it. Not a second later, there was banging on the cabin door, and the Sharm surrounded the house. Erya was disappointed with himself. It looked like they had been following him. Fami slapped Erya across the face, then told him to come to his senses. Erya calmed down and said the only way to destroy it was to say his name as you are holding it. However, he also told her that the cost of saying the Enlightened One's name was the speaker's life. Fami immediately said she would do it as Row had problems with that decision. In all that arguing, the Enlightened One walked into the cabin, looked at Erya, snapped his fingers, and set him on fire for his betrayal. The Enlightened One laid eyes on the beautiful Fami and demanded her to give him the orb. When Fami refused, he snapped his fingers and turned her into a block of ice. The orb fell to the ground. Row dove after it and grabbed it, and Erya, while on fire, yelled a name out as the orb lit up. When Row grabbed it, instead of the orb exploding, the silver orb was transported to your side of the world."

I looked at Vanya and asked, "What happened to Row?"

Vanya said, "The only thing I can think of was that he was consumed by the silver orb, since it has an identity of its own."

I looked at Vanya and asked, "What exactly are you saying?"

Vanya said, "I can communicate with the orb. It has a voice of its own. You, Brownie Kickfinger, just don't have the ability to hear it yet. Right now, it is not saying much in hopes that its master finds it before we destroy it."

"Wait, so, Vanya, you're telling me that you do not actually know the Enlightened One's name, and the only one that has heard the name is the silver orb who does not want to speak to us? Let's not forget the fact, Vanya, that you are one of few that can hear it speak and communicate with it!"

I got so frustrated that I stepped outside to get some air to calm down. When I closed the door, I saw why Varmington's population was so little. It was a little town living within the ruins of what used to be an advanced megacity. I could see where the city's downtown used to be by all the skyscrapers that lay piled on top of one another. Some of the ruins were still standing, but the rest of the city was nothing but craters and debris. I found myself coming across the remains of cars, ships, planes, and so much more scattered throughout the city, rusting away. The further down that I walked, I began to see new homes hiding within the rubble. The town did have about two thousand people living in it, and I found it very resourceful how they built their homes using what was around them. I must have caught the attention of someone because I saw the light of their home come on as someone exited the front door, making their way to me. As the person approached, they asked my name. I yelled out, "Brownie!" As they got closer, I could see they were wearing a white mask and a full winter onesie to stay warm. They told me to follow them because it was cold outside. I had not noticed until they said something. I walked inside, and the individual told me to take a seat as they gave me some coffee to warm up. The coffee was so delicious that it made me forget about everything that was going on, and a warm feeling began to brew in my stomach. The individual took their white mask off and presented themselves as Catalan Strongleaf, mayor of Varmington.

"You don't look like anyone from around here," she said, pouring herself a cup.

I lied, "I'm from out of town to visit Vanya.

Catalan raised an eyebrow as she shared some homemade desserts with me. I asked her, "What happened to the ruined city?"

"I'm not really sure. It happened so long ago that few have the answers. The people that live here now in what we named after the founder of this town only came within the last hundred years." I spent what felt like hours talking with Catalan. We talked about my earliest memories as a baby to my hardest moments growing up. I told her how I loved to eat a variety of foods like pizza, lasagna, seafood, and much more. I had gotten so comfortable talking with Catalan that I told her everything that has happened until now. Her eyebrow raised again as there was a knock on the door. Catalan opened the door, and there stood the trio, wondering where I had run off to.

Catalan invited everyone in as she passed around more coffee and sweet bread. Catalan, more serious now, asked the trio why they had not brought the silver orb to her attention. The trio looked at each other and pointed fingers, trying to find the right words. Catalan ordered everyone to be quiet.

"I have been receiving text messages from my scouts throughout the town with reports of an unusual amount of Riller activity. What's worse is that several of my scouts have been found decapitated, and just a few minutes ago, I was informed that the Third had been spotted lurking around. Varmington itself may not look like much, but we built this place with our own hands. We're surrounded by mountains, but the problem is that we are in a valley, so if an enemy were to come attacking, they would have the high ground, and there wouldn't be many avenues of escape for them to cover." My stomach growled like a bear, and Catalan chuckled.

"Hungry?" she asked.

After a delicious dinner, we all lingered around the living room, trying to avoid falling asleep. Catalan had come into the living room, turned off all the lights, and told us, "I have received a text message that several Sharm had been spotted not too far from here." Catalan told the group, "I know of a route out of town that will make it hard for them to track us. There is only one problem with this route as to why no one uses it anymore."

I asked, "What is the problem?"

"A single cyborg, the old remains of the ruined city, inhabits much of the Eklund Route we will be traveling."

"And what is the problem?"

"It hunts everything and anything that comes within its region, and if we happen to come across it, there is no telling if we could stop it."

Varun stepped forward and told Catalan, "At the rate at which we are being pursued, it looks like we have no choice."

Catalan looked at all our determined faces and told us, "Suit up! We head out in ten minutes."

Lata asked, "Once we make it through this path, where are you intending to take us?"

Catalan said, "There's an old village, Trivoli, that I am aware of north of here. Living there is a very old mage that I hope is still alive, for she can help in figuring out our dilemma with the silver orb."

Vanya asked, "How could you be so sure?"

"Because the mage used to have a silver orb of her own at one point. Let us hope she's still alive. We were friends at one point, and I got to learn more about her. She was from…ancient times."

We packed everything we would need for the journey. Our backpacks weighed a good seventy pounds, and each of us carried a rifle as we made our way. We used the ruins of the city to make our way through the shadows. I saw the remains of structures spread out in every direction up close. Every step we took was carefully placed as not only glass lay scattered everywhere but rusted chunks of metal too. As we crept through the city, I looked through the shattered windows and noticed bats watching. It was kind of creepy making our way through a dead city. There were enough rats that I was sure they were the true lord of the city. We took our time to make sure to not be spotted until we came upon the Eklund Route. I had a bad feeling about going through this route. Something about it made me cringe. We had to make our way through brush, and it all smelled like death as animal parts were scattered throughout the route. Varun had packed a device he called the Stick. When he would activate it, it would make the group invisible for thirty minutes at a time, giving us time to rest. Catalan called for Varun's attention, asking if he could connect her to a tower so that her phone could get service. Varun asked for Catalan's phone and inserted one of his personally made chips. Within minutes, Catalan's phone had service. Catalan thanked Varun, giving him a kiss on the side of his cheek. Catalan's phone beeped, and she said, "I have received a text indicating the enemy has a tracker with them, and they are making their way towards us." Catalan had us move out, trying to cover as much ground as possible.

That night, there was no moonlight, and it was extra cold with heavy wind and snowfall. After walking for several hours, we took a break as Varun brought out the Stick. He stood frozen in place and raised his right hand in the air, turning it into a fist. We all got quiet as multiple Sharm made their way past us. Catalan was surprised how quickly they had caught up to us. We stayed as still as stones the entire thirty minutes before we cautiously made our way out again. Varun really had some ingenious devices with him. He pulled out his backpack with what he called the Box. It would show him everything around us for approximately a mile. With Catalan's knowledge of the route and Varun's device, it became easy to maneuver around the enemy for many days. The enemy got so frustrated that they put explosives in the mountain to set off avalanches, hoping to bury us.

Things were getting dangerous quick. The enemy let loose a horde of Rillers onto the route, getting impatient with not being able to locate us. The Rillers were so loud that we could hear them coming. In my perspective, they were useless after a while because they would get bored and start killing each other. The Sharm began to agitate the wildlife around us. Bears, wolverines, lynx, you name it, could all be seen with flaming red eyes, bearing the gold dot known as the mark of the Enlightened One on their foreheads. Luckily Varun was a genius. He sprayed each of us with one of his special bottles that would eliminate our scent completely. When we took our break, Catalan told us that Trivoli was only a good day away now. We were told to rest as much as we could and eat, for this may be one of the final breaks in order to make for a final push.

We got careless, and we forgot to check our surroundings. When the thirty minutes ran out, we saw ourselves looking at a handful of Sharm. All I could hear was Catalan yelling out "run!"

Varun had quickly grabbed his rifle and shot a few of the Sharm in the head as he yelled at me, "Follow the group. I will catch up."

Lata touched me and said, "Let's go!" I found myself moving behind her, but as we ran, we had lost sight of where Catalan and Vanya had run off to. To the right of us came out a giant grizzly bear that had been fighting off Rillers. Several Rillers looked at me and came after me. Lata touched me on my back and said, "Be a brave soldier." I aimed my rifle and started killing as many Rillers as I could. Then the wildest noise I have ever heard in my life scared everything in the area, sending goose bumps all over my body. From out the brush came the cyborg Catalan had been speaking of. It grabbed the grizzly bear, picked it up in the air, and split it in half. Lata touched me and said, "Run fast." We ran away from the cyborg as I saw it annihilate the Rillers one by one. As we were running, we did not notice the dip and fell straight down several feet. We were grabbed from behind, noticing we had caught up with Catalan and Vanya. No one knew where Varun was.

A thunderous clap could be heard echoing all around us. We all turned to look behind us and saw the Third perched atop the only sugar pine tree in the area. With a deathly gaze, he extended his left forearm. His palm bore the Enlightened One's gold dot mark, and it began radiating a bright gold. The Third spoke out, "Before the end of tonight, I am going to personally brand each and every one of your foreheads, for everyone and everything belongs to my master. Even this pine tree is now his servant."

I reached into the safest pocket in my coat and pulled out the silver orb, telling the Third, "Don't harm my friends, and I will hand it over." In that moment, the orb caught the attention of the Third, and it started glowing red with the Enlightened One's mark appearing all over it. In that moment, the Third, with his right foot, stomped on the pine tree, breaking it perfectly down the middle. The Third landed gently on both of his feet, walking toward me while extending his left arm. As he got closer, I could see the Enlightened One's mark in one of his eyes. The Third stood before me, demanding I hand over his master's orb.

I gave it to him, and as it touched his hands, I could hear a terribly loud vibrating sound. I was wondering what the heck that awful sound was. From behind me, Catalan said, "The silver orb is speaking. It sounds almost debilitating to you, but I could hear it just fine." Somewhere during the entire scuffle, we all had lost track of the reality around us, and the cyborg found itself standing behind the Third. The Third did not have time to react by the time he noticed. The cyborg picked the Third up in the air, causing him to drop the orb. I grabbed the orb and quickly stashed it in my pocket, then hurried up to pick up my friends and make a run for it. None of us looked back. I was so scared I could hear my heart beating. Lata touched each of us and told us to "run superfast." Before we knew it, we had come to a river.

Everyone looked at each other, and we all knew we had to get across no matter what. The good thing was that the water was not moving too fast. We started making our way through when we all heard a vicious yell echoing for miles. The cyborg had begun speeding toward our direction, uplifting entire trees, rocks, and debris. We moved as fast as we could as the yelling got louder and louder until the cyborg appeared on the riverbank. We all stopped in an instant, dead silent in fear. It tried putting one of its feet in the water but quickly backed away. At that moment, we understood that the cyborg could not come into contact with water. It looked directly at all of us as if to let us know the hunt was on. We quickly gathered ourselves, making our way completely across the river. We figured it wouldn't be long until it got creative and found another route to get to us.

We kept a tight group as Catalan led the way forward. We were all wet and wishing that Varun was with us because he would most likely have some special device with him to dry us. We quickly realized we were in a game of cat and mouse with the Cyborg. Every so often, we would find half the body of a moose or a deer, almost as if they were being used as a marker. We had a strange feeling that the cyborg was finding pleasure in all this and that it had been waiting a long time for an event like this. I almost tripped on a wire when Lata touched me and told me to stop. She pointed up, and as I looked up, I saw a thick log dangling over my head, swaying side to side supported by a weathered rope. Then the daunting question hit all of us: how many more traps were out here, and how did the cyborg manage to quickly set these traps? We concluded that this particular cyborg must have been a special forces cyborg in its time used to infiltrate and sabotage its enemy with quick and vicious strikes.

We all heard loud rustling and quickly took cover. We were all so nervous that each one of us was shaking as I noticed the sweat coming down the side of my comrades' faces. After a few minutes, the cyborg emerged from the trees and brush, checking its traps. When it noticed they were all still intact, the cyborg got mad and appeared to be getting frustrated. It ferociously punched the tree next to it, knocking it down. We continued very slowly. Minutes felt like hours with our current pace as we slowly made our way through the terrain. At last, we came to a system of rivers with Catalan letting us know we were not far from Trivoli.

We continued through the woods, stepping with care to make as little noise as possible until I heard a heart-dropping snap. Vanya began screaming in pain and fell to the ground, pounding the ground and making a ton of noise. Lata and I tried to assist when, from atop of the trees, the cyborg dropped down. It came after me until a metal spear went through its hip. I looked toward the direction that the metal spear came from, laying my eyes on Varun. He loaded another metal spear into his spear gun, shooting the cyborg through the neck. The cyborg screamed out in pain as it ran off into the woods like a wounded animal. Meanwhile, Varun asked, "How are you all doing?"

We looked at him, and I said, "Better now that you are here." He looked at us and apologized that he had gotten lost. Varun quickly disabled the bear trap and picked up Vanya, who was still screaming.

She started pointing in the direction we needed to run. "To the left, quickly, before that thing comes after us again."

We had gained a good distance and thought everything was going to be all right until we could hear the cyborg coming after us. I began to pick up my pace as I noticed the cyborg had managed to pull out those metal spears, but it definitely took some heavy damage. Varun called me over to him, telling me that he had some sticks of dynamite in his pocket. Varun tossed me a lighter and said, "We only have a handful. Make it happen, and end this thing." I lit up a stick, fumbling with it as fast as we were moving. I barely managed to toss it. It fell on the ground next to the cyborg, who ran past it as it went off, blowing off its right left leg and arm. The thing was relentless as it came hopping our way, even more determined. Varun yelled at me, "Destroy it already!" I lit up another stick and tossed it, and another big explosion went off. I decided I would use two sticks of dynamite at the same time now. As the cyborg continued hopping at us, I threw one directly at the ground and one in the air where it might jump. Like I planned, I got the cyborg in midair. Metal parts flew in every direction. I grabbed my last stick of dynamite, lit it up, and put it inside the mouth of the cyborg, walking away as it blew up.

I turned around one last time, and, in the distance, I thought I saw someone with green robes standing over the cyborg. I made my way back to everyone with the sheer adrenaline of survival coursing through my body. I asked Varun if he had anyone else with him. Varun said, "No, just me."

"You didn't see him?"

"Who?"

"The guy in green robes!"

Varun placed a hand on my shoulder. "Young man, your mind just needs rest. There's no one else here. Come on, let's catch up to the others.

When we took a quick break with Trivoli visible in the distance now, we all laughed at how scared we were. Catalan pointed at me and said, "Brownie Kickfinger, you had made me feel like a young woman again. I will forever be a friend to you, and wherever adventure takes you, I will go with you." I could see why Catalan was a mayor. She was smart, funny, and knew how to talk. The words Catalan used brought strength and charisma with them. Every time Catalan opened her mouth, she immediately had my undivided attention. I was glad to have met Catalan, and I was glad she was part of this team. The other major benefit of having Catalan around was she was a specialized chiropractor, and she believed that she was a fighter pilot in her previous life.

Varun finally spoke out and said he enjoyed thinking up stuff on how to improve the quality of life for all of Devansh. Varun told us how he used to own his own business. Varun had a contract with the government to build dams throughout Devansh. Eventually, it became a battle with the local politicians about money, and he was forced to work with cheaper and cheaper materials. One day, he got a job to build a dam right outside the capital, Anika, for a city twenty miles south called Green Valley. In that city lived about a million people, and the nearby river was ferocious. The locals called it the Wild Horse River. He had instructed the politicians and the powers that be that in order for things to be done correctly, it would take five years. They stopped Varun right there and said it was to get done in three years or he would not get paid. Varun admitted he was frustrated and, at this point, just wanted the job off his hands. So Varun rushed like they wanted him to with the cheap material provided, and he had the dam they came to call Tamer Dam done in three years. Not even a year later, on a night clouded by heavy rain, the Tamer Dam cracked, and the river ripped through Green Valley, wiping out the million inhabitants. When Varun found out about what had happened, he lost interest in building for others and decided to focus on himself, selling the business and moving to the Brady Mountains. Varun also mentioned he was a fourth-generation engineer, so there was nothing he couldn't build or design.

Varun stretched and yawned like a tiger. "Well, we're not far now, so we may as well finish while we can." He slowly picked up Vanya. She winced with a groan and held onto his neck tight with both arms. Her leg was bound tight with a bloodied bandage. It shimmered red, and it would need to be changed soon.

Chapter 4

We arrived in the village of Trivoli, exhausted and hungry. It was warm out, and the sun was right in my eyes. I could feel the sun's rays against my brown skin, and boy did it feel rejuvenating. Varun put Vanya down and continued working on her leg to make sure it did not get infected. Lata touched her, telling her, "Relax. It won't hurt much longer." To Vanya's astonishment, the pain suddenly wasn't so bad. I saw a big rabbit hopping along the path that caught my attention. I followed it, and as I came to a hill, I saw the entire village for as far as I could see. The buildings were charred, and the trees were scorched. Anything that was alive was burnt to a crisp. I called the group over, and they looked onward in disbelief.

Catalan wanted answers, so she wandered down and dragged us along to see if the mage's house was still standing. As we walked through the village and through some of the burnt homes, they looked like they had been like this for a while as vines and other forms of nature started taking over the establishment. When we got to the heart of the village, several large craters were spread throughout. Catalan was at a loss for words. Tears began to run down Catalan's face as she began to wonder if her friend was alive. After about twenty minutes of walking, we finally came to the mage's house. I asked the others, "Does anyone have any snacks on them?"

Lata came to me and touched me on the shoulder, telling me, "You are fine." Varun kicked down the entrance door with his steel-toe boots. Catalan made her way into the mage's home. Vanya was limping in with a big stick that she had found on the ground for support. As Catalan looked around, she eventually spotted dried blood on the living room floor. I examined the room, spotting holes in the walls, holes on the floor, overturned furniture, and broken glass everywhere from the window and smashed television. Catalan continued making her way through the house, looking for more clues.

I had decided I needed some air. It was too stuffy inside. When I walked outside, I came face to face with the mage. She put a blue staff in my hand that began to glow brightly. I looked at her, and she was completely covered in blood. The mage was stumbling, but she kept forcefully backing me into the house until we were both inside. Everyone's eyes were directed our way when the mage slammed the door shut. I looked around the room and saw that everyone was a bit tense seeing all the blood the mage was covered in. Catalan asked the mage, "What happened?"

The old mage said, "My fear was that the great locks that prevent us in Devansh from going to other parts of the world were destroyed." The mage flipped over a seat to take a load off her feet and told Catalan to bring her a cup of water. The mage took her time to drink her water, but when she was done, the mage continued, "The longer that silver orb stays in this country, the more danger we are all in. Now if the Enlightened One gets his hands on the silver orb, then the problem becomes that more troublesome. We would have to defend Devansh and the rest of the world from invasion. A few days ago, the Third came here with his Sharm, and they demanded answers. When they didn't like what they received, they wiped out this entire village. They wanted to know why you guys were heading in our direction. We had no idea. I was sitting here eating with my fellow disciples when we were attacked. Everyone in this village was killed except me. I chased after the Third for what he did to my little village of Trivoli. I destroyed all the Sharm one at a time, nice and slow, as I forced information out of them. That is when one of them told me that the silver orb was back, and this time, there would be no stopping the Enlightened One from entering other parts of the world to conquer. It scared me enough to travel far northwest where one of the great ancient locks was only to see that, indeed, it had been destroyed."

The mage walked my way and said, "It has begun again, and by bringing that silver orb here, you have endangered the entire world, Brownie Kickfinger."

Catalan stepped forward and told the mage, "The reason we came was because we needed your help in destroying this thing."

The mage looked at Catalan and said, "Unless that thing decides to befriend you and reveal the name of the Enlightened One, then I hate to tell you that no one in this room could destroy it."

Catalan asked, "Then how did the other orbs get destroyed?"

I had gotten tired of waiting for a response and decided to ask the mage, "Why did you hand me this staff?" The mage looked at me, leaning forward, looking into my eyes, licking my face and ears, and smelling my clothes. I looked at the crazy old mage asking, "What the heck are you doing?"

The mage quietly began to speak. "It would appear that your bloodline originated from Devansh," Everyone in the room got quiet, the level of interest skyrocketed. "It would explain why someone like your father is so strong, even while being shadow-banned. I see right into you, Brownie Kickfinger. I see all the limitations you have placed on yourself from being bullied. Ostracized by your family and your community, your greatest power within you is screaming and yelling to come out. No wonder you have no confidence in yourself." I got a bit angry and told the old mage to shove the air tubes going up her nose where the sun doesn't shine.

The mage gave me the stink eye as she said, "This staff, Brownie, belongs to your family bloodline. I had a vision not too long ago to take a journey to a little island southwest of here called Duster Island, where I would retrieve the tool of the ancient bloodline. Your bloodline, Brownie, has untapped potential, but you're so damaged from the life you lived that you may never be able to truly help us, let alone the world. Place the silver orb atop the staff. Place it in the middle until it locks into place." Once I did as instructed by the mage, for the first time in my life, I felt connected to something. I looked at the mage, wondering what this feeling was. She smiled and said, "There might actually be hope for you yet, Brownie."

I said, "What do you mean?"

The mage said, "For now, let us all eat," as she spoke the words "restore," and the home, including the foundation, went back to its former self.

Once everyone ate their steak dinners and their bellies were full, Catalan, with a glass of whiskey in her hand, asked, "What is the next course of action?"

Varun was still licking his chops, wiping his lips, when he said, "I'm going to check on the condition of the remaining locks."

The mage's eyes locked onto Varun's eyes, and he said, "We might as well see what we are working with and see if there may be some way to buy us more time."

Vanya blurted out, "I'm ready to go back to Varmington. I don't want any more part of this journey. I want to go back to my cozy home and continue living out my life."

Lata looked at Vanya and told her, "Not only is it dangerous for you to go back but you can't turn a blind eye to what is in motion."

Vanya hit the table with her fist and said, "Come tomorrow morning, I will be heading back home to Varmington. I have contributed all I can to this journey." Vanya excused herself from the table and limped away to find a vacant room to fall asleep in for the night. Lata made it clear that she was behind me until the end.

Catalan said, "I can't let Vanya return home by herself. Not with that leg. I'll escort her back to Varmington, take care of a few things, and rejoin you at a later time."

The mage smiled and said, "Very good. You are all dismissed for bed, except you Brownie." I looked around and wondered what else the mage wanted.

I had been sitting several seats away from the mage when she told me to come sit next to her. I walked slowly over to her as I was a bit frightened without the others present. Upon taking my seat, the mage told me, "There is a collapsed space tower northwest of here, a several days journey. I would like for you to accompany me there."

"What will we be looking for?" I asked.

"Answers, of course. There once existed four space towers that predate Devansh. It's been said that in those towers, there is ancient knowledge far older than even this planet. Each tower was placed in a random location. It was said in the ancient scripture of the mages that these four towers were the first space vessels that brought the very first people from space to Devansh. Before the demise of the four towers, the mages looked at them as the pinnacle of civilization."

"So how did the tower you want us to visit meet its demise?" I asked.

The mage looked at me and said, "I will tell you along the way."

I made my way off to bed, but I did not feel tired. There was just too much on my mind. So I placed the staff against the wall and began staring at the silver orb. I was finally ready to call it a night when I heard a voice. I looked at the silver orb, and I began to hear a whispering voice. It was faint, but for the first time, I heard it. The orb was desperately trying to call its creator, to no avail. There was a pause until the orb began to focus its attention on me. It called me by my name, Brownie Kickfinger, demanding that I return it to its rightful owner. The silver orb began to open up like a cantaloupe cut into four sections. Everything around me went black, and I began to see a dark shadow walking toward me. The dark shadow hypnotized me and said I must only mutter these words, and death will come swiftly to me. The dark figure began, "I, Kickfinger, forfeit my life."

I felt compelled to repeat his words, and as I began speaking the words, I could feel a part of me slowly dying until an old man covered my mouth. The black shadow was furious, and the man stood in front of me, telling me that I must never come back here. The man, distracted by attending to me, was consumed by the black shadow. As I began to fade out of sight, I yelled, "Who are you?"

I could barely hear the man call back as the black shadow had all but consumed the man. "Row."

When I came back to my senses, the mage stood over me, telling me, "You must be very careful how you handle the orb, for it will do everything it can to be free of your grasp."

I told the mage, "I saw Lata's grandfather Row!"

"How could you be so sure?"

"Because he was the one that stopped me from speaking the words, and he yelled out his name to me." The mage lit her pipe and stood, thinking for a bit, then she told me, "It is time for bed," as she put a blanket over the orb and walked away.

In the morning, everyone went their own direction, and I began mine with the mage, scarfing down a sandwich she had made for me. My backpack was a little heavier than before, this time making sure I prepared for anything. I even had some special items that Varun gave me. Since we had time on our journey, I began to tell the mage how much of a failure I was back home. I told her about how the Kickfinger family fell apart the day my grandfather, Remo, disappeared. It was as if he had completely vanished from the face of the planet. Several other family members saw this as a great opportunity to purge the Kickfingers, and while I escaped with my life, I am not certain if all my siblings survived. What made it easier now was that my father had already been shadow-banned, and without the protection of my grandfather, we were open for attack.

The mage stood quiet. It almost looked like she was thinking several things through and wanted to say something. We wound up taking a rest near a few trees that were staggered next to one another. The mage pulled out an apple and asked me to continue telling her about life back home. I informed her that the dominant family, being the Wiohez, must have had all twenty families bowing before them by then. My cousin, Moy Wiohez, had most likely been named the new head over all the families. He had a great sense of leadership, knowledge, wealth, and respect. Many people also feared my cousin Moy because of his family. They were such a large family that I think I counted a thousand total family members, and they were heavily invested in multiple things within the economy. I am sure that if I was to ever return, my cousin would immediately have me killed for fear of being challenged. The mage tossed me a pear and said, "I knew your grandfather Remo."

I looked at her and said, "There was no way!"

She shook her head, smiling at me, telling me, "You are still too closed-minded." The mage continued, discussing the cult of wizards, "From recorded history, the wizards were actually the first ones to meet the people that came from the four space towers. Now much writing has been lost, but I gathered enough details to know the wizards were known for their power of pointing and sending people to other dimensions. One of them, as you know, is the Shadow

Dimension. Well, as the new inhabitants began to get smarter and grow in the way of science, they began to see the wizards as something unnatural. So they began hunting them down. Some time ago, for I myself am ancient, being kept alive by these special air tubes I created that are running up my nostrils, I met a wizard named Remo. This wizard was the one that got me interested in becoming a mage. He spent a few years teaching me in exchange for me helping with various tasks."

I asked the mage, "Who am I?"

"That is for you to find out, because if you don't, then I fear this planet will perish."

I had been so focused talking about myself that I had completely forgotten about Lata. I began to freak out, and the mage told me to calm down, informing me that she was fine.

"Why isn't she with us?" I snapped. The mage told me that she sent her on a mission, but I felt there was more she was not telling me. The mage looked at me again and noticed there was no fooling me, so she said the plan was for Lata to stay behind and distract the Third while we make our way to the ruins.

"I left a decoy version of you back at my home that Lata will be watching over, buying us time to get to the ruins without distraction."

I asked, "What happens if things get out of control for Lata?"

The mage told me, "She will be okay. Have confidence in Lata." The mage looked at me and added, "You should smile more, it fits you better."

As we continued our journey, we eventually came to a hill that looked over a land full of ruins. The mage pointed me to where the tower used to stand, and as I made it out, the tower was huge. We made our way down the hill and found ourselves among the ruins. I was surprised to see how much bigger the ruins were close up. As we made our way to where the tower had fallen, I asked the mage, "What exactly are we looking for?"

The mage said, "An entrance." I continued walking, looking around, and I did not notice how dark it had gotten when, in horror, I looked up into the sky and saw a black moon. I began to hear heavy stomping footsteps. I turned my head slowly in fear. In the darkness, I saw nothing except the shadows of crumbled walls. I could hear stomping that got louder and clearer, making its way toward us. The mage grabbed me and told me to run as fast as I could to the tower. When we got on top of the ruins of the tower, the mage, with her hand outstretched, began to mutter something I've never heard before nor could understand. It looked to me, with her staff in hand, that she was trying to command her surroundings to do something. The mage said she was trying to see if something would open for us. I looked over the ledge only to see the walls creeping with dark shadows. I then saw the dark shadow begin to crawl their way up the walls. I saw my father emerge from out of the group with a burnt face.

It began raining as the mage told me to prepare for battle whilst she continued to work on finding us an entrance into the tower. I reached into my backpack and pulled out a pack of gum that I began chewing ferociously, along with some grenades that I began tossing like a madman. I even found a machine gun that was nicely packed for me by Varun. In true Varun fashion, he modified it so that each shot fired was electrifying upon impact. I loaded my extended magazines and went to work on anything and everything that moved. I began shouting at the mage, "Found anything yet?" The mage said she needed more time. I was already doing the best I could as I came face-to-face with my father. I finally was able to see my father for what he was: a monster. I reached into my backpack and just happened to grab the staff. When I pulled it out, it shined a bright-blue color, and all my enemies before me stopped as I could see my father's surprised expression. My father had seen this staff before.

"I found it! I found the passage!" the mage shouted. I backed my way toward the entrance, and as I put the staff away, our enemies quickly advanced on us until the door closed shut.

The mage told me to stay close to her as we made our way through what was left of the space tower. We had to be careful with every step we took because this place looked like it was ready to collapse all at once. There were parts of the tower that were completely gone, walls that had collapsed long ago. It was big inside, though as the darkness got heavier, I pulled out the staff for some light, and, slowly but surely, the light began to appear on the walls and all around us. I even felt like the silver orb was directing me. The mage let me lead. As we continued walking, we began to see piles of skeletons spread throughout the area. The silver orb eventually led us into a great hall that looked like a giant library. I looked around and was amazed at how high the bookshelves were, let alone how many books there were. In the deep heavy darkness, a creepy dark voice spoke out. "What…do you…seek here?" It was a bit much for me to hear a moving voice in the darkness. I took a step backward and almost tripped over a pile of old books. A place known for educating oneself now looked like something suited for a dark lord.

The mage spoke up, "We came to find out more about the Enlightened One and how to destroy the final silver orb." I swear it sounded like the voice was behind me one second, then on the other side of the hall the next second. The mage told me to remain calm. "Whatever remains here in the dark must be ancient, so we must be careful." The voice shifted to an authoritarian tone; the words alone began to create a spiral of darkness around us.

"I have been waiting for you…in particular," the voice said.

I yelled out, "What do you want with me?"

"As the one dark god, I can give you power…oh, so much power." The voice's sneer made by stomach churn.

I yelled out at the voice, "I don't care what you're offering me! I want nothing to do with it!"

I stood back-to-back with the mage as the voice spoke, "You came for knowledge…so I shall grant you knowledge. The Enlightened One…was originally a human who managed to make his way to the final standing space tower to the northeast of Devansh that the wizards were on the verge of destroying. This human, on that day, came across forbidden knowledge. Not knowing exactly what he was doing, he performed the ritual that would…sacrifice his will and spirit to be replaced by the appointed successor of the Fect."

The mage forcefully told the voice, "Explain yourself!"

"On the home planet of the Fect, they appointed a sole ruler known as the Successor to ensure their race lived forever."

The mage said, "There is no such thing!"

"The Fect have been around since about the beginning of time. Creating orbs as vessels is what they do in order to create a new successor."

While listening to the voice, I had a bad feeling that the Fect did not have the greatest plans in mind for the planet or the cosmos. The voice got louder as it revealed, "When the new dark successor arises, we will begin to eradicate all imperfect life in the universe." The voice began to laugh louder and louder and louder until the mage grabbed me to follow her. Just then, a loud bang could be heard. The one dark god's words could be heard. "I am Gilsavel, I gave you a chance for power, and you denied me. You could have been one of my strongest dark wizards, but instead, you will now drown in here in a ruin of knowledge."

We ran as fast as we could, but we could not outrun the water that came pouring in from all directions. By the time we managed to get back to the door, we were nearly out of space to breathe. For whatever reason, I pulled out the staff, and the door opened. We came shooting out, water spilling into the surroundings. We did not stop running until we got up the hill and saw the entire ruins covered in water.

Chapter 5

I was so happy to have made it up the hill that it was not until I took a seat on a random boulder that I saw acres of dragon bamboo a hundred feet tall. I looked at the mage and asked, "Did we go up a different hill?"

The mage looked around and then up to the night sky and said, "It would appear so." The mage came to a complete halt. Suddenly, I heard some footsteps clanking our way. We quickly ran inside the dragon bamboo fields. My heart was thumping so loud I thought it would give me away. As the clanking got closer, two six-foot-tall Cassowaries bearing the bright gold mark of the Enlightened One on their foreheads arrived at the boulder I was sitting on just moments ago. The mage looked at me and told me, "It would appear the Enlightened One has many servants looking for you, Brownie Kickfinger, not just his Sharm."

I asked the mage, "How come you do not have a mark?" The mage went quiet, and she began to explain as we walked deeper into the dragon bamboo field.

"When I was a little girl, my family lived further north of here in a farmland community called New Water. The entire community was related to me in one way or another. We had chickens, cows, and all kinds of animals. My father, Spark Nugget, was respected for being both a great teacher and a great leader. In fact, he taught everyone how to farm the land. My mother, Avalon Nugget, had come from a city a hundred miles east of New Water called High Bolt City, which was run entirely by foreigners. They would arrive in their massive spaceships early in the year, and by the end of summer, they would leave. They would take everything with them, using the location primarily as a swap meet. The foreigners believed the region was prime for the many trade routes it was connected to in Devansh. The city would remain uninhabited until the foreigners returned the following year. Some would arrive a month or so early to begin the process of cleaning the city, setting up the markets, and then tearing everything down at the end of summer. They loved to trade all kinds of things from all over the world and all over the cosmos. Well, my mother happened to be a human who was being sold in one of the markets. One day, a fight broke out over a major gambling bet gone sideways that led to a violent riot with multiple fires, shootings, killings, and explosions. My mother used the fire to set her bound hands and feet free." The mage took a second to clear her throat, collect her thoughts, and rub her hands together.

"My mother made the best of her situation and ran for her life. She had no idea where she was going, but as long as she was free, she did not care. Eventually, my mom got so tired of running and going days without eating that she fainted on one of the muddy roads. My father just so happened to be passing by to go sell some of his cows in the city when he saw my mother. He picked her up, nursed her back to health, and allowed her to say at his farm. She helped him around the farm and learned the trade. She decided she didn't want to leave and then shortly thereafter, they married. My parents hit it off pretty well. My mother was intended to be a gift to the Sharm as a token of peace to the Enlightened One. She was exotic, the first human ever seen in Devansh. My parents figured after thirty years that if they had not been discovered by now, then they must have just moved on from worrying about my mother. When my mom first told me and all of my siblings her story, we all laughed and thought our parents were just trying to be funny. We never took it seriously, and life continued.

"Time was spent milking the cows and helping my family maintain the farm. The work never stopped, but boy did my mother's cooking make up for it all, especially the apple and peach pies she would make. We would always get on Mom to tell what her secret recipes were so we could write a cookbook, but she would not give up her secrets. My father loved to hunt, and he would always bring me along with me. He showed me everything he knew, and eventually, he made me in charge of going out and bringing something back to eat for the whole family. One day, while hunting for a while, a nice-sized moose finally appeared. I shot and field dressed it all by myself. Coming back home with all this meat put a smile on my face, until I saw the mile long stream of black smoke rising over the trees. New Water was on fire. All the animals had been killed, and its residents had been executed in front of their homes. Screams were coming from my aunt Pelos Proudhorn's home. The Sharm had killed all my aunt's family, and I shot the three Sharm in the head. My aunt was so happy to see me. I asked if she had seen my parents. She shook her head, but she did tell me that the Sharm were all heading toward my parents' home. She said they came looking for my mother.

"By the time I got there, the house was surrounded with Sharm, and my aunt and I hid in the distance listening to what was being said. My entire family was on their knees, and a hooded Sharm calling himself as the Third was passing judgment on my father. The Third told my father that for taking what belonged to the Enlightened One, he was to be executed, and his entire bloodline was to be branded with the mark to serve when called. Then I watched as they hacked my father's head off. I screamed out, but my aunt Pelos had already covered my mouth, telling me to calm down or I was going to get the both of us killed. The Third walked up to each one of my siblings and put his palm on their foreheads, branding them with the mark on their foreheads. My mother was then taken away on a small spacecraft with the Third. I do not know what overcame me, but in anger, I started shooting and killing as many Sharm as I could until one finally shot me in the stomach. They dragged me and put me in front of my siblings. They easily captured my aunt Pelos. One by one, starting with my aunt, they murdered the rest of my family.

"In the end, I could not stop crying. I asked that they finish me as well so that I join my family. They were going to oblige until an individual with a blue robe was making his way toward us. The Sharm all told this individual to stop in his tracks or he would be shot. Well, the individual kept walking until he must have gotten tired of hearing them. He stopped and pointed at all of them, telling them all to stand still. All the Sharm stood frozen in place, and the next thing I know, he pulls out a staff and starts complaining about his back. He uses it to make his way to me. Finally, once in front of me face-to-face, I asked the man, 'Who the heck are you?' He loudly said, 'You can call me Remo.'"

The mage whispered to me as she could hear the footsteps of the two cassowaries lurking around, "We are going to stay put for a bit while the enemy lurks in the darkness."

I smiled as I looked at the mage, telling her, "You really did know my grandfather."

The mage looked at me and said, "I guess so. The mage took a breath through her magical air tubes and reminded me that she was ancient after all. The only reason she is still alive is because of her specially created air tubes pumping air into her lungs.

The mage sighed and continued, "From that day forward, I spent years with him traveling all over Devansh. The adventures we had together were out of this world." I looked at the mage very enviously, and she could tell, but she quietly continued as she put her red robes over us. The mage led with how mesmerized she always was of listening to Remo talk about the Cult of Wizards. To her, they sounded like complete badasses. "Remo would tell me how much he enjoyed traveling and coming across new things in the cosmos. The cult had apparently been founded when one of them pointed at a tree and it exploded. This wizard came to be known as Abir. Well, Abir spent years trying to understand what the heck he was doing when he pointed at something. Abir spent time writing down about his feelings, thoughts, emotions. One day, Abir was alone in the forest, starving and cold. He had run out of food, and he forgot to go hunting that morning. He watched a squirrel pass by him with a walnut in its hands. With envy, he pointed at the squirrel and told it to stop. Then it did, and it held the walnut out to him. On that day, Abir came to terms with the fact that he could use his thoughts to command his surroundings. He began to wonder if there were others like him, so he spent much time focusing his thoughts and projecting them in every direction. He figured that if there were others like him, one of them would hear him.

"Years passed by, and Abir began to lose hope. During that time, to stay positive, he continued to explore his mind and gain a better understanding of his ability. One day, it hit him. He had been tapping into the cosmic language, and sure enough, he would discover that there were others that used the cosmic language in different forms. So instead of just pointing, Abir began snapping. Shortly after, Abir would be greeted by five newcomers, one of which was Remo. It would take another two hundred years to build the Cult of Wizards, and many issues arose in that time. The biggest problem, according to Remo, was the cult's war with the beings from the space towers, the Fect. Remo told me how the cult was viewed as a threat to the future plans of the Fect." I felt like a little kid grinning hearing about my grandfather. I wanted her to tell me everything. She knew she had my undivided attention by the way she kept looking at me, deciding what to tell me now or hold off for later.

The mage took a couple deep breaths and began again, "By the time your grandfather had met me fifty years prior, Aziza, who was one of the last remaining wizards, had passed away, making your grandfather the last surviving member of the cult. Your grandfather took me to a temple where he put Aziza's body to rest. I was told Aziza was concerned that they would all die out before fulfilling their duty."

I jumped in while the mage was taking another breath, "What was the Cult of Wizards' duty?"

The mage finished her breath and answered, "I did not know. Remo never told me. That said, the fact that your grandfather built an entire temple for Aziza, and Aziza alone, implies how important he must have been. We spent years at that temple, and now that I think about it, it is where I need to take you, Brownie Kickfinger."

I looked at the mage, drooling all over myself, asking, "Where is the temple located?"

The mage thought hard about it and told me, "About a four-day walk east of here." I wanted to know more, and I motioned for the mage to continue. She shook her head and stretched her shoulders. Through a deep yawn, she said "Not tonight. There will be plenty of time for stories tomorrow." I was disappointed, but I would be tired too after talking for so long. I tossed my backpack on the ground and stretched out, the stars partly obscured from the tall dragon bamboo fields we were in. I prayed in my mind that I would not snore loudly so that I would not draw any unwanted attention from the two cassowaries from earlier.

In the morning, we both woke up starving. I wanted an omelet, and the mage wanted a skillet. We walked faster and faster through the dragon bamboo fields, joking about stumbling onto a nest of eggs. The mage's stomach began to growl when she told me how much she loved rambutan, kiwano, jaboticaba, lychee, durian, and mangosteen.

"The northeastern part of Devansh is abundant in animals, exotic plants, and some of the most amazing views of the ocean. One of the last times I was with Remo, he said he loved jackfruit, so we would locate these jack trees and start collecting as much of the fruit as we could. Well, after a while, these elephants would come storming in, eating all the jackfruit like there was no tomorrow. So we found ourselves having to bull-rush our way out of there with all this jackfruit. Pretty much the entire eastern region is known for its splendor, including some of the most beautiful marine life and active volcanoes. That land is called the Land of the Gods, and it's where the Enlightened One built his temple.

"There was a time when Remo went around Devansh collecting exotic plants like the flower king or the Dutchman's-pipe, and many more. Remo's crown jewel was the Middlemist red flower. We spent months in the islands off the upper northeast regions of Devansh to locate that flower. When we found it, it brought such a smile to your grandfather. I think, in a lot of ways, it reminded him of someone special to him. He would just never tell me, but I could read it all over his face. I enjoyed the garden and all the unique additions he added to Aziza Temple, including all the capybara that roamed the area freely. It is funny, because they like to spend a lot of their time swimming in the river that flows through the rear of the temple. In those days, I saw Remo more of a collector, trying to leave something memorable behind while taking the time to teach me the ways of the Cult of Wizards. I am not sure if he was just exhausted and had decided to go a different route with me, but his teachings were more stories than anything else. I did everything to the letter as he would describe it to me, yet I never managed to connect with the cosmic language in the way he intended for me to." The mage rumbled through a small bag and took a long swig from a bottle of water.

"I truly believe the war with the Fect haunted Remo. From what I saw, I would say he suffered from post-traumatic stress disorder, because at night, it was the worst. I could hear him screaming out the names of his brothers. I could hear him sleepwalking and acting out different parts of the war on different nights. It would get so violent at times that he would wake up to things broken around him. This world does not know, Brownie Kickfinger, but I do. If it was not for the Cult of Wizards and the stand they made, then none of us would be here right now. The Fect would have wiped out the entire world's armies and then began massacring its inhabitants to make rise for their own people and purpose on this planet. While the Fect were all wiped out, thanks to the Cult of Wizards, we have to ensure that we destroyed the First, the Second, and the Third."

I looked at the mage, who had a serious face, and asked her, "Why?"

The mage took a second to respond and told me, "It is because they are the only three that survived the war. They were then transformed into higher beings by the Enlightened One's powers."

I suddenly felt scared. I began to ask myself, *How in the world are we going to stand toe to toe with the Fect if all the wizards are gone? It took them years to defeat the Fect, and here I am now in the middle of all this with no power.* I began to shake in fear until the mage slapped me across the face. The mage reminded me that fear was the most powerful enemy of reason, and for me to trust her, she is going to do all she can to try and give me a fighting chance.

"Darkness arose once in Devansh, and, thanks to Remo and others, it was defeated. You are of his bloodline, and now Devansh is asking you to stand like your grandfather did. You need to know that the wizards were dealing with two enemies at the same time. Gilsavel, the one dark god, appeared out of nowhere with his dark wizards, looking to eradicate us. Remo had managed to shadow-ban many of them, but Remo began to become unhinged himself. When the dark wizards were thought to be defeated, nobody saw Remo for a while. There were dark forces that still searched for Remo, but they could not find him, so Masta became the next best thing. Masta had been going around Devansh doing as much good as she could from bringing running water to the villages to providing food to the poor and refugees. Masta, at this point, was more popular than Remo since he was spending time with Aziza. Masta spent years being involved in all kinds of humanitarian work."

The mage tapped her wrinkled old head. "I recall reading everything I possibly could about Masta from the wizard archives. I was obsessed over her. Masta loved adventure and had gotten involved with Devansh's politics, helping the first woman become president. Masta even tried starting her own school of wizards, but for some reason, the students she would take on never managed to display any sort of abilities or connection to the cosmic language. This concerned her a great deal, and she wondered if there was a problem that the Cult of Wizards needed to address. She was running around looking for Remo when, one day, she came face-to-face with a dark wizard by one of the active volcanoes in Devansh close to the great barrier reef to the far east."

I interrupted, "How do you know of all this? It's like you were actually there."

"At death, every wizard leaves a little magic behind that is collected, analyzed, and sorted in the wizard archives, accounting for every detail that wizard experienced from birth until death." The mage's eyes turned red like a raging bull as she continued, "That day Masta battled with the dark wizard, and she lost. He killed her and took her orange staff. After Masta's death, a familiar darkness began to take rise again in Devansh. The locals started to tell stories of how their neighbors had begun to disappear and how black wizards had begun to be spotted throughout the land." The mage needed time to breathe and took another sip of water.

"Remo was crushed when he finally heard what happened to Masta. At Aziza Temple, Remo placed a giant rock eight hundred feet high in Masta's honor. After several years, he would use it as a punching bag to take out his frustration, eventually breaking a piece of the rock. It put a toll on Remo knowing both Aziza and Maska were gone now. One day, he was outside in the woods, eating some king coconut. I noticed he had put his staff against a tree. Remo kept walking, and I asked him what he was going to do with his staff. Remo ignored my question and acted like he did not hear me. Instead, he told me to hurry up. He wanted to get some cotton fruit. I did not make much of it until we kept walking, and every time I asked him when we would be going back, he would change the subject or ask me how far we were from my home in Trivoli. We finally stopped because he was hungry and had brought a lot of amazing vegetables with him. I could see him smiling again, so I did not say anything for a while. He was not lying when he mentioned he had packed vegetables the day we arrived. Remo was so hungry that he cooked up some nopales with eggs and salad.

"Two weeks had passed since we had left Aziza temple. The next morning, I had plans to sit down and have a real conversation with Remo, but when he never came out of his room, I went to check, and he was gone. I just knew that I would never see him again, and I felt he was ready for a new life. When he left Devansh, I took it that he found his peace in his wife and grandchildren.

We power walked all the way to the outskirts of Aziza Temple from the side of the hill. The mage pointed in the distance to the section of the woods where the dragon fruit trees were telling me, "That area is part of the temple." I was so excited. The closer we got, the more I was able to make out the miracle fruit, durian, red fruit, hog plum, and all the fields of vegetables that included Romanesco, birdhouse gourd, purple corn, yuca root, and so much more. As I was one step away from entering paradise, the Third's voice called out to us from behind. I took a step back. The mage told me, "On my mark, you're going to run as fast as you can."

The Third began to speak, "Aah, I should have known this is where you'd end up. You're lucky you've made it this far." As I looked around, I began to see the Sharm hiding in the shadows of the trees and brush in front of us.

The mage told the Third, "It was a good thing that we have quick feet."

The Third gave a light chuckle to that and said, "Either way, it does not matter. The moment you step foot over into its boundaries, we cannot touch you. We are aware that the entire region that belongs to Aziza Temple is protected." The Third, this time, took a few steps forward and looked directly at me and told me, "This place is going to be your demise. For the moment that you step out, I will be waiting for you. I hope for your sake, Brownie Kickfinger, that when you decide to walk out of the protection of this sanctuary, that you have awakened something within you to at least make the fight a little more interesting before you perish." The Third took one more step, and the mage grabbed onto me tightly with her left hand. The Third snapped his fingers, and thousands of arrows, bullets, and laser fire were quickly coming our way when the mage forced us back another step, and the projectiles turned into flames, and the lasers fizzled into nothing.

The Third told me one last thing. "Remember this clearly, Brownie Kickfinger. Even if you do become a wizard, I have killed my fair share of them. It won't help you as much as you hope. Your friend there can tell you, in detail, the times I snapped a purple wizard's neck like a twig, or the last moments of a gray wizard's life when I plunged my dagger into his chest…for the eighth time." I was a little shaken up, so I trembled my way forward, forcing myself to turn my back on the Third.

Chapter 6

The mage grabbed my shoulder as I swayed back and forth. I stopped wobbling and came to a halt. The mage said, "Raise the staff as high as you can." I grabbed the staff out of my backpack, and when I raised it into the air, nothing happened. Then, after several seconds, I began to feel the energy emanating from all around me, making its way toward me. It was then that I felt something within myself again, a monstrous power within me ripping my insides apart, fighting to make its way to the surface.

I asked the mage, "What is this feeling inside of me?"

It brought tears to my eyes, and she looked at me and said, "Follow me." I could feel the staff radiating with power. I could feel it trying to connect with me, but I was not ready. It had too much power that made it difficult for me to wield. I could hear it speaking to me. It wanted me to call out its name. It wanted me to hold it up and scream out its name. It was asking too much of me, so I threw it into the field of tiger melons. I could tell that the mage had her concerns by the bewildered look on her face, but she kept them to herself. She grabbed the staff and told me she would hold onto it for now.

As we continued walking to the center, I could see birds, squirrels, elephants, and so much more. I was awestruck, but I was also getting hungry again. I saw some white asparagus that I grabbed and started chowing down on. The mage looked at me and told me, "Hurry up. We will eat when we arrive." I could not help myself. I even grabbed some June plum that I was biting into like a little kid smiling away. The mage, struggling to catch her breath, told me that everything within the temple is magically powered, and it allows the growth of practically anything. When we arrived at the Temple of

Aziza, I was amazed. It was huge, and at the front was a statue of Abir greeting all those who arrived. I noticed that the mage yanked something bright, cheery yellow off this eight-foot tree. The mage told me, "Every time you come to visit from here on out, make sure you pluck some of Buddha's hand and place it at the base of Abir's statue as a sign of appreciation for his welcoming hand into the temple."

I started walking toward the steps of the temple when the mage turned around and told me to stop. "This is where you will begin your training. Also, the only people welcome inside the temple to enjoy its many paradises are the ones who know who they are."

I looked at the mage and said, "That's not fair! Who are you?"

The mage looked at me and said, "I am Vanas the mage, and who are you, Brownie Kickfinger?" I felt an immediate internal struggle and could not answer. Vanas looked at me and said, "Until you find out who you are, you will be sleeping, training, eating, and bathing outside."

The first thing Vanas ordered me to do was take a bath in the river. Man, when I jumped in the water, it was freezing, and my skin started to turn blue. I scrubbed and washed off as fast as I could. I put my towel on, and before I took another step, I noticed I was surrounded by multiple purple frogs. They were all staring at me with wide bug eyes, slightly slanted, as if they were judging me. I had also noticed Vanas had left me a black fitness suit to put on with some black tennis shoes. I returned to the front of the temple where Vanas had some halibut and salad ready for us. Vanas served me using jerk teak leaves, while I used a banana leaf as a plate. After the delicious meal, Vanas took me to the giant rock where I saw where my grandfather had broken a piece off the enormous boulder. Vanas told me, "Every day, you're going to be pointing at this boulder until you make a connection with the cosmic language that will awaken your ability to break a piece off it." I was at it for hours, pointing at the giant boulder, getting nowhere fast, and I began to get distracted by my surroundings.

To my right, I saw a red panda eating some bamboo, looking at me with what appeared to be a wave in my direction. I looked to my left, and a sloth bear was hanging upside down, eating mangoes.

It almost felt like they were watching me with a purpose, almost as a scout would. I decided to go on my ten-mile jog for the day. I was trying to tap into this cosmic language Vanas was speaking of by running and pointing, but nothing was working. It was weird for me, but after my running and stretching, Vanas would have me hugging trees for about thirty minutes. She told me it would reduce my stress, improve my immunity, and lower my blood pressure. She also claimed it would accelerate my recovery from illness or trauma, but I am curious if there would be any kind of side effects. There were days she had me running through some arduous obstacle courses, as if it were set up for special forces.

A month had passed, and Vanas did not let up for a moment. She was being ruthless with my training. Since I arrived, she has pushed me hard. At this point, all my fingers were in pain from poking trees all day. Vanas told me, "I expect for you to make holes into the trees one day soon and to be able to do the one-finger handstand."

I was getting frustrated with Vanas and was telling her, "You're full of it. There's no way I could make a hole in a tree with my finger." Vanas, with her left index finger, made a hole in the tree, then easily began doing one finger handstand push-ups. I was flabbergasted, so I decided I would not complain anymore and just do my best at whatever I was instructed to do.

The next training activity was one of the hardest for me. Vanas had me meet her at the river. Vanas then explained to me, "In order to complete this particular training, you are going to have to run on water." I looked at Vanas like she was demented. I looked around, and yet again, I caught sight of a few elephants looking at me, making me nervous. Vanas saw my hesitation and reminded me why we were here by telling me, "For one thing, it's your duty to your bloodline to become a wizard. On the other hand, if you don't try, the Third is going to rip your head off, so, for your sake, learn." Vanas instructed, "The idea is to run and point in front of you using your connection to the cosmic language to create, say, an idealized plywood plank." Well, I ran across the river, pointing, and quickly found myself going into the water. After an hour, Vanas disappeared, and my doubt began to kick in. I felt like I was hearing voices in my mind telling me that I am nothing special, yelling at me, calling me a loser, making me feel like a nobody. I tried all day until night had fallen. I pulled myself out of the cold river and looked up. I saw an amazing visual of our galaxy. It was truly magnificent watching the twinkling specks of light that dominated the dark sky.

The next morning's training started at four o'clock, like usual. I began my typical stretches when I noticed a green glowing figure walking through the woods. All I was able to make out in the glow was a pointed hat and a flowing cloak. I did not hear much of anything as it poked a staff in the ground with each step. I really started to wonder if something was wrong with me.

When Vanas met up with me for the morning, she wanted me to bear crawl all the way down to the river from the flight of stone steps in the back. After a few attempts at it, Vanas then wanted me to do handstands making my way down to the river. By the time I was done, I fell asleep at the bottom of the river. I was exhausted. I didn't even remember falling asleep. I know I passed out with a lot of doubt in my heart, and I felt the darkness trying to overcome me in fear. I remember having my eyes closed and then seeing my grandfather. He poured some fresh cold water into my mouth and grabbed my hand, telling me to get up. I remember standing there, finding nobody around at four in the morning, listening to the birds sing. When I turned around, I saw Vanas was looking at me. She said, "Are you ready to continue with the next exercise?"

I told her yes! She took me back to the big stone, and there stood two big pots that came all the way up to my waist. The first pot was filled with water, and the second was filled with sand. She told me that I was to start with striking the water first, then the sand, alternating an hour at a time. I found it more tiring and painful striking my palm into the sand than into the water. What made it worse was, that day, it decided to rain, and it got a bit chilly out. I began to feel miserable, but I knew I had to keep going. After many hours, with each strike I made into the water, I finally felt like I was making a connection. I could hear the voice of the water getting louder in my head, and I could feel all my dark thoughts being washed away. I kept pushing and striking until I felt like an empty vessel, ready to take in quality thoughts. I felt a cosmic awakening within me, so I pointed at the water, telling it to explode out of the pot. The water exploded out, shattering the pot into pieces. As I looked around me, I started to feel connected to something more, as if a bolt of lightning had struck me. Vanas was standing behind me, telling me how very pleased she was with me.

"But much more work is still ahead," she said as she tossed me some finger lime fruit.

The next day came, and Vanas had me stand in front of a giant boulder, and the first exercise was putting my hands in between a machine with two giant stone rollers. The following exercise was driving nails into a wood plank and pulling them out with three fingers until I was doing it simply by my command from pointing. I was feeling it that day, and I could see a few pangolins looking at me to see what I was doing. Suddenly, an enormous bang echoed out from behind me. I turned around, and Vanas came storming out the temple. I ran in the direction of the sound. I ran so fast that I didn't even notice that I passed Vanas. When I heard that bang again, something inside of me went off as though I could sense there was someone that needed help.

I ran outside the barrier to see Lata, who was in trouble. Several Sharm had just grabbed her and tossed her to the ground, kicking her violently. I lost control, as if a cosmic force came bursting out of me. I pointed at one of the Sharm and made a hole in his head. The other three I froze in place, and the fourth one was consumed by the ground. I never considered how draining this would be on my entire body. That's when I came face-to-face with the final Sharm, but I was out of gas. The Sharm grabbed me and repeatedly slammed me to the ground, punching me in the face with all its might. I could feel a part of me calling out. It sounded like a beating drum, a heartbeat that exploded in my mind, and I came to my senses again. My staff was suddenly in my hand, and I pointed it at the Sharm, blasting it into outer space with a beam of light. I picked up Lata, who had been knocked out by the Sharm. She was full of bruises and cuts all over her body. Some blood had gotten onto her white hair. As I brought her behind the barrier, I could hear the Third's voice yelling back at me. "This one is special to you, I see. I thought she might prove a good distraction for you."

I turned around, looked at the Third square in the face, and stared him down until Vanas showed up, touching me, and commanding me, "Let's go."

The next day, Vanas had me hugging trees all morning again. I was annoyed because I wanted to speak with Lata. Since she took her inside the temple, I could not go to her. Well, I had had it. I started hugging the biggest trees that I could find and pulling them straight out of the ground. "That's it!" I screamed. I made my way to the steps of the entrance, and the very first step I took led to an explosion that sent me flying. When I finally landed, I was in bad shape. I quickly began to panic out of desperation for survival. I worked on calming my mind, trying not to think of the parts of my body that were bleeding. My left hand was still mobile, so I touched the dirt, and, with my thoughts, I connected with my surroundings. I asked the trees, plants, and everything around me to provide me with some of its natural energy. This was a good start, but I still needed more juice. I looked to my left and saw a ton of giant forest ants. I pointed at them and finally managed to connect my pointing with my thoughts. I asked the ants if they could throw me into the river so that I could fully heal. The ants immediately got together, picked me up, marched me over to the river, and tossed me in. When I popped my head out of the water, Vanas was shaking her head at me.

"You could have been killed by the barrier protecting the temple," she said. Vanas did give me a little smirk. "At least you're getting better at tapping into the cosmic language." Vanas told me to follow her to the temple. When we got to the front of the temple, Lata was there waiting for us, wearing the same uniform as me.

I screamed, "Lata! What happened? You look like you haven't been scratched!"

"Vanas is one heck of a healer. She used her powers to heal me. Look, not even a scar." I told Lata to stop talking as I hugged her so tightly. She pleaded for me to let her go because I was suffocating her.

Vanas said, "There are a few things that I feel it is time for me to let you know." I looked at both women, a bit surprised, as if waiting to hear something bad. Vanas started, "I taught Lata years ago how to use cosmic language. One day, during her training, she had a vision that she would find the last wizard. You, Brownie Kickfinger, came to Lata, and now here you are, still working out the details for yourself. The final thing from here on out, Brownie, is that you will be training with Lata. There are a few matters I need to attend to."

Later, I suddenly awoke to Lata having some coffee ready, along with a few omelets with some juice, fruit, and some cereal. Lata told me, "You better eat up, because we are in for a long day." After breakfast, she wanted my mind clear, so she had a table outside ready with two chairs. On the table, Lata had a chessboard ready, and for about a solid hour, we played chess as elephants, giraffes, giant tortoises, and many other critters pulled up alongside us as spectators. After several matches, Lata asked me to find an elephant and start doing squats with the elephant on my back.

I looked at Lata and asked, "Are you kidding me?" Lata touched one of the elephants next to her, and it immediately got on her back, and she started carrying it on her back. I guess she was improvising for not having a squat rack. Then she grabbed the tortoise and started using them like dumbbells. I got under one elephant, but it did not want to listen to me and walked off on me.

I lost track of time. At one point, I had grown a full beard that came down to my neck. One day, Lata had me training with a bear. She told me that the bear had beef with me ever since I knocked down the bear's honey tree a few days ago during my training. I was pointing at the bear and sending it commands, but I kept getting yelled at by Lata, saying I was sending the wrong commands. The bear wrestled me to the ground and finally sat on me. I was wiped out from the workout. Lata smiled at me, telling me, "I won't ever tell anyone that you lost to a bear." She then touched me on the shoulder and said, "Rejuvenate." She helped me up and said, "Follow me."

When we got to the river, Lata pointed at the river and said, "Do you hear the river speaking, Brownie?" I shook my head. Lata said, "Let go of what is holding you back inside. Let yourself become vulnerable to the world around you, and become unshakable by unlocking yourself." Lata pointed at the river again and said, "Listen, Brownie. The water is using the cosmic language right now to talk to you, commanding you to look at its beauty and to wade into its waters. Since the day you walked into this place, it has been calling to you, Brownie, and you have just been letting the phone ring. The birds sing to you every morning, telling you to wake up for your training. They have been your alarm without you even realizing it, and at the same time, they have been trying to get you to sing with them. Think about the trees you have been hugging. Vanas didn't have you doing that for your health. The trees here told her they wanted to get up close and personal with you to get to know you. The way they really feel someone out is with a great big hug. These trees have been sending you commands, Brownie, and you have only been doing them because you had been instructed to. Everything around you is here to protect you. I know you lived a hard life, Brownie, but when you touch something, you have the ability to see its beginning in this cosmos for the sole fact you have wizard blood running through your veins. Your greatest power is still locked away because you have been hurt over and over again by the people you loved or who said they loved you. Trust us, Brownie. Trust me!"

I did not know how to completely let go. I wanted to and had been trying. Lata came up to me and said, "You're not alone anymore. You are home. You just don't want to believe it yet. You'd rather self-sabotage and run off somewhere like you have before." I began to feel that calling again within my heart. I began to hear the voice clearer as I let go of another lock within me, and when I opened my eyes, I had my staff in my hand. I felt my power flowing through the mighty staff, and as I lifted the heavy staff with my own might, I directed a great beam of blue energy at the giant boulder, blasting a piece off.

I had been so caught up training with Lata that I had not taken the time to notice that I had not seen Vanas in months. When she came back, she would stay for the day, talk with Lata, and then be gone for months again. I had just finished jump roping when Lata threw me a blue milk mushroom and informed me, "Today, I am going to wrap you in towels so that when I touch them, they will become freezing cold. You will also be standing on two pillars in a squatting position while doing this, but you will be holding bowls filled with water on each hand. Your job will be to tap into the cosmic language to use your mind to heat the freezing towel and warm the bowls without dropping them."

She had me wrapped up like an uptight monk. I was freezing and was finding it hard to focus. I was annoyed by the exercise. My legs started to feel like butter after about six hours. My shoulders were on fire, and that was the thought I went with. I began to think of fire, and after a while, I felt like I had connected to something. I could feel the warmth all over my body. When I opened my eyes, Lata looked at me in amazement. She said, "For about an hour now, you have been floating in the air in your squatting posture as a bright-blue flame encircled your entire body, drying you up and heating up the water in the bowls."

Lata got serious with me and told me, "In one hour, meet me in the dojo that is in the woods." I went to the table where the chessboard was and ate all the blue milk mushroom that was left, including the akebi. I drank down the blended gấc fruit and ate all the pan-roasted Romanesco that was left for me. At that moment, I began to realize I had no idea where the dojo was in the woods. I honestly had never seen it nor heard about it from Vanas. Then it dawned on me.

Let's see if all this training has paid off, I thought. I pointed at the trees in front of me and asked them if they could tell me the direction of the dojo. After a few seconds, the trees that I pointed at leaned over to the left until I saw a trail to follow. I told the trees "thank you" as I began jogging my way over.

When I arrived at the dojo, it was nothing like I had ever seen. It was huge, and outside of it was a statue of my grandfather pointing his hand at the wizard Aziza. Aziza was pointing his staff at my grandfather. Lata was standing in the dojo courtyard, waiting for me as I arrived with five minutes to spare. "It's good to see that you are finally using your brain, because if you would have been late, I would have had you doing push-ups and pull-ups all night." Lata got serious, and it went dead silent to the point that I was able to hear a single leaf hit the ground. Lata said, "This is where I am going to show you how to use what some call a wand, cane, staff, or what I like to call a pointing stick." Lata raised her hand, and a marvelously crafted brown staff came to her. Lata could see that I was mind blown by the magnificence of the staff.

I took a long second and asked Lata, "You're a wizard?"

Lata smiled and said, "Yes, Brownie! But I am also glad that I have found the last wizard so that we can help bring an end to the Fect once and for all." Lata looked at me and said, "Now stand in front of me, and call your staff." I tried calling it, but nothing happened. Lata asked me, "Do you know why you are having problems?"

I said no!

Lata shook her head. "Because that staff is an extension of you, Brownie. You have been treating your pointing stick like it is just some item or thing to be left lying around. That pointing stick has a name. Call your pointing stick." I closed my eyes and began to focus, letting my mind reach out. Then, slowly but surely, I could hear it. A vision formed in my mind, and I was able to see that I had left the pointing stick by the chessboard. Finally, I called its name, Alaric, and before I knew it, it was in my right hand. Lata said, "Good, because now that you have called its name, Brownie, you may finally begin to take your place amongst us. From here on out, you will be known as Alaric the wizard. Now listen, Alaric, you are aware of your finger-pointing attacks, but those same attacks are quadrupled with your staff in hand. The same goes for your defenses. This staff should never leave your sight. Your staff is your tool to create or your tool to destroy. When I say 'begin,' the two of us will commence in battle. Do not hold back, Alaric." Lata quickly turned and hopped to the other side of the dojo. She readied her staff, and, seeing the look of steel in her eyes, I brought mine up as if I was going to block whatever she planned on throwing at me. My heart started to pound with each passing moment of silence.

"Begin," her voice ranged out with ferocity. The two of us clashed as if we were holding swords. After so many clashes, Lata yelled out to me, "Your pointing stick can do so much more! Open your mind!" Lata took a step forward and sent a sizable brown blast of energy my way. I sent a large blue blast of energy her way, and the two waves of energy hit each other with such force that they emitted a shock wave after leaving a crater-size hole. Lata was emitting a colossal amount of brown energy around her that it amped me up, having me dig as deep within to unleash more of my blue energy. Lata raised her staff, and brown balls of energy the size of garbage trucks came down on me from the sky. I used my pointing stick to erase as many as I could. There were so many that I was stuck using my pointing stick as a shield. Lata yelled, "That is not good enough, Alaric." Lata aimed her pointing stick directly at me, and I could hear what sounded like a rail gun being fired from a battleship. I panicked and jumped out of the way of the beam zipping toward me. When I looked in the direction that I had been standing, there was complete destruction the likes of which I had never seen. Lata told me, "Look at me, and understand that this is still child's play compared to the kind of power your grandfather possessed with the very staff you now have in your hands."

Lata kept pushing me. I began holding my staff like a rifle, firing rapid energy blasts at Lata when she said, "Enough playing around." Lata raised her staff in the air, and brown lightning immediately surrounded her. A giant brown bolt hit her staff, making it look like she had a lightning rod in her hand. Lata had decided to give me a glimpse of power I had yet to even wrap my mind around. Lata threw what looked like three brown lighting rods at super speed, hitting three massive hills in the distance. I saw the whole thing. Witnessing her display of raw power was making me wonder how powerful of a wizard she was. Lata had noticed she had caught my attention with her display. "That's enough for today," she said. My head was still spinning, trying to process the display of power I just witnessed.

Chapter 7

The very next day, I was supposed to have breakfast inside the temple for the first time. I woke up at four in the morning and felt excited, like a little kid. At four thirty, I took my first steps onto the temple stairs, and nothing happened. As I continued up the stairs, I reminded myself of the last time I was here. I tensed up, waiting for something bad to happen, preparing my body for the feeling of being midair just before landing on the hard ground beneath the stairs. When I got to the top of the stairs, I turned around and gave a sigh of relief. I did it. I am here right now at this very moment, and I'm not lying in the dirt this time. I took the time to see all the holes that I had made around the temple to sleep in. I had some chess pieces in one of my holes to keep me entertained, along with some cherries that I left for a snack later in the day. There were days that I could not sleep. I was too anxious about becoming a wizard. I would grab a stick and make drawings all around my sleeping hole. I had clay designs of football players, and family, things that this land did not have. I gave another sigh and turned to grab the door. Then I made my way into the temple.

Once inside, I made my way through a tunnel into a great hall that had a giant picture of Abir with the head of his staff levitating off the ground. Abir was shown doing a single-finger handstand on the end of his staff. I continued down the hall where I saw a picture of what must have been hundreds of wizards. Part of the hall was set up to show the history of the cult's wars, the later ones showing the Fect. I recognized the purple skin, with the golden mark over their foreheads. I saw a picture of Magni the wizard, the second-in-command, at the time of the war. I also saw that there was a picture of my grandfather, Remo, meditating in a full lotus position upside down with his bald head hovering just off the ground, with a golden staff levitating next to him. There was a picture of Abir bowing his head while on his knees next to a golden staff levitating in front of him surrounded by fire. In the very next picture, Abir was standing on top of the head of the golden staff, rising toward the heavens.

At the end of that hall was a cafeteria where Lata was waiting for me. I noticed there was a chef wearing red robes. I hadn't realized that there was anyone else in the temple. I never saw anyone come or go, nor anyone harvesting any of the dozens of fruits and vegetables surrounding the temple. Lata saw my curiosity and told me, "He was one of the last remaining mages that got the opportunity to serve out his time here. He's continued to serve the Cult of Wizards despite there not being many left to serve. Aside from Lugii, there are a total of four other mages in charge of the upkeep on this enormous temple."

"How come Vanas does not just claim the title of wizard?" I asked.

Lata looked at me and said, "Because there are rules and laws that govern us. Vanas swore to the wizards she would fulfill her duty in training the last wizard when the time came. Vanas is very happy to have earned the title of mage, for she will forever be known as the greatest mage of all time. Without Vanas, there would be none of us left. We are the last two wizards, Alaric." Lugii chimed in the conversation as his white teeth sparkled. He slowly began to put on his white gloves. Lugii, as he began to speak, would clap his hands repeatedly after so many words.

Lugii said, "It is the highest honor in this life to be a wizard," as he clapped and smiled. Lugii clapped up a storm. "You know, not everyone has the potential to be a wizard. It's truly an honor you should relish in!" he said. Lugii looked directly into my eyes as his eyeballs sparkled a bright white, and he said, "Vanas tried to become a wizard, but she did not have the potential within her. Not like you!" Lugii got closer to my face as he used his white gloves to wipe my forehead. "Vanas was taught by the wizards, and they saw her natural abilities as a teacher. So the wizards tasked Vanas with learning every bit of wizard knowledge that she could in order to teach the final wizard one day." Lata spoke up and told me that was why it was important that I continue to learn everything I can here. Lugii brought us our plates of sticky bean fried rice with some prawns and fresh donut peach with some water. Lugii looked at me with a heavy bright smile, and I got a bit creeped out.

"What are you smiling about?" I asked.

Lugii clapped ten times and said, "Ohh, because it is such an honor to serve the wizards! My services are at your disposal, Alaric!" At the end of our meal, Lugii presented us with some chocolate smoothies.

Lata had me follow her after our meal as she informed me it was time for me to have a change of clothes. I found myself in a section of the temple that was highlighted with a sign that read Wizard Clothing. Lata was talking to a man that she introduced as Mayoko. Mayoko had his entire face covered in tattoos. Mayoko was the type of person that never used his inside voice. Mayoko loudly told me, "I will be your tailor." After measuring me out, he handed me some blue robes, a blue hat, and some blue boots to go along with my blue staff. I was beginning to notice a pattern. I was also given what they call silk weight undergarments, a blue top, and blue bottom with long blue socks. Mayoko looked at me, yelling, "When you put this uniform on, wear it with pride!"

I smiled and said, "Thanks." When I presented myself to Lata and Mayoko, they both agreed the uniform looked good on me. I was not a fan of the hat, so I put it around my neck to hang off my back. I felt like I could kick a hole in a wall with these boots.

Lata took me to the section of the temple where the mage Hardrock ran his business of tuning up wizards' pointing sticks. Hardrock had half a body that was very muscular, and the other was slim with no special bulky muscles. When Hardrock would speak, he would get his saliva all over his red robes and face I kind of got a bit grossed out. Hardrock wiped his face and caught sight of my pointing stick and gently smiled. He called out my pointing stick's name right away, and it made its way toward him. He grabbed the pointing stick, and, just by gripping it, he knew there was a lot of work to be done. Hardrock looked at me and said, "How dare you misuse this beautiful blue pointing stick!"

Lata looked at me and said, "Hardrock is a walking stick whisperer."

Hardrock looked at me and said, "Your pointing stick needs some therapy." Hardrock went so far as to say, "Your pointing stick feels disrespected by you in the way you treat it and never talk with it."

I looked at Lata, who whispered to me, "Look, Alaric, he is the pointing stick whisperer. He has earned that title around here." Lata looked at Hardrock, who seemed to be in deep conversation with my pointing stick, and said, "We will be back tomorrow for the pointing stick." Hardrock paid us no attention as we continued on.

Lata looked at me excitedly and told me, "Now for the best part of this experience!" We walked down a spiraling marble tunnel that led to the temple hot spring. Lata looked at me and said, "I want you to relax and recover for the rest of the day. I will see you bright and early first thing in the morning." I got into the hot spring, and the moment that I did, I felt at peace. I allowed the heat from the planet's interior to work on me, and boy did it feel damn good after so much training. After so many hours, a man came to me, presenting himself as Kali the massage therapist.

He asked, "Would you like a deep tissue massage?"

I immediately said, "Yes, please!" The moment I lay on his massage table, it was over. He tapped on my back and said he was done. What felt like seconds was three hours.

Kali looked at me and informed me, "You should be as good as new." I honestly did feel renewed. Kali then instructed me to follow him for my final stage in recovery. Kali had a presence about him that was very dominating. Kali looked like he was going to burst out of his robes from too much muscle. When Kali spoke, his voice was so heavy and strong that he demanded and got your attention. Kali told me that one of these days, he would like to test out my powers in his weight room.

I nodded and said, "Anytime," while I stared at him banging his bald head up and down. I noticed something in his ears.

"Kali, what is that in your ear?"

"Oh, this?" he said, pulling one out of his ear. "They're headphones!"

I stared at him blankly. "I can hear it from here. How can you hear me with music so loud?" Kali shrugged. I asked, "What are you listening to?" He motioned me over and placed one of the sides into my ear. I couldn't understand what they were screaming about, but it was an odd combination of someone sounding angry, but they weren't. I took it out of my ear and handed it back to him.

Kali hit a button in one of the halls and had me walk in. All I saw was a bed! Kali said, "Rest as we monitor you to make sure every-thing is okay." I did not want to, but the more I thought about it, the more I thought that I wouldn't mind finally sleeping on something other than the floor. The moment I lay down on whatever that bed was made of, my body became like Jell-O, and I passed out.

When I awoke, I felt like I had slept like a rock, but my body, mind, and spirit felt fresh again. I noticed my robes, hat, boots, and staff were placed neatly on a small table on the right-hand side of the bed. A note was left by Lata, telling me to go to the dojo and keep training. There will be someone there waiting for me to work with. I did not like it because I felt that there was something being kept from me, but I carried on with my instructions. I ate a quick break-fast and made my way to the dojo. When I got there, someone was waiting for me. It felt odd since I hadn't seen anyone except Vanas or Lata since I entered the temple yesterday. She presented herself as Kogi the mage. I looked at him, and the first question I had was, "How are you going to spar without a staff?" And second, "Are you blind?"

Kogi informed me, "Everything is going to be okay. May we begin the training?"

I looked at him and said, "All right. It's going to be your funeral." Kogi got into his stance with both of his fingers pointing my way and his body parallel to mine like a martial artist. I pointed my staff at him, and after a few seconds of staring at each other, a leaf from one of the trees around the dojo slowly fell in front of us until it hit the ground, and we commenced. I shot out a beam of light at Kogi, and, with one finger, he deflected it. Then, with the other finger, he shot my chest with what I am going to call wind bullets, knocking the air out of me. "H-hold on a second," I said, gasping for breath. Kogi stopped dead in his tracks and moved back into his stance as he fixed the bun on his head.

When we started again, at the drop of a second leaf, Kogi came at me so fast that I was stuck defending the entire time with my staff. It almost felt like he could read my every move, and at one point, he broke through my defenses and landed a punch square in my face. I was getting frustrated. My training made me feel untouchable, but I was getting beaten by a blind man. I was so annoyed that I lost it. I powered up my staff with every ounce of energy that I could gather around me from the soil, the wind, the sun, the trees, and the plants. I hit my staff on the ground with such force. A violent blue vortex of energy went spinning toward Kogi, who remained calm and focused as if nothing major was happening. I saw him take a stance like a tall firm tree and then, with both his fingers, as if he had chopsticks, he grabbed my vortex and spun both his fingers really quickly. I watched as my vortex dissolved itself. This was insane. I was not going to be bested by a blind mage like Kogi. I dropped my staff to the ground and pointed my two fingers at Kogi, pouring my thoughts of annihilation toward him. With his fine-tuned senses, Kogi picked up on my ambitions toward him and canceled it out by pointing only one finger at my attack. This began to boil my blood. This mage was overpowered as my mind began to go dark. I thought I had matched what he sent my way, but the next thing I knew, I felt the force of what felt like a car hitting me, sending me flying into the woods.

Kogi pointed his left finger toward me, and, with his right finger, he flicked it his way and commanded me in his direction. My body came moving through the air toward him. Koji played with the bun on his head and asked me, "Why did you lose to me, a blind mage with no staff?"

I told him, "Because you're clearly better than me!"

Kogi looked at me and said, "No. It is because you have not yet used the cosmic language to connect it with your fighting style."

I asked, "And what style is that?"

Kogi shook his head. "I can't believe Lata has not taken the time to tell you. It is called Bodhia, the consciousness of the self. We call upon the cosmic language using different means, whether it's our pointing sticks, or our fingers, to direct it. However, it is used differently by each person. A true wizard with the gift can just use the cosmic language with enough training, but its full potential is locked within each individual, and every individual must access it within themselves and tailor the cosmic language to work for them. How you ultimately use the cosmic language will be different from how I do, or how Lata and Vanas, Lugii, or Mayoko do. Bodhia manifests itself in each of us differently. Keep gaining understanding of yourself, your pointing stick, and the cosmic language, and then you may be ready to use Bodhia. Do not be discouraged, because your training was to set the foundation for this next step in becoming a wizard. The best of them, like Remo, understood Bodhia as something that was a part of himself, which allowed Bodhia to naturally come to him. A true wizard will not even need a pointing stick. True masters need but a single finger. Through my invisible, magically powered eyes, I have even seen Aziza the wizard and Maska the wizard square off, and I would only ever see them sparring with their fingers. They would make special occasions where one would use a rock as their pointing stick and the other a branch. They got so good at speaking the cosmic language that it came as something natural and effortless while still being conscious of their actions."

I am not going to lie, I was a bit discouraged, and it did not make me feel any better when Kogi told me, "If we were to use a scale from one to ten to compare where I was right now, I would be at a three. Lata would be at four, Vanas and the Third would be at five."

I asked, "And where would I be?"

Kogi slowly told me, "Three." I did not understand how he could be that much stronger than me but at the same level.

I said, "With how you just kicked my butt, I would have said you were a nine! How are you only a three?"

Kogi told me, "It's because I have been practicing Bodhia a lot longer than you. You are way stronger than me in every aspect. You just have not allowed your full potential to reveal itself. You just need to practice more in understanding your connection with Bodhia."

A year had passed since I had last seen Lata, and I really wanted to know what was going on. Nobody would tell me where she went, but it must have been important enough that she didn't have time to say goodbye. I had got so caught up in daydreaming that I did not hear a word Kogi had just told me. Kogi told me, "Read it again." He had me reading a short book that Abir the wizard wrote on Bodhia. His and my definition of short were two very different things, it seemed.

"Abir goes on to say that the cosmic language, for one, selects you to come in connection with it. Second, it is your job to find out how to complete that connection. Abir goes on to say that he meditated on a river for a whole year until, in a single thought, the concept of Bodhia came to him. So if he pointed at a tree and the visual he had in his mind was destruction, the command would be for the tree to destroy itself. Abir also talks about Beadong, ensuring to always have a clear mind when you are meditating, sleeping, or in some sort of trance state, because you do not want to be giving commands while you sleep and wake up to problems. Abir mentions how he had trained one day to the point of exhaustion that it was not until the mind came back to its senses three days later that he came to realize he destroyed the entire valley he was training in, leveling it all out void of life. Abir highlights the sense of control over your abilities, even when not in control or in a state of rest. Abir describes it like putting a lid on a bottle so that the liquid does not pour out. Abir continues with Sechu, the idea that everyone needs a good defense. Abir admits not being the greatest at it, but with the combination of his staff, he formed a defense that worked for him. Abir mentions how he would command the river to fight with him to work on his Sechu sparring with him. Abir states it took him a solid year of nonstop training to master Sechu. Abir went on to talk about attacking, which he coined Wadah. Abir understood in his time that one day he would have to defend himself by attacking. So he went to a valley known for tornadoes and all kinds of devastating weather and trained on his attacking, defending, his state of rest, and his connection with it all through his consciousness." As I turned the page, I saw that the next several pages had been torn out, almost in haste, as there were some jagged edges remaining.

Kogi interrupted my reading. "There are several other forms, but as you can see, the pages were torn out of this book. Abir did not want us to have knowledge of these other forms, for whatever reason."

"Torn out or stolen?" I asked.

Kogi raised his eyebrow at me and asked, "What do you mean by that?"

"Look, I'm not stupid. You've been hiding something from me the whole time. Tell me the truth!"

Kogi took a long pause while playing with his hair bun, as if looking for the correct words. He finally said, "Yes, they were."

I told Kogi, "Tell me what happened."

"Shower up, and meet me inside the temple in the conference room."

I said, "Okay," but then realized I had no idea where that was in the temple. After another amazing shower and a fresh pair of robes, I made my way to the conference room with the help of Kali, who was vibing out and banging his head back and forth to whatever he was listening to on his cool-looking red wireless headphones. When I entered the doors, I was amazed at the presentation of the room. The walls were finely carved wood with openings that had a glass case displaying the hats of the greatest wizards of the cult. At the center was a great rectangular table made of glass with Kogi standing beside it on the far side.

Kogi said, "As you may or may not know by now, every single wizard in existence, before they die, leaves a minuscule amount of their magic that finds itself to this temple and is collected by me to interpret and add to our archives. What I am about to show you is detailed accounts from the very wizards that were present at past events. Let us begin." He waved his hand over the glass table, and images appeared of Abir with his second-in-command, Magni, standing next to him. Then it showed Remo, Aziza, and Masta, all the original wizards who looked to be outside in the middle of night.

They had all been arguing about how many wizards had been killed fighting the Fect. Masta shouted out and kept shouting until she got agitated, raising her orange staff in the air until an annoying sound emanated from her staff, drawing every wizard's attention toward her.

Masta used her piercing orange eyes to stare each wizard directly in the eye and ask them all, "What the heck is wrong with you all? You let so many of our people die, and for what?" Masta's face began to turn red as she pointed out the fact that most of the wizards were not even dying from battling the Fect. Masta punched Aziza in the shoulder and said, "Our brothers are dying from battling depression, alcoholism, and suicide, to name a few. Some have become so psychotic they can't even control themselves anymore! If this war continues, it will be the end of us all!"

Magni, having heard enough, threw his canteen to the ground and said, "This war was at a tipping point! We have lost many, yes, but those losses have been worth something! We have destroyed three of their four space towers. The enemy is on the run to protect their last tower, and we can end this if we push now!" Magni ran his fingers through his horseshoe mustache as he adjusted his robes that were half-gold and half-silver, the only wizard with such a feature. Magni continued, "We just have to figure out how to get through the Fect's final defenses without any more casualties."

Remo chimed in, "What about Caden? He has been studying the Fect in great detail. He has a few ideas that may help us. In fact, he is eager to go through the ceremony. He wants to become a wizard. He wants to fight with us." Remo had been training Caden at the time, who he saw as a great addition to the Cult of Wizards because of his natural connection with the cosmic language and his natural abilities of being a quick learner. The Cult of Wizards were impressed by Caden, but they felt that he was much too young to become a full wizard at a mere eighteen years old. They still saw him as immature and impulsive, which could lead to recklessness and much more. Abir was concerned over the fact Remo would not tell them anything about Caden, yet he made grand promises about him. Aside from the fact that Remo tried telling the Cult of Wizards that he had been training Caden since he was eight years old, and while still not a fully developed adult yet, he was fully capable of doing anything he was instructed to do.

Abir began to pace in his burgundy robes, eventually taking off his hat. "No, Remo. I stand by my earlier decision. In due time, young Caden shall join our ranks as an equal, as a wizard. Until that day, however, he has much to learn. I realize that there is little glory in study, but he will learn, in time, and with wisdom, that there is more to life as a wizard than glory and heroics." Remo hung his head down and nodded, his face curled into a frown of disappointment.

The holograms disappeared, and Kogi said, "Caden was Remo's prodigy. He was always strange, and some days, it looked like his face was drained of life. And other days, he'd be just fine. When Remo broke the news to him, he was furious, and something snapped in him. He said he'd wasted enough of his life, and he was going to earn retribution for all that time. It was clear that he wanted revenge. While Caden was studying the Fect, he also learned of our key battle plans, and he decided to sell that information to the Fect. Then he changed his mind because he learned of something that even we don't fully understand yet. He snuck into the Fect's space tower and discovered a book that explained many things, one of which led him to the process of creating a new Fect successor." Kogi took a breath and gave me a moment to process all of this.

Kogi continued, "Caden had to hurry because it was looking like the wizards were going to win the war. The wizards had pushed for weeks on multiple fronts now, having made their way through the Fect's final defenses. Caden was inside the tower when it finally fell. There were lots of reports, including Remo's, that said they saw him."

Kogi waved his hand again, and a new series of holograms appeared. This time, it looked like a party. All the original wizards were there, including many I did not recognize. They were celebrating that the tower had been destroyed and that the war with the Fect was over. Aziza got all the wizards drunk that night, and light-yellow robes were soaked in beer, and he was chanting and screaming with two other wizards. They had their arms locked, and they were kicking their legs. I thought they were going to fall over. As Abir left the party, the hologram switched to him, and he went to his bedroom.

As he entered, he saw his desk was ransacked, and several pages were torn out of his book.

Kogi started speaking again. "Abir was sure it was Caden's doing, and he ordered a unit of wizards to find him. Remo pleaded with Abir, but Abir had had enough. He denounced Caden as being too dangerous, and he ordered that he be killed. There was one survivor out of that unit. Her report said that they found him deep in the woods, but that he was no longer Caden. She said he had begun morphing into something as purple hands began appearing out of his body. When they were found that day, four wizards were found disfigured, with their body parts lain out in a pattern. The report also noted that when Caden had finished arranging the body parts, Fect soldiers arrived and took orders from him, and they left together. By the time Remo and the others arrived on the scene, Caden was gone. The next day, an important meeting was held. Abir told everyone that it will be the remaining wizards' duty to bring a complete end to the Fect by killing Caden. The wizards looked all over Devansh for Caden, but they could not find where he was hiding.

"As the years passed, the wizards became discouraged. Remo, over time, began to become concerned, so he held one final meeting. Remo said that he had a dream that one final wizard will be born, and that wizard will be the one to bring an end to all of this. Some wizards took Remo seriously, while others thought he had gone insane after the war. A lot of wizards found it difficult to believe Remo, knowing how much time he had been spending drinking his thoughts away. Remo admitted to everyone he had a drinking problem, but that didn't help him make his case. Remo was one of the cult's deadliest wizards, and he possessed powers that few other wizards could even pull off. But after what had happened with Caden, along with the toll he took during the war, his abilities weren't doing anyone any good.

As the years passed, more and more wizards slowly died off, and no one took to training new recruits. The threat became more serious when five wizards took their lives from severe depression."

I knew the rest and told Kogi, "I've seen enough. Tell me the truth! Where have Vanas and Lata been?"

Kogi gave a sigh and slowly began to say, "They have been laying their lives down to give you as much time as they could for you to keep training. The Third has been going around Devansh burning down villages and destroying entire cities, butchering all in his path until you decided to come out and fight him. Well, the battle intensified as the Third attempted to destroy the final lock that blocks the bridge that blocks our land from yours. Varun sent word that they needed more help or the final lock would be destroyed. So Lata decided to go. From the last letter I received, the Third has become quite formidable ever since his master granted him Masta's pointing stick. The fact of the matter is that everyone is putting their hopes on you to come through and be the wizard they believe you to be. The Third is leading an army of specially trained Sharm. These Sharm are sharp fighters solely bred for war. Varun and Catalan gathered forces after speaking with President Nilla of Devansh, who understood the severity of the matter and provided them with three brigades of soldiers. At this point though, it might not be enough."

"I've heard enough! I'm going!"

I stormed out of the conference room, grabbed my backpack with all my items, and walked out the temple. I walked toward the doors to see Kogi blocking my way.

"You cannot go yet. You are not ready."

"And when am I going to be ready? When this is all over and everyone is gone, my home will be the next to be destroyed."

Kogi thought long and hard and finally said, "I will let you pass if you can get through me." I quickly ran at him, and he threw me to the ground. I pointed my finger at him, and he deflected me. He pointed his finger at me. This time I deflected him. I powered up my staff to district Kogi, sending out a beam of light his way while I made a run for it. He redirected the light and had the trees block my way.

I finally said, "Fine!" I closed my eyes. I let myself breathe and then I felt that sensitive tingle at my core that brought tears to my eyes. I said to myself, *I have to stand up and fight before there is nothing left. I won't be afraid anymore. I am Alaric the wizard.* As a blue aura surrounded me, my eyes turned blue, and my blue staff began to shine. With my left hand, I pointed out beyond the temple stairs, and, with a snap, I found myself outside the barrier. I had done it, but I saw that everything around me had been destroyed. There was nothing left for miles but ash and embers. The sight was depressing compared to the temple that now looked like an oasis in the middle of nowhere.

As I began walking, Kogi popped up behind me and said, "You're going to need all the help you can get. I am coming with you."

"You're not going to try and stop me this time?"

"You got past me, didn't you?"

I looked at Kogi and smiled. "Let's go, then," I said. The good thing was that Kogi brought a backpack filled with star fruit, Gấc fruit, durian, and dragon fruit along with plenty of other amazing veggies and food.

"I like the way you travel. Well, since you're here, I don't suppose you know the direction?" I asked, laughing.

"Yes. Southeast of here, about a good week's walk."

I looked at Kogi and asked, "Do we have a week?"

Kogi yelled, "No!"

I said, "What are we waiting for?" as we began running.

Chapter 8

Lata the wizard was sitting on a chair next to Vanas the mage's bed. When her eyes weren't closed, they looked glazed over, but it was clear that she was still alive, and she was listening, at least. She hadn't been the same since the ambush. Lata informed Vanas, "The Third's reinforcements are starting to push our forces back. The Third has been using genetically enhanced gorillas and grizzly bears bearing the mark to make them stronger and wilder to break through our frontline defenses, along with a new breed of Sharm. Our soldiers are starting to get restless, tired, and hungry. Honestly, this mix of tactics is starting to wear them down. They're used to fighting regular Sharm, but these ones seem to feel no pain, and the animals have no regard for their personal safety. The number of wounded is rising, and morale is down since last night's losses that pushed us back. I put a strong barrier around the final lock so that the power core won't be destroyed, but if they break through our defenses, I do not know how long our forces will stand for."

Vanas said nothing, but a couple blinks reassured Lata that she was still there. Lata continued, "Varun has put multiple turrets around the power core to ensure the lock is not exposed without defenses, along with five hundred entrenched soldiers. Varun managed to get us some tanks as well, and about a hundred robots he built for battle, each bearing a machine gun and some bazookas. It's certainly held them back so far today. Catalan has been tending to the wounded as our full-time medic. She has not been taking time to sleep, and we need her to stay focused because she is our professional surgeon. I never realized how many skills Catalan had until now. I always just thought of her as the mayor of Varmington. She really is an amazing woman that I am glad is on our side. I am struggling to help provide support to this army without your help. President Nilla never intended for the last few magically powered to get involved. We're not generals, Vanas."

Vanas finally shouted a single word, "Alaric!" Her breathing rapidly increased, and Lata placed a hand softly on her chest until her breathing returned to normal. Vanas snapped out of her trance and looked at Lata.

"I'm sorry, Lata. I just can't stop thinking about him. It's been a year, and we never told him what was really going on. What if he left the barrier?"

Lata said, "He's probably still training with Kogi. He's safe as long as he's at the temple." Vanas nodded and closed her eyes before softly falling asleep. Lata stepped out of the room and made her way to the command building.

When she entered, President Nilla of Devansh was present on video, as well as all of the other officers. President Nilla started the meeting stating, "As I speak, I plan to be dropping care packages for you guys in giant crates. In the crates are medical supplies, packaged food, ammo, and much more. We understand the severity of protecting the final lock. With that being said, I currently was only able to send you one battalion. As you know, Anika, the capital, is being attacked as well, and I am having to use all the forces I can to keep the Sharm from entering the city. It has not been easy as of late, as intel has informed me that the Second has recently joined in leading the assault on the capital."

Lata was surprised. "And the First?" she asked.

"We are not certain," President Nilla said. "You are to protect the final lock with your lives. If the power core is destroyed, the entire foundation will come tumbling down. All will be lost. The other lands don't know how grave the threat is, and some do not even know of it at all! The Sharm cannot be allowed to leave Devansh and spread out. Now return to work, and we will rejoin in three days." Lata did not like their military position. The lock was placed inside what looks like a hydroelectric dam, which had them fighting on two sides. They have not been able to stop the Sharm from pushing their ground forces back. If they overrun the ground forces and make their way into the dam, then how long would we actually be able the interior before the lock was destroyed? Lata had never seen these kinds of tactics before. The Sharm had been using the marked animals in suicide assaults, like a banzai charge. On top of that, the Sharm had resorted to chemical weapons, and the expanding gasses were wiping out everyone in the trenches that couldn't get their masks on in time. Lata mulled the situation over in her head as the chatter of officers buzzed in her ear.

If we stay in defensive positions, they'll grind us down, and they'll just gas our positions. If we meet them in the open, the infantry will be slaughtered. We don't have enough tanks to justify a direct counterassault. What can we do? I know how to hunt, I know how to garden, hell, I can rebuild my cabin in no time if it was torn down in a tornado, but... I don't know how to play general.

Lata's personal advisor, Zow, was the only off-world being that she knew of besides their enemy. She did not dare ask from where in the cosmos she was from, out of respect. Zow was about six feet tall and had no ears, but she was fully capable of hearing whatever she desired. Zow told Lata one day that she was four thousand years old and actually could speak the cosmic language in her mind. She did not know Bodhia, but they wished she did. Zow described the cosmic language as the language beyond anything that exists within space and time. Apparently, she learned it from another group she met beyond our solar system. Zow was impressive, and her understanding of the cosmic language was as good as any wizard's. Zow took her duty as an advisor seriously, and while many of the command did not trust an off-worlder, it would be a waste to not use her brain power, which, according to her, equaled that of the power of five hundred human brains. Nobody could say whether she was serious or if she was stroking her ego, though she could make calculations faster than any of them, and she could remember details that most found irrelevant.

From the cameras in the command room, Lata saw that there was an advancing battalion coming from both sides of the dam. The defenders had begun to take fire from several enemy platoons, including artillery from the mountains and hulking vehicles that resembled robotic spiders. Lata told the communications soldier that she needed to get in contact with the commander on the ground, Captain Raider, but communications were down. Captain Raider was one of the best officers they had on the ground. All the soldiers gave him the nickname Achilles. Morale stood high in his section, because every soldier knew there was no one better than Captain Raider. All the soldiers respected him for his leadership and bravery. Captain Raider had so many scars on his face people were scared to look at his face, let alone directly into his eyes. That, and they had heard the stories of how he killed several Rillers with his bare hands.

Captain Raider was leading the ground forces on the right side of the mountain while also trying to instruct the left side through signals on a spotlight whenever the dust from a landing artillery shell didn't obscure the view. Captain Raider threw down the radio when he found out that communications were down. He had his soldiers get into formation and had one of his lower-enlisted soldiers shoot up a green flare to let the other side prepare for the next wave. It was dark and cold outside. Not even the moon and stars lit up this night, but Captain Raider had his soldiers locked and loaded, huddled together for warmth behind barricades and sandbags. Captain Raider could sense something big was coming, so he began yelling as loud as he could, telling each and every soldier that they would forever be immortalized through their bravery. At least they could feel good about themselves when they bit the bullet, sometimes literally. The line grew quiet. Each man and woman could barely see the next few beside them. Flares lit up the midnight landscape, and the Sharm and their animal soldiers stormed over the bodies of the dead, rushing toward the trenches.

"Hold!" Captain Raider shouted. One of the soldiers beside him began to shake. He struggled to hold his rifle steady, and he stood straight up, stiff as a board. Captain Raider placed his hand on the soldier's shoulder and gently pushed him toward the barricade. He grabbed the man's rifle and pressed it against the edge of the barricade.

"Relax. Use it to your advantage. Save your energy for those ugly bastards." The soldier nodded and relaxed his shoulders a bit.

Captain Raider looked toward the force rushing toward him. He raised the clicker that was pressed into his palm, and he squeezed hard, setting off the explosives that were set in the field.

"Fire at will!" he screamed at the top of his lungs, and bullets and lasers enveloped the field, cutting down the closest Sharm that weren't killed by the explosions.

Varun sat perched in his sniper's nest above the trenches as he screamed into the radio, "Lata! They're dropping in troops from the sky!" He waited for the crackle, but no voice came through. "Lata! Come in!" There was nothing besides the crackle. "Piece of crap!" he shouted as he tossed the radio. He picked up his sniper rifle and eyed the Sharm plunging into the craters left by the artillery. They were dressed in special jumpsuits, distinct from the other troops. Varun squeezed the trigger, and as soon as the first one dropped, he started shifting his aim and firing at every Sharm he could see that landed on the field. Varun hit some buttons on his wrist device and had several of his battle bots with rifles began targeting the halo jumpers in the sky. Lifeless bodies began to hit all over the battlefield, and tracers filled the night sky like a shooting star, but there were too many halo jumpers, and some landed on the top of the dam, engaging the defenders with swords. Varun saw that they quickly began to make their way inside, and he picked off the ones fighting with the defenders, but Varun had no other choice now but to leave the rest of them to Lata. Varun focused his attention back on the ground forces, cursing at his failure.

Captain Raider had gotten into a Humvee, firing off the fifty-caliber gun, taking out as many Sharm as he could until a giant cybernetic gorilla flipped the Humvee over. When Captain Raider pulled out the soldier with him from the Humvee, they had discovered the enemy had their backs to them, focused on incoming fire. Captain Raider and the soldier drew their sidearms and began shooting the Sharm in the back, taking cover behind the wreckage. Captain Raider was focused as if possessed by the god of war, making his way through the field of Sharm, killing every one that came into view. Captain Raider began screaming like a madman as he gunned them down or choked them out with his bare hands. The ground forces caught sight of the siege that Captain Raider and the other soldier were delivering behind enemy lines, and that rallied them to advance and support Captain Raider.

Captain Raider felt that tingle of suspense crawl all the way up his spine, and he pulled out a sword he had picked up along the way. Captain Raider showed no fear on the battlefield. He showed no sign of exhaustion, only excitement for more. His family bloodline came from the old shogun figureheads before the rise of democracy in Devansh. For Captain Raider, war was just another way of communicating. In his opinion, the thing about war was that it allowed him to unleash the beast within him, and all his intentions and feelings, without any sense of regret at the end of the day. Captain Raider had mastered every form of combat. He was a weapons expert, explosives expert, and one of the best commanders in the nation. Stories are still told about the battles he has won and the countless lives he has saved.

Zow informed Lata that several halo jumpers had managed to get inside the facility and said she was going to form a response force to hunt them down. Lata tried the communications again, but they were still down until Zow said, "Touch my shoulder and relay your message to the people you need to." So many long hours of bloodshed had passed. It was five thirty in the morning now, and the soldiers were beginning to be pushed back now that the Third had shown up on the battlefield. Captain Raider had all his forces firing everything they had at the Third, but nothing was working, so he had his troops concentrate on the Sharm while he faced off with the Third.

Captain Raider came face-to-face with the Third and told him, "I know exactly what you are."

The Third sneered at him, "Knowing is not going to prolong your life."

Captain Raider brought out another sword, pointing them both directly at the Third.

Captain Raider's soldiers did their best to make sure he was not disturbed by any of the Sharm soldiers and could just focus on the Third.

The Third then asked Raider, "Are you ready to die?"

Raider told the Third, "After you harmed Vanas, I've been wanting a shot at you."

The Third said, "Am I supposed to care about who that is? You'll all end up in the same grave eventually."

Captain Raider began swinging his blades at the Third who was using Masta's orange staff like a sword to block everything Captain Raider threw at him.

Catalan had decided it was time to get active in the fighting. She wanted to do more than just play doctor. There were too many people dying, and she thought she could do more by trying to prevent any more casualties. She put on an exoskeleton combat suit and sprinted toward the battle. Lata communicated with Catalan through Zow's telepathic ability, asking her, "Can you support the air force and help take out some of the enemy's aircraft?"

Catalan acknowledged, "No problem." She stepped outside and waited until one of the enemy's aircrafts got close enough, and she jumped on. She unloaded her shotgun on everyone until she jumped out onto another aircraft. She put away her shotgun and pulled out her assault rifle, unloading the magazine into the crew while the other aircraft plunged into the ground like a fireball. The Third, while fighting with Captain Raider, noticed all the havoc that Catalan was causing in the air. The Third powered up the orange staff, blasting Captain Raider with a whirlwind of orange energy, sending him into the ground in a bloodied heap. The captain was fearless as he managed to lift his battered body back up. He did not care if he died right here right now. He was going to take the Third with him, one way or the other. As Captain Raider picked up one of his broken swords, he continued on his path toward the Third, who fired multiple orange blasts of energy at the captain. Raider took them all square in the chest like a brick wall, but even he couldn't take all of that energy. He was knocked out cold when his head slammed into the hard ground, blood staining his hair.

As the Third raised his staff to bash in Captain Raider's head, several soldiers nearby unloaded their machine guns into him. The Third took some bullets from the soldiers and then he beamed his way up to the aircraft Catalan was on, surprising her after she had just snapped the pilot's neck. Several soldiers ran over to Captain Raider and immediately yelled for the medic. Captain Raider had some severe open wounds. The soldiers did the best they could to stop the bleeding with some of the medical equipment they had on them like bandages and tourniquets as they kept yelling out "medic."

The Third told Catalan, "It's rare for someone to catch my attention so fast, but you're worse than a fly who refuses to leave."

Catalan told the Third, "I'm flattered," as she immediately shot an explosive round at his chest, which he stopped by snapping his finger. As the round stopped dead in midair, suspended above the fuselage, she had already thrown five grenades at him. He spun his staff in a whirlwind, knocking away four of the grenades, while the fifth clanked on the fuselage and stopped at his feet. The aircraft jerked sideways, out of control from the blast, as Catalan laid down every ounce of firepower she had at her disposal. As the aircraft went crashing down, she jumped out at the last minute. From the massive explosion that sent hot metal flying around, slicing through everything like hot butter, a metal piece made its way into Catalan's left leg. While the suit gave her the power to stand herself up, she was in agonizing pain.

The Third slowly made his way toward her, saw the state she was in, and said, "That's all the fun we are going to have together." As she struggled to stay standing, the Third pointed the orange staff toward her, and a black ball of energy flew out the end. It kicked up dust as it sailed across the ground and slammed into her chest, sending her into the dirt.

A Humvee flew over the hill just as Catalan fell to the ground. Lata slammed on the brakes and came to a stop. She turned to Zow, who was in the passenger seat, and said, "You are going to be left in charge while I go down to face the Third."

Zow told her, "Not alone you're not. I've sworn to protect you."

Lata snapped back, "You have, and now help protect everyone that is fighting and lead us to victory." Lata grabbed her brown staff with her brown wizard hat and blasted off in the direction of Catalan. The Third advanced on Catalan until he laid his eyes on a prize he had been wanting for quite some time. Now it was right in front of him.

The Third asked Lata with a smirk, "How is Vanas doing?" Lata did not respond and readied her staff. "When is the coward, Alaric, going to come out and face me?"

Lata looked at the Third dead in the eyes and told him, "Today, your fight is with Lata, the grand wizard!"

The Third clapped. "Ooh, it's been long since I've had the pleasure of fighting a fully-fledged wizard." The Third said mockingly, "What happened to the Cult of Wizards? Where are the so-called heroes and peacekeepers and the destroyers of my people, the Fect?" Lata watched the Third's eye twitch at the mention of the Fect.

Lata told the Third, "It looks like this wizard's hit a soft spot."

The Third told Lata, "You will pay for the sins of the wizards." Lata, tired of words, shot a brown blast of energy at the Third as the two engaged in battle.

Lata spun her staff, delivering heavy blows to the Third's body, shredding his uniform. Both had the sensation of battle in their eyes. The Third began to thirst for blood. Lata pointed at the side of the mountain and commanded massive boulders to tear themselves from the mountainside and hurl themselves at the Third. The Third pointed his staff and shot out several black beams at the boulders, crumbling them to dust. The Third directed the orange staff at Lata and shot out another black beam. Lata stopped it in midair with a brown beam, and they both fizzled out. The two were now close enough that Lata smacked the heck out of the Third with her right hand and rammed the head of her pointing stick straight into his face. The Third turned his anger into rage, losing focus of his original intent to just inflict pain on Lata. Lata powered up her brown pointing stick, forming brown clouds in the sky. Lata, after raising her pointing stick in the air, dropped some massive brown lightning bolts on the Third. Upon impact, massive blasts went off, and when the dust settled, the Third had taken substantial damage. Lata found it a bit odd that the Third was not panicking even after taking a beating. Lata, after a sequence of moves with her pointing stick, landed three powerful blows, sending the Third six feet deep into the ground. The Third took a few minutes to rise to the surface, dusted himself off, and became wild, aggressive, and unpredictable.

"How grateful I am for Caden to have betrayed the wizards, for I would have never had learned the snap that the great Abir had created," he said. The Third did a triple snap, and Lata wondered what he had done. The Third said, "I have canceled out all snapping and pointing for the next fifteen minutes. We will now truly see who is more versed with their fighting style and magic powers. What you wizards call Bodhia is a load of garbage." The two squared off, running at super speeds and exchanging blows with their pointing sticks. They both ran up the side of the mountain, firing blasts at one another until they reached the top. The Third, with the power of the orange staff, eventually created an opening. He took the opportunity, and he kicked her furiously into the mountain. She sailed through the rock and into the command bunker. She dusted herself off as she stood up in the cafeteria room.

The Third zoomed his way into the cafeteria and told Lata, "You see, we embrace your stupid Bodhia to inflict pain on our enemies and to break their mind, body, and spirit, as I am going to begin to break yours." The Third fired multiple blasts that Lata dodged but left her open to a kick to the face that had Lata seeing stars and spitting out blood. Lata did not know if she had become slower or if he had become faster. The Third could tell what Lata was thinking and said, "Yes, it is that I am getting faster, Lata. It's one of my natural abilities as a Sharm." Lata did not like the sound of that. Lata pointed her staff to the sky, drawing in as much lightning as she could until it was channeling through her entire body and her brown staff was electrically charged. Lata gave a blast with her staff that the Third blocked. Lata followed up with a bigger blast, which the Third could not block, sending him flying down to the battlefield into a tank. Lata did not hold back on any of her attacks. She grabbed the staff with both of her hands, pointed the front of her staff at the Third, and fired a barrage of heavy blasts of energy until a giant crater formed. The Third's purple body had begun to bleed out as one of his eyes had swelled up, and both his horns on his forehead had been broken off by Lata's attack. The Third told Lata, "It is a shame that the dark wizards want you dead. I very much would have loved to have made you my personal slave. But, for everything you've done to the Fect, your life is forfeit."

The Third had his fun with Lata, but he knew for now he had to complete his mission to destroy the final lock. The Third raised his staff and sent out a black beam toward the sky, which lit up like a beacon. Four giant cybernetically enhanced lions made their way toward them, hauling a piece of the Fect tower that had fallen long ago. The Third pointed his staff at the crumbling tower and made it rise. The Third looked at Lata and told her, "While you wizards were busy doing whatever it was you were doing, the remaining Fect excavated the remains of our space pillars to find technology that we could still salvage to one day defeat you wizards and conquer this world." The Third shot a black beam of energy at the tower, and, as surge of energy rose from the base to the top, metallic constructions creaked to life and extended their barrels toward the battlefield, and the turrets fired upon Devansh's soldiers. The Third told Lata, "It is a shame of what I must do next in order to break your spirits. Funny how cruel fate can be when the initiative is on the enemy's side. I will say that we, the Fect, are an amazing, technologically advanced race, while you wizards managed to prove more than we could handle the first time around. We knew that with enough strategic planning and patience, we could catch even you wizards off guard. Behold, Lata, some of your own—Aurelio the wizard and Kiato the wizard."

The two cybernetic wizards came out of the tower, wearing all black robes as black rods pierced throughout their entire body. The two wizards bore the gold mark on their foreheads. Aurelio walked forward, holding a black pointing stick in his metal hand. Lata looked on as Aurelio looked more like something you find dead on the side of the road. Lata took a good look at Kiato and got a tingling feeling.

"Toward the end of the war, instead of just killing you wizards, we began to capture and experiment on you to see what made you so special. We chose to combine our technology with these two wizards, and, out of all our participants, they were the only two who survived." Lata was at a loss for words as the Third continued his way toward the dam, leaving Lata to face her former brethren.

Zow, witnessing everything that was going on in the battlefield, activated all remaining offensive and defensive weapons, focusing half of their firepower on the tower and the other half on ground and air attacks. Lata ignored the Third for now and pointed her staff at the shield protecting the dam, focusing all her energy into it. This bolstered the shield for several moments, but as Lata's strength faltered, so did the shield's power. Zow got in contact with Varun telepathically, telling him to let his robots loose onto the battlefield. Varun yelled out, "It's about time!" As Varun prepared the robots, he also prepared the new drones he had built, which were armed with machine guns. Varun released the horde of robots down the mountain. Zow tried getting in contact with Captain Raider but could not get in communication with him, so she tried Catalan and managed to get in contact with her.

Zow asked, "Catalan, are you all right?"

Catalan responded, "Yes, I just finished patching myself up. I took a hit to my leg."

"Will you still be able to help?"

"Yes. What are my orders?"

"Take a unit with you and some explosives to destroy that tower."

"Consider it done."

Catalan made her way to the tower, and on the way, she just so happened to come across Captain Raider, who was sitting still as the medic finished working on him. Captain Raider asked, "What is going on?" Catalan filled him in. Captain Raider said, "We are coming with," as he whistled sharply. Captain Raider's platoon showed up hollering and cheering, ready to blow some stuff up.

Catalan yelled out, "Well, follow me. We need to take out that tower now."

Captain Raider yelled out, "You heard your orders! Let's go!"

Lata stood face-to-face with Aurelio and Kiato, neither of whom could speak since their mouths were sealed shut. Lata, in tears, said, "I'm sorry for what you must have had to endure." The two pointed their staffs at Lata and shot beams of black energy her way. Lata deflected one with her finger and the other with her staff. Aurelio sprang forward and tried to wrap his arms around Lata to tackle her down to the ground. Lata dodged and pointed her left finger at Aurelio, sending a beam of energy at him, pinning him to the ground. Kiato sent a boulder flying at Lata, which she split in half with her finger. Aurelio broke free from the ground, springing forward to smash his staff over Lata's head. Lata created a brown vortex of energy that she directed at Aurelio, crushing half his body. Lata's energy dwindled, and her attention was split between fighting and maintaining the shield. Shame and pity swelled in Lata's heart as she fought her former brethren, and her strength continued to wane while she shunted the rest of her energy into her attacks. Lata's grief consumed her, and she began to lose her focus. Since the two wizards were more machine than organic, they did not have a sense of fatigue. They had no conscious thought, nor did they feel any pain. All they had was their mission, which was to pulverize Lata.

Aurelio lifted his staff in the air and slammed it down to the ground, sending pieces of space rock from outer space spraying all over the battlefield. As Kiato battled Lata, he eventually kicked her through one of the giant space rocks that landed nearby. Lata incinerated the giant rock and nearly dropped her staff from fatigue. The two wizards touched the heads of their staffs together, and a colossal black ball of energy formed that they sent hurtling toward Lata. Her life flashed before her eyes. In those final seconds, she saw a garden with flowers, a beautiful green cabin home with acres of land out in the field, and a man wearing green robes showing a teenager in orange robes how to use her pointing stick. Lata came to her senses as Kogi placed his hand on her back to bring her back into a state of balance as he began to restore her energy. Lata's sight was still blurred, and she was not completely sure if she had just witnessed Alaric the wizard absorb the oncoming attack with his staff and drop the two cybernetic wizards within seconds, each with one blow using his staff. Lata finally took a good look and said, "You guys finally decided to show up, huh?"

Kogi smiled, saying, "Alaric ran the whole way here."

Lata looked at Kogi and said, "And you let him?"

Kogi smiled. "Relax, he is focused now."

Chapter 9

A heavy fog rolled in, and Catalan was making her way into the tower with Captain Raider and his platoon. Upon entering the fortress, they were met with heavy resistance from Sharm soldiers. Catalan told the captain, "Lay down ground fire for me so that I could start laying down the explosives." As Catalan had made her way around, planting all the explosives they had, she noticed a blue light and decided to follow it, finding herself in some sort of nursery. Catalan continued to look around until she spotted a girl who was cowering in the corner. She sobbed in fear with her face buried in her arms. Catalan called to the girl, but she would not respond.

Zow got into Catalan's head and asked, *What is taking so long?*

Catalan responded, *I found a girl who looks to be about fifteen. I'm trying to get her to come to me.*

Zow said, *Make it quick!*

Catalan reached out her hand one more time, telling the girl, "Please, trust me," until the girl finally grabbed her hand. Catalan told everyone, "Fall back," as they ran out the space tower at full speed. When she was a good-enough distance away, she jumped into one of the trenches, then yelled out, "Fire in the hole!" and hit the switch. The explosion sent bits of the Space Tower in all directions, catching the attention of the Third. He also finally noticed the blue wizard that'd been watching him.

The Third finally appeared before me, telling me, "I thought you would never show."

I told Kogi, "Hurry up and take Lata into the mountain to get her off of the battlefield."

The Third said, "Not quite," as he pointed his staff directly at them, sending a black energy blast toward them. I stepped in its path, absorbing it with my blue staff. The Third gave a surprised look as he began ranting nonsense.

I asked him, "Are we just going to talk?"

The Third responded, "Eager to die?" I took a step forward, extending my pointing stick in his direction and hit him square in the chest with the head of my staff. The Third was delighted, screaming, "How glad to see that you have a better understanding of what it means to be a wizard. This makes killing you much more exhilarating for me."

I looked at the Third and told him, "You don't deserve to wield Maska's orange pointing stick."

The Third told me, "It's a shame that you could not do anything about it." I was not completely sure at the time, but I felt like I could hear a voice. The more blows I exchanged with the Third, the clearer it became in my mind until I realized Maska's pointing stick was trying to communicate with me. The Third clenched his fist into the air and yelled out "Enough of this!" The Third closed his eyes, and when he opened them, they were glowing bright purple.

I was focused, clenching my staff tightly, sinking my boots into the ground when the Third started yelling toward the sky. The Third's purple eyes turned to me, and he slowly raised his left index finger and touched the golden mark on his forehead. The mark began to seep blood until a line of blood ran down the middle of his face, and the two sides of his face separated. What separated them was nothing but a dark void. I did not like the feeling of this as I gripped my pointing stick even tighter. From the darkness came out the heads of what looked like previous wizards, I presume ones he had killed in the past. I had to take a second to take in what I was seeing. Before I knew it, the six heads opened their mouths, and blasts of energy cut through the ground toward me. I ran as quickly as I could, trying to close the distance with the Third, when one of the heads extended outward, its mouth widening to devour me. I nearly missed becoming its meal. Their dismantled and contorted faces stared at me, their necks stiffly extended, biting out toward me like a dog locked to a leash.

I extended my blue pointing stick into the sky until its bright-blue aura covered our surrounding area. I pointed in the direction of the Third, and a relentless wave of powerful blue arcs of lightning struck the Third. I watched his body convulse and twist with the loss of control of his muscles. The heads screamed in unison and shriveled away. The Third was on his knees, screaming and hollering, and part of his face looked as though it had peeled away. There was little blood seeping as the lightning had cauterized whatever wounds it had created. I ran up to Third and put everything I had behind my punch, slamming it dead center into his face, sending him flying into the woods and through several trees.

The woods were filled with heavy fog that had begun to rise because of the morning sun. As I took a second to concentrate, I found myself making a complete connection with Maska's pointing stick, telling it, "I understand." I took a few steps forward and powered up my blue aura around my entire body. The Third lay at the base of a tree, shards of bark impaling his body, fresh wounds seeping across his purple skin. He gasped for each breath, and he could barely pick his head up to look at me. He had to turn his eyes upward to see the rest of me. Maska's pointing stick lay a few feet away from him.

"Do you surrender?" I asked him as I summoned Maska's pointing stick to me.

"Never... Let me die...with my honor."

"You have murdered countless numbers of people. How can you have any honor left?"

The Third spit out the blood that was pooling in his mouth.

"War is war... And death in war is as honorable as any. Failure in battle that ends in death is still a good death. Take your victory... and finish it..., wizard."

That word filled me with energy. "Wizard." I extended both pointing sticks, and the blue aura slowly creeped along the ground toward the Third. As it enveloped him, he closed his eyes, and his mouth hung open, blood trickling from the corner of his lips. And then the aura glowed, and he began to finally feel what was happening to him. What started as screams became silence as his skin began to bubble, blood began to simmer, the blue aura exploded, and there was nothing left of the Third.

Lata reunited with Zow, introducing Kogi the mage in the process. Zow reported that all remaining enemy forces were withdrawing. Lata said, "Good. Let us get the wounded off the battlefield and set up a strong perimeter on both sides. After that, have the soldiers eat and then go back to their duty stations."

Catalan had made her way in with Captain Raider and his platoon at her side, letting Lata know, "These soldiers were responsible for helping bring down the space tower."

Lata gave an astonished look and suddenly noticed there was a teenage girl standing behind Catalan. Lata asked, "So care to explain who this is?"

Catalan whispered to Lata, "I would like to talk in private regarding this matter." I had decided to quickly stop by to make sure Lata was all right before going back to support the troops when Masta's pointing stick, which I was carrying on my back, flew out of its binds and made its way to the teenage girl. Everyone got super quiet.

After a few moments, I broke the silence and told Lata, "We need to talk. Right now. Bring the girl."

I slammed through the door to an empty room with a single light above, away from the ears of the troops. Lata stopped in front of me, and, from behind her, Catalan dragged the girl inside. I asked, "Who is this girl?"

Catalan responded, "I found her in the tower, but she refused to speak a word."

"I thought that pointing sticks tend to gravitate to wizards, not random people, or the enemy?" I asked.

Lata said, "They do!"

I asked, "Are you telling me this girl is a wizard?"

Lata responded with a shrug. "I am not sure."

"I thought you said there weren't any more wizards left outside of us?"

"So did I!"

Catalan asked Lata, "Couldn't we ask Zow to enter the child's mind?"

Lata said, "That is a good idea. I will make sure everything else is taken care of while she helps you."

Zow entered the room looking to be in a hurry. Comparing her to the girl, Zow was no more than four feet tall. Her skin tone had changed color to all yellow, and she wore what looked like a gas mask on top of her head.

"My apologies for my change in appearance," she said. "My race goes through drastic changes throughout the day, and they become more pronounced with exhaustion."

I asked Zow, "Could you help us?"

"Of course I can, wizard."

"Good, because the girl seems to not want to talk for whatever reason."

Zow approached the girl and sat next to her. Zow, at first, tried to place her hand on the teenager's head, but she bit her. The girl looked terrified. So Zow took out a candy bar from her pocket and slowly gave it to the teenager. After she finished nibbling on a piece of chocolate, Zow would hand her another, and another, and she would get closer with each piece until she could finally place her hand on the girl's forehead.

For half an hour, it looked like the two were meditating. Zow finally returned to us, tears dripping from her eyes as the teenager threw up all over the floor, gasping for air. Zow asked, "Which version do you want to hear first? The bad one or the not so bad?"

I said, "The bad one," as I looked at Catalan, who had a sad look in her eyes.

"This girl can speak. She is just terrified," Zow said.

Catalan asked, "Of what?"

Zow said, "Save those questions for the end. Her name is Honovi. She was artificially created in the Successor's laboratory using Caden's DNA. The Fect had originally been experimenting on wizards they had captured, but they kept ending with the same result—a failed test subject. The wizards' bodies could not handle Caden's DNA now that it had been intertwined with that of the

Successor's, which led the wizards' bodies to decay. When Honovi came to life, the Successor's plan was to sacrifice Honovi and consume her genetic material to enhance his power."

It took a few seconds for me to process everything. I paraphrased my understanding of what Zow just told me, "So you are telling me that not only do we have in our possession the only remaining silver orb but we also have the perfect host for the silver orb."

Zow said, "That is correct."

The next thing I said was "We need to separate the two as quickly as possible, and we have to find a way to destroy this orb."

Zow continued, "Honovi had been tired of being held in a room every day and being used as a test subject. She showed me that, not too long ago, she was able to somehow tap into some of her wizard powers and escaped. At that time, she said she was held in Caden's laboratory, which is located to the far east of Devansh in the region known as the Land of the Gods. Now for some more bad news!"

I looked at Zow and said, "What now?"

Zow took a deep breath. "The Successor wants Honovi back at all costs, and he has sent his entire army throughout Devansh looking for her. He will destroy anything and everything to get what he wants." Zow suddenly placed her head in her hands and groaned, sitting on a nearby chair.

I told Zow, "That is enough for now. Go rest, and I will watch over Honovi. Follow up with Lata to ensure that the power core, the lock as everyone calls it, is still intact. In the meantime, I will make sure Honovi gets something to eat and a change of clothes, along with some rest." At the end of the night, I closed the door to the room where Honovi was sleeping, and I made my way to one of the balconies facing outside. I started looking up at the stars, wondering what in the heck just happened. One day, I am training to learn to use powers I never knew I had before, and now my head is racing in all directions, wondering how I'm caught in the middle of this crazy war and the mad science experiments that came with it.

The next day, Lata called us all over to one of the conference rooms where the president of Devansh was seen speaking on a projection Captain Raider had set up. President Nilla reported two hours ago that the Successor reached out to her directly, demanding the return of his experimental property. To make things clear, the Successor nuked a city directly north of the capital, killing over two million instantly, and he will do it again every seven days, after which, he will attack the capital with a nuclear device. "I believe you are smart, President Nilla, and care for the people of Devansh. Don't let others die for a cause you know very little about!" the president quoted. The president admitted to us all, "The message was disturbing to me, and, for the city of Dots and its two million residents, they will be avenged. They did not die in vain."

I pulled Lata out of the room with Honovi at my side and told Lata, "We have to split up the silver orb and Honovi. We are asking for problems by keeping the two this close together."

Lata looked at me and said, "I agree, but I do not know what to do. There are six major cities that go further north of Dots in a straight line, eventually leading to the capital. We cannot let six cities worth of people die."

"Well, what is to stop the Successor from nuking this place right now?"

"Don't be dumb. Aside from us wizards, I even went so far as to reinforce the barrier."

I asked Lata, "Would Vanas be able to help us?"

"Maybe, but she is still in critical condition."

The three of us went to Vanas's room and saw that the mage was still not doing too well. Lata looked at me and said, "She might not make it."

I got next to the mage and said, "I took care of the Third for us, but I need your help in figuring out what to do next." Lata looked at me with a discouraged face as she wiped her face on her brown robes. As I put my head down, Honovi grabbed Vanas's left hand. An orange glow appeared as if giving life to Vanas. The orange wave of light spread throughout her body, giving her enough strength to speak. Lata and I looked at Honovi with the same expression of astonishment.

Vanas coughed, "It took you long enough to come and lend a hand."

I joked with Vanas, telling her, "Maybe if my teacher would not have just up and left me, then things might have turned out differently."

Vanas said, "I see you have not changed. But regarding your situation, Honovi has brought me up to speed telepathically. And, yes, she can do that. You could go far southeast to the Island of Wizards."

I said, "We got an island too?"

Vanas rolled her eyes at me. "It is where Abir first discovered his connection with the cosmic language."

Vanas began to recount, "Abir's connection with the cosmic language got so deep that he began to unveil some of its mysteries. One of them took the form of a golden staff. This staff is actually a very small embodiment of the cosmic language itself. Abir used its powers during the final push through the Fect's remaining forces to help win the war. At the end of the war, Abir was worried that, in the wrong wizard's hands, the golden staff could destroy Devansh, or even the planet. So he left, never to be seen again. It wasn't until your grandfather, Remo, had a vision of the Fect's return that he went to the Island of Wizards. Remo spent a year on the island, and when he returned, he said Abir rode off into the heavens on top of the golden staff. In all honesty, Alaric, I believe Remo was onto something when he disappeared. He became so obsessed over what Abir told him once pertaining to the idea ancient dark magic had been possibly used on the Cult of Wizards somehow. For a dark voice existed in his mind that called him to take his life. The dark voice poured guilt into his mind, calling him to the bottle, drugs, and other vices. I believe that with Remo's ability to be able to go into different dimensions, he sought out this green wizard for help. Abir would tell Remo that during his first connection with the cosmic language, a wizard wearing all green robes appeared to guide him. The Cult of Wizards always thought that Abir had simply envisioned a green wizard as his way to communicate with the cosmic language more easily, as if he had created a character for him to visualize and talk to. But when Abir showed up one day with a golden staff, the commotion died down. During the last night he stood in my house, Remo kept talking about a green wizard in his sleep until it sounded like he was talking directly to the wizard. The next day, he was gone, but I had a suspicion that he somehow managed to figure out how to get in direct contact with the green wizard."

I asked Vanas, "What makes you so sure?"

"Because I am a mage, and I know my wizards. On that day in my home, I sensed this green wizard's energy that was so strong that they left a trail of green footsteps everywhere they had walked. I also know that this green wizard exists because after the war, I would speak to various wizards attempting to archive the war. A lot of them recalled looking over their shoulder and seeing a green glow, and others would recount seeing the green wizard himself. So much happened so quickly with the war against the Fect that no one really had time to reflect, because if they did, they would have known in the Cult of Wizards, there has never existed a green wizard."

I looked at Lata and said, "I will take Honovi with me to the Island of Wizards, and I am giving you the silver orb."

Lata said, "Okay. And what about this green wizard?" I thought about it for a bit, remembering when my grandfather saved me from my father just before I knew that I was a wizard. There had been an interesting glow.

I told Lata, "Whatever the situation may be about the green wizard and my grandfather, I'd imagine my grandfather knew what he was doing, and we have to trust in him and his decisions. Honestly, I do not know if he is alive, in another dimension, or whatever the case may be. Knowing my grandfather in the way that I did, he never did anything without thinking it through and having a plan." I squatted next to Vanas and told her, "Please, regain your strength."

"Make sure you stay strong yourself."

Lata said to me, "The power core and everything here will be fine for now. Make the trip quick!"

I asked, "Why?"

She replied, "Because I will need your help in defending the capital. While you make your way to the Islands of Wizards, I am going to gather all remaining forces to go defend the capital. When you are done, come immediately!"

Later that day, after packing everything we needed for the journey, Honovi and I made our way with our bellies full and our minds open. In my backpack, I had placed Masta's staff, but it was so tall that it was sticking out like an antenna, making it seem like I had a radio with me. I noticed Honovi kept eyeballing the staff for days. Along the way, I would try to stir up a conversation, but she did not seem like she was ready to trust me. I even began to tell her where I came from and the experiences I have had while in Devansh. It took us four whole days until finally reaching the ocean. It was as beautiful as Vanas had described it, leading to Honovi's first word: "wow!"

The magnificence of the blue ocean matched Honovi's blue hair. Honovi had been given a pair of blue robes by Lata, so we kind of matched. Honovi appeared a lot taller to me now that the sun was shining down on us. I could see on her face that there was a lot on her mind as her eyes continued to analyze everything about me. I looked around the beach and noticed a fishing vessel in the sand. I pointed my finger at the fishing vessel, and it came out of the ground. With my finger, I traced the sky toward the water, and the boat slowly lowered itself into the water, some of the years of sand dissolving into the waves. I inspected her closely, and I was impressed that for something the beach had begun to claim, she still was functional. Honovi had already boarded the green fishing vessel by that time as I looked around calling out her name.

We set sail, letting my pointing stick do the navigating. Vanas reminded me that my pointing stick is alive and that I need to give it attention. Before we left Vanas's room, she grabbed my pointing stick, grabbed the head of it, and whispered something to it, covering her mouth with her hand. I asked her what she said, but all Vanas would tell me is that she told my pointing stick how to get to the Island of Wizards. I felt she may have left out certain details. I noticed Honovi had a smile on her face as she looked out into the horizon, bringing her a sense of peace. I came to stand next to her, looking out into the distance. Then, breaking all the suspense that built up within me since we began our journey, enduring days of silence from her, Honovi finally spoke her first sentence to me.

"You know, I'm actually sixteen, thank you very much."

I was surprised how quickly she began to open up. Honovi began to tell me of the horror she witnessed at the laboratory as each day, they would take samples of her blood to try and create more like her, but after a few hours, the test subjects would die. Honovi told me she found out who her father was when one day, she escaped and logged into one of their computers.

"It was titled 'Caden Bastard Child.' I did not get to find out who my mother was because by the time I navigated through the system, the Sharm had found me. Caden, that day, came to see me and told me that if I ever ran away again, he would never tell me who my parents were and that he would slowly begin to make their lives miserable." Honovi continued with telling me how she was scared of Caden because he was a psychopath who, at times, was unhinged and would act like a complete lunatic. The Successor, on the other hand, only cared about regaining the silver orb and consuming her genetic material. Honovi told me how Caden would pace and talk to multiple other voices that were not there.

"At times, he said he could hear the voices telling him to kill every remaining wizard as if he would tap into a serial killer's personality. Caden knows better than to lay a hand on me. The Successor ruled it as such, but there were days where I could see a stone-cold killer looking at me as he began to name off all of the wizards that he had put down. One day, I saw Caden come back completely covered in blood. He was ecstatic in a sense of bliss, laughing with such a sinister tone. He told me he pleasured himself today by the thrill of killing another wizard. Caden bragged how he managed to defeat her and decided to take her staff as his prize." Honovi talked about how terrified she was that day, because when Caden got into those kinds of highs, he was very unpredictable.

"The thing I wanted to tell you about, Alaric, was that same day, later that night, Caden was screaming, and I could also hear the Successor's voice asking him what was wrong. Caden yelled and cursed saying, 'That damn green wizard keeps meddling in my affairs!' The Successor's voice went silent, as though looking for some kind of answer." Honovi said it was interesting to her when she overheard Vanas talking about the green wizard, seeing as she had heard the name before from Caden.

I looked at Honovi, and the first thing I said as I gave her a hug was, "I'm sorry you had to go through all that by yourself."

When I let go, Honovi had tears coming down her face. As I wiped the tears off her face, she pointed in front of me and said, "What the heck is that?" I turned around and laid my eyes upon the most beautiful bowhead whales I had ever seen in my life.

The smiles kept coming as Honovi almost appeared to be somehow drawing all these animals to her. They would not stop, as dolphins came next and began to talk with her. There was even a great white shark that came to protect Honovi by following our boat. At that point, I was even impressed. As nighttime crept over us, I turned on some of the boat's lights, which guided us through the vast darkness of the ocean. I pulled out some goodies, and we ate some Romanesco and king coconut I had packed, but I could tell Honovi wanted something else. Not even a few minutes later, a giant tuna jumped on the boat, looking at me directly in the face, telling me, "Cut me up, and feed me to her."

I was thinking, *I must be losing it.* Well, I did as I was told and used my pointing stick as a knife. Then I passed my pointing stick over the tuna to heat it up, and seconds later, I was serving seared tuna to Honovi. While she ate, I thanked the tuna for offering itself, chopped up the rest, and put it away in my backpack for later. That night, when Honovi went to sleep in her sleeping bag and closed her eyes, I watched over her, and she looked like she finally felt free.

In the morning, I was beginning to wonder what would be for breakfast as both our stomachs growled, when out of nowhere, a blue whale came to the edge of the boat, opened its mouth, and spit out shrimp, crab, and lobsters all over the deck for the two of us. I was feeling like I was living the life of luxury the way that these animals kept bringing us food. I had no problem cooking it all up for the two of us. Honovi seemed to really be enjoying the experience. There was a night where Honovi had pulled guard duty. I felt like I needed to rest so that I could be ready for what lay ahead. I got into my sleeping bag with my pointing stick next to me. I was feeling lazy and decided to leave Maska's staff in the backpack. I closed my eyes, and what felt like five minutes later, Honovi had the staff and had sent a giant orange energy blast into the sky. Orange streaks of lightning lit up the sky, each blast being a flare to light up the blackness around us. I told Honovi, "Hand the staff over," but she was too far gone as her eyes had turned completely orange. I went to grab the pointing stick from Honovi when it blasted me backward. After a few minutes, she finally calmed down. She dropped the pointing stick to the ground, and she fell over unconscious. It was at this moment that Honovi left me wondering how powerful she could become.

After she awoke, hours later, Honovi came and sat directly in front of me and asked why I never came looking for her. She wanted to know why I let a schizophrenic psychopath who called himself the Enlightened One raise her in a laboratory. She wanted to know whether it was because she was not worth saving. Honovi said all the memories in her head were put in there by Caden's scientists, so she knows she cannot believe her memories when it comes to looking for answers.

"One day, at the dinner table, Caden was so frustrated that he had the Sharm bring in captured soldiers from the capital and would have them line up against the wall in front of us. Caden would have a drink and toss it across the room just to watch the soldiers crawl for whatever refreshment they could get. He'd make me watch, and he'd have a random one or two executed. He'd do this over and over again. The soldiers never knew which one of them was next. And sometimes, Caden spared them all just for a day or two. The Successor would take control once more and ask me how unhinged Caden was today. I tried to joke about it and responded, 'Very.' He didn't like that very much. Over the years, it appeared to me that the Successor was losing the mental power struggle that was going on in Caden's head, because he would not be around for as long. Caden lifted up his black robes and showed his entire chest had been heavily bruised, and, from his stomach down to his legs, he had deep wounds. On this particular day, Caden asked the soldiers where the green wizard was. All the captured soldiers looked at each other and did not have a clue about what Caden was talking about. Caden, desperate for blood, used a dark magic blast on each one of them. One by one, they each dropped dead to the floor. That day, Caden grabbed me and tossed me in the pool of blood. It was a while before they managed to capture any more soldiers for him to torment."

Toward the end of the next day, I was taking another nap when Honovi woke me up, pointing and telling me, "Look!" When I lifted my hat from over my face, I was mesmerized. How could a giant stone wall go completely around an entire chain of islands? Now at this distance, the wall did not look that big, but as we got closer, the wall must have been ninety stories high, and who knows how far down into the ocean. It was circling the entire chain of islands that included the Island of Wizards. I could not help but be humbled by its magnificence. It truly was quite the site as Honovi stood quietly, looking straight up.

Chapter 10

As we grabbed our belongings, I asked Honovi to grab my blue robes as I pointed toward the peak of the nearest island and snapped my fingers. When we got to the top, I looked over and saw ten islands surrounded by blood orange water that radiated with the sunset. There was a darkness that appeared to be lingering on each island. I could not make it out, but it seemed like someone may have beat us here. I took a moment to breathe and collect my thoughts when I noticed one of the islands appeared to be sinking. I looked at Honovi and really began to wonder if I should just leave her on the boat as I saw the sinking island disappear into the ocean. My hand quivered as my pointing stick started to push my hand up. It wasn't trying to free itself from my grip but as if it was possessing my hand. My muscles gave in, and my hand shot upward. The pointing stick's tip faced the largest island of them all.

Honovi looked at the island my pointing stick had selected and immediately put her hands over her head, saying, "I don't like that island."

I asked her, "What is it?"

"Something terrible happened over there."

"Stay close."

I pointed directly at the Island of Wizards with my other hand and snapped my fingers, bringing us onto the beach. The moment my blue boots touched the beach, I could sense that, indeed, something was terribly wrong like Honovi had indicated. I looked up and down the beach but couldn't make anything out that seemed special, so we picked what I thought would take us inland soonest, and we started walking.

The further we walked up the beach, I began to make something out on the ground spread out all around. At first, I noticed tiny red spots in the sand that became bigger red spots. It was not until I got up closer that I realized dead bodies surrounded us. There must have been over a hundred bodies lying on the beach. From the burn marks on the bodies and the looks in their faces of contorted scowls, attempts to scream, and gritted teeth, it looked as though they all died in agonizing pain. I told Honovi to follow me as we made our way into the island, looking for the temple. I did not like what we were walking into. As I took another step, I became light-headed and began stumbling around, throwing up black vomit. Honovi began freaking out. I tried to calm her down as my insides felt like they were on fire. It had been a while since I threw up black vomit, and it was hitting me stronger than ever before. After a good half an hour, I regained my strength, and Honovi stood quiet.

At first, there were green leaves all around us, and after a mile, everything was blackened, as if this part of the island had been scorched. With every step I took, the hairs on my back shot up as I gripped my pointing stick to keep moving forward. I could sense the pain and hear the screams of those that were vaporized. As I probed the area, I began to make out black spots spread out the barks of the trees where people stood. We came to a point on the island where if you looked to your left, it looked like a war had taken place, and if you looked to the right, there was nothing but footsteps running away into the woods. I decided we should follow these steps to see where they might lead us. I looked at the mountains in the distance and thought that they were covered in blood. The mountains were sliced through, and the trench came its way to where we now stood, like a beam had cut a deep scar into the ground. The trench continued for a mile down and then it looked like it completely destroyed several other mountains. I began thinking out loud, "What could have done all this?"

Honovi said, "Another wizard!"

I jerked my neck thinking, *But who? There aren't any left besides us and everyone back on the continent.* As we continued walking, we came across a whole acre of land filled with dead animals that had been caught by whatever beam made the trench. I began to wonder if this journey might have been a mistake. Everything was covered in blood, even the leaves on the trees. I looked over at Honovi, and I could tell that she was scared. I asked Honovi, "Do you like to whistle?"

She said yes!

I told Honovi, "Awesome. You can be our whistling person that will give us strength to continue the journey."

Honovi looked at me and said, "You are so lame. Did you think I was ten years old or something?" as she continued walking. I stared into her eyes, whistling a joyful little tune. I couldn't tell exactly how close she was to smacking me, but I assumed she was close by the scowl she made.

We slowed our pace as we stumbled across a giant crater on the ground. From examining it and grabbing some of the burnt dirt, it let me know this happened recently. It appeared as though something had lifted a chunk of the ground out of the planet. The sky began to turn black as we continued walking. It started to become clear to me that some dark magical force was lingering around. Then a massive bang could be heard with a shock wave that came our way. Honovi was petrified. The shield I put over us didn't protect us from being knocked down. The very next second, a black beam of energy was shot at the enormous wall, causing it to crumble. It was then that it became crystal clear that whoever had done all this was still here! I looked at Honovi, and I was determined to not let her feel scared. I looked around and spotted an opening in one of the mountains. I made my way in and checked around to make sure no one else was inside. I told Honovi, "Wait for me here." I also gave her the orange staff and told her, "If I do not return in twenty-four hours, find a way to get out of here. Okay?" Honovi gave me a look to let me know she understood everything that was going on. I left my backpack with Honovi and told her, "Don't be shy. Have at it. There's plenty of fruit and tuna I had packed. Take a nap and recover."

"You don't have to treat me like a little girl and hide things from me. I know I look scared, but I'm worried about you too! I know you are scared because whatever is causing all these problems must be pretty strong."

I told Honovi, "You are correct, and I do not know if I can protect the both of us."

"It's fine," she grumbled.

As I turned around to walk out, Honovi said, "You better be careful!"

I looked back and said, "I will be." As I walked away, I was not sure why, but I teared up a bit after thinking of the sad face Honovi had made at the end. Was it because I cared for her well-being?

I walked for quite a bit longer as I began to hear agonizing screams getting louder and louder. I came to a point where I spotted something as I got closer. I saw it was a temple. There was nothing left of the temple aside from the little wall standing with a window still open. Its remains were scattered in different directions. As I got closer to where the temple once stood, I heard a voice, and out of the darkness of the woods came out a terrifying figure.

I asked, "Who are you?"

The black figure said, "You already know the answer to your question."

The voice made my skin crawl. I recognized it. I yelled out, "My father was shadow-banned, and there is no black moon out. So state your name and your business."

The black figure's voice croaked, "You were never one for formality, were you, son?"

"You are not my father."

The hooded figure pulled back his hood, and there stood my father, in the flesh, with a burnt mark across his face from when Varun got him some time ago. I was frozen in place, asking, "How in the world are you here? No one escapes from being shadow-banned. It is not something you can do from that dimension."

"You are correct, wizard. I see the side you have chosen."

I asked my father, "What did you mean by that?"

My father shook his head and told me, "You are still as naive as ever. Even as a wizard, you still can't tell. Could you?"

"Tell what?"

"You know, your grandfather who you believed loved you so much. It was more so to monitor you once he shadow-banned me."

"You're lying!"

"No, Alaric the wizard. You are lying to yourself!"

"I don't have to listen to this. You were always filled with lies, even now."

"You truly are blind, aren't you, son?"

"Stop calling me that, because you are not my father."

"You are correct, Alaric. I am not your father. I am now more than just that. Your grandfather always feared what the mixing of our bloodlines may do, but I didn't care, as to why I tricked your mother into loving me."

I began to get impatient and told him, "Get to the point!"

"The point, wizard, is that you are too dumb to notice your true bloodline."

"And what is that?"

"The warlock blood that runs through your veins. For whatever reason, son, you always had a stronger connection to the wizard bloodline, which is fine, because it's been a while since I took the life of a wizard."

I told my father, "You did not answer me. How is it that you are here without a black moon?"

"Well, you see, wizard, after seeing you with your grandfather's staff at the ruins, I decided to use my brain, seeing how you had been developing toward becoming a wizard. I realized it was time to use my ace. While you were training, I managed to get in communication with Caden using old dark magic. With the power that he possesses, he broke me free from the shadow dimension. I consumed just about everyone that had been shadow-banned with me, helping restore my full power. Caden, in return for setting me free, wanted me to bring him back Honovi. So Caden sent me here to get the place ready for your grand welcoming. The bonus is that I get to destroy my own son."

I looked at my father disgustedly and told him, "You do not deserve the right to say you're my father."

My father said, "Be respectful and address me as Lumusi the warlock."

I told him, "That is never going to happen!"

Lumusi said, "I see you are still just a hardheaded kid in the mix of things. I bet your grandfather never took the time to tell you anything the wizards did wrong, right? The wizards were the ones that decided the warlocks were a threat to this planet, and we were their first enemies before the Fect. The wizards never liked how we used more unnatural resources to tap into power they have absolutely no idea about. But then they felt they were the superior beings and deemed it wrong or evil. So what? For me to maintain my power as a warlock, I have to take someone's life. It is just one life amongst an overpopulated planet. And so what if we had to destroy a mage, a sorcerer, or even a wizard to acquire our power? It is considered a blessing in our perspective to give a warlock your life for the greater purpose. In fact, we're helping the planet. We're removing the unwanted squabble that takes up too much space! Speaking of which, I was thanking the residents of these fine islands for sacrificing their lives for my greater good."

I looked at this warlock and said, "You mean butchering."

"I am thankful because their lives have allowed me to tap into more of that unnatural power you wizards deem evil."

I looked at the warlock and said, "I am ashamed of what you chose to become."

"Do you know the real reason I was shadow-banned?" I stared at the warlock. He said, "Of course, you do not know, because I bet your damn grandfather would have never told you. I tried taking his life one day when I discovered he was a wizard. My grudge against you wizards is like none other. I had prepared to take his life. I just did not know how strong of a wizard he was until I attacked him and came to find out when he shadow-banned me. Don't get me wrong, we had one heck of a fight, but age and experience proved to be on his side, but now the tables have turned, and I am going to end you wizards. Warlocks will rise again and join the Fect in taking over this entire planet."

"How naive could you be? Don't you see by now that the Fect alone plan to rule this planet? Once you help them get what they want, they will eliminate you."

Lumusi said, "I think not," as two more hooded dark figures slowly came out the dark woods. "I forgot to mention that I brought along a few warlocks that were also shadow-banned by your grandfather. I should really be thanking your grandfather for giving me an army, giving us time to plan and to make moves from the shadows. I don't think he ever believed we would have ever come out of that pit he put us in. And now look! Only two wizards are left. It looks like the joke is on the wizards, and don't forget, wizard, today makes seven days that have passed. By now, another city has been nuked because of your stubbornness about returning the girl." Lumusi's black pointing stick appeared in his hand. "This is the end for you, my son...the wizard." He snarled at having to say that word again. I drew my pointing stick as a mighty storm was approaching us.

Lumusi threw something in my direction so fast I did not have time to react until it hit me square in the face, almost knocking me out. I was a bit dizzy as I felt something warm running down my face. I touched my head and noticed blood. Lumusi told me he was going to break me.

Lumusi said, "How about another lesson, boy. Do you know how warlocks get their pointing sticks?"

"No, and I don't want to know!"

"Pity, but children must learn, or what good will that do this world?" Lumusi licked his lips and said "The dark gods grant us one after we have killed a grand wizard. I wonder what they will give me this time when I kill Lata?"

"Don't you even dare think about it!" I snarled. Lumusi stared at me as a smile grew on his face, and his eyes turned black.

Lumusi told me, "The last dark god will give rise to the true dark wizard that will topple your entire little cult!"

"You've lost your mind!" I screamed.

"Perhaps...," Lumusi said as his pointing stick began circling around him until a black energy completely surrounded his body. I stood firm, patiently waiting for whatever would happen next, as a black hand emerged, and out came Lumusi. I took notice that his entire head had a black flame around him, and it looked as though some of his flesh burned off his face. The darkness around him became heavier as the black flames made it harder to breathe. With every step he took, he left a black imprint on the ground. The black flames spread throughout his entire body as the smell of burnt flesh made its way into the air as bone began to show itself, revealing his entire jaw.

I choked on the rising smoke emanating from his body, but I croaked out, "You went through all this effort, regained your face, and just burned it off again? Are you stupid?"

I watched as one of the warlocks turned their hands into fire, and the other began to contort his fingers into signs. Lumusi came at me with his pointing stick, screaming how he was going to kill me, my blue pointing stick matching his blows. Lumusi pulled out a dagger as I knocked him back, but he managed to cut across the chest of my blue robes. I looked at Lumusi and said, "You warlocks really have a whole style of your own, huh? I had no idea," as the warlock with a fist of fire popped up on me. I dodged his moves, and right when I was going to blast him with a beam of light, the other warlock shot me with a black blast that really packed a punch. I got up, pulled myself together, and before fully gathering myself, Lumusi shot a blast at me, which I deflected. This time, I pointed twice with both my index fingers and sent two shock waves at one of the warlocks. I wasn't moving fast enough, as the fist of fire landed ten punches on me, and the warlock ended it with a blast that sent me to the beach. When I got up again, I knew I was in trouble. I was outnumbered, and as much as my ego wouldn't want me to believe, Lumusi was more skilled than I.

As the three warlocks appeared before me on the beach, two other warlocks stepped from the shadows and removed their hoods, revealing that they had six black eyes. Lumusi said, "Let me show you the unnatural abilities that your fellow wizards feared about war-locks." Lumusi walked up to one of the warlocks and touched his forehead, turning him into a black plum. Lumusi ate the black plum, and four more eyes appeared on his face, making six. Lumusi walked to the other warlock, and when he touched him, he fell into Lumusi's palm as a black apple. With a crunch, Lumusi's forehead became riddled with a veil of black tattoos, and matching runes were etched into his pointing stick. Lumusi shot a black blast of energy my way that I deflected with my pointing stick, and it hit the far side of the great wall, completely obliterating a chunk of it. Lumusi used his new powers with the power of his pointing stick to raise the water and direct it at me. I snapped my fingers to teleport away from the massive force of that wave. As I reappeared, he hit me with a blast of black energy he had prepared for me. I sailed through the air and smashed into the ancient wall. I felt my body aching after that attack, and my left hand was shaking. I noticed a few dislocated fingers that I painfully popped back into place.

As I stumbled to my feet, dusting myself off, I found myself inside the wall itself on a flight of stone stairs that led further upward. I followed the steps up as quickly as I could, and I found myself outside again, on the top of the wall. As I stepped out of the interior, the darkened sky flashed with streaks of lightning dashing off in each direction. I raised my staff and powered up, drawing as much natural energy as I could. Over the island and the water below, Lumusi levitated higher and higher, his small figure growing larger as he approached. I was about to blast him back into the island when I was suddenly grabbed from behind. My muscles froze and clenched up, my veins pulsed, and my vision frizzed as electricity ran through my body. I could barely feel anything when I fell forward onto the ground. I fought my muscles, which were slowly loosening up, to stand, and above me was another warlock with hands pulsing with electricity.

With all my attention focused on the warlock, I had forgotten that Lumusi was on his way, and I barely noticed as he levitated over the edge of the wall. I quickly turned and pointed my pointing stick at Lumusi when someone from underneath me suddenly pulled me down toward them. Next thing I knew, I was surrounded by warlocks. I struggled with their grip on me, but I quickly triple-snapped my fingers to cancel out all their spells, and then I powered up my blue aura. I unleashed a massive blast emanating from my body. The warlock holding me down flew off my back, and I scurried to my feet. I turned around and pointed my pointing stick at Lumusi when a warlock sprinted toward me and slammed into me with his shoulder, pushing me off the edge of the wall. I hurtled into the water with a hard splash. As I was sinking, I could faintly see blasts of energy fly into the water after me. Each blast of energy pushed me further and further. I tapped my mouth with my pointing stick, allowing me to breathe underwater.

I took a few minutes to think of how I was going to deal with these warlocks and Lumusi. After a few minutes, I had an idea, and I resurfaced. I snapped my fingers and flew out of the water and high into the air, landing on both feet on the beach of one of the other islands. When I arrived on the beach, a huge boulder came flying my way. I split it down the middle by pointing at it. From the woods came a crunching sound interrupted by footsteps. Lumusi came out of the trees. His mouth was stained with black juice as he held another black fruit in his hand.

I yelled out, "How many more of your comrades have you eaten?"

Lumusi smiled and said, "Let me show you."

He pointed his pointing stick at one of the smallest islands, lifted it out of the ocean, and hurled it at me. I have never experienced having something so massive being thrown in my direction. I managed to cut through it using every ounce of energy I had, but large chunks of rock were still coming. Lumusi appeared behind me and sent six black balls of energy my way. As each hit me in succession, I sailed further from the island and higher into the air until I flew across the bay and landed on my back on the furthest island. The entire upper portion of my uniform and robes were completely torn.

One of Lumusi's warlocks teleported above me and lifted me up on my shoulders. Lumusi slowly levitated over the water toward me. Lumusi smiled as he raised his hands to the stars and drew the streaks of dark lightning to his fingertips. As he pulsed with electricity, he shot a stream of it into my chest. I felt like my organs were burning, and the pain only grew as my muscles contracted. Lumusi stopped as he watched one of the warlocks fly backward and disintegrate into ash. He followed the beam of light down the beach to Honovi, whose hands were glowing bright with energy.

Lumusi dropped to the beach and grabbed the remaining warlock, turning him into a black fruit, and devoured him. I screeched, "Run!" at Honovi with my last bit of energy as my body suddenly went limp. All I heard was a snap, and Lumusi's smile widened as he dropped his hands to his side. I tried to lift my arm, but I couldn't. I tried to snap my fingers, but even they felt dead. I couldn't even pick up my head. Lumusi twirled his pointing stick in a circle around me. Black ropes of energy wrapped around my body, locking my hands and limbs against my body. I couldn't even move my fingers. Lumusi finally said, "What's wrong, my boy? Can't move? It is a shame you were not taught by the wizards of old. Instead, I hear your teacher was a mere mage, one bested by the Third, no less. I'm surprised that you managed to defeat him, but he was a fool, and it was bound to catch up to him eventually." Honovi shot a beam of energy at Lumusi to get his attention away from me. Lumusi told her, "You need to wait your turn…, but I will indulge you," as he made his way toward her. Honovi aimed her staff at Lumusi once more, and she sent out an even greater blast of orange energy, which he deflected as if it were a feather in the wind. Lumusi squeezed both of his hands together. Then he separated them slowly from one another as a black aura of energy began to grow between his palms. He shot it at Honovi, knocking the pointing stick out of her hand and capturing her within a black ball of energy. Lumusi walked up to Honovi and said to her, "Be a good girl, and wait until I am finished with this one. Then we can leave." When Lumusi turned around, he was pummeled into the sand as a barrage of energy blasts struck him in the chest.

"Sorry I'm late," Kogi joked. "I got lost with the coordinates for a bit since I don't have a pointing stick, and I had to get creative."

Lumusi growled as he stood up and stomped his feet, infuriated. "That's hardly sporting!" Lumusi snapped.

Kogi told Lumusi, "How dare you speak in lies!" Kogi noted, "I may not have been able to see it happen, but I heard your lies of how the wizards killed off the warlocks as if they were committing genocide. You deserved what you got. Your desire for power drove you to madness and evil. You kidnapped wizards and ordinary people to force them to join you, and those who refused or failed, you consumed. You felt threatened by all other sorcerers, so you began to hunt us all down, hoping to be the last sorcerers left in the world. You started the Hundred Years' War, and you brought ruin upon yourselves!"

Lumusi began clapping. "Finally, someone around here who knows their history. Nonetheless, now that I am free, the warlocks will rise again, and the world will be as we make it." Kogi giggled and looked over Lumusi's shoulder into the forest. A grin stretched across his face, and Lumusi's grin disappeared.

"Maybe you should ask him what he thinks of my history lesson," Kogi said. Lumusi turned around and he quivered in fear when he saw the tree line bathed in a bright-green glow. All he could make out was a pointed green hat and flowing robes, and he fired every ounce of energy he had into the trees, screaming in panic. Kogi came over to me and snapped away the weakened black ropes.

I asked him, "Is the green wizard here?"

Kogi told me, "Let's worry about getting you free." Kogi noticed the death mark on my chest bearing down on me, so he powered up his left hand, and it began radiating white. He rammed his palm into my chest, destroying the death mark once and for all. Kogi winced in pain as his hand shriveled and blackened.

I tried to grab his hand as I said, "Let me take a look at it."

He pulled his hand away and said, "We have no time. Don't forget the girl."

Lumusi had gone mad, firing indiscriminately into the trees, blasting bits of the island away. When we got to Honovi, Kogi summoned the orange pointing stick toward him. He placed the head of the staff into the black ball of energy containing Honovi and drained it of its power. When Kogi was finally done, he had been severely weakened and dropped to one knee. He grabbed onto me and said, "Let's get out of here." We all held onto one another when Lumusi shot into the air. His voice grew hoarse as he continued to scream. Lumusi barraged the entire island with black energy blasts that emitted from his body in all directions. One of the blasts landed in front of us, knocking Kogi out. Honovi went flying forward, and I flew backward, landing facedown in the sand.

I lifted my head and only saw a dark blur. I think I could make out the forest beyond the beach, and another blur moved closer toward me. "I'm done with toying with you. I'm going to enjoy finally watching you die." His voice croaked as he tore up his vocal cords. Lumusi grew closer, and his staff withered and contorted into a sword. With no strength left, I simply closed my eyes and thought of home, of my mother, of my siblings. I thought of the deer grazing in the lush meadow around Lata's cabin. I thought of Lata's home-cooked meals, and I wished I could smell it once more before the sword came down on my neck. Then the footsteps stopped, and I felt as I did before, so I opened my eyes, and Lumusi stood just in front of me but was looking over me. "How could it possibly be? You shouldn't exist!" he squealed. I kept trying to turn around to see who he was staring at, but I couldn't move any muscle in my body. Lumusi cried out and stepped back as a green orb of energy blasted him in the chest. The glow hurt my eyes, and I was forced to blink. Lumusi cried out again, and when I opened my eyes again, I saw the energy of another blast fade away. Lumusi stood, poised to scream again as a final blast of energy struck his chest, engulfing him in a green glow, disintegrating him. My eyes closed again, and I didn't have the energy to open them again. Before my mind let go and my consciousness faded, I heard footsteps scurry toward me, opposite from where Lumusi had been standing.

I heard a gruff voice cry out, "Alaric!" Then I felt nothing.

I found myself walking toward the light. When the light got bright enough, I found myself looking at the temple on the island. The island looked beautiful, like it had never been touched by anyone. Not even animals nor insects stirred. Nothing. There was a sense of peace and balance that I felt connected to. I began to wonder if I was dead. If this was the afterlife, I wasn't going to complain. Suddenly, the doors of the temple slowly swung open, and Abir stepped forth, clutching his golden staff. His wrinkled face and thick gray eyebrows were shielded by his glowing pointed burgundy hat. I bowed my head, and Abir said, "No need for the formalities."

I asked Abir, 'Where are we?"

Abir said, "You are at the temple that I built on the Island of Wizards."

"But…that temple was destroyed by my father."

Abir smiled and chuckled, "You are funny. The temple that I built for the wizards is not the one in the physical world. We are in a metaphysical dimension, separate from the mortal world that you know, and you must learn how to master your connection to the cosmic language in order to arrive here next time."

"Well, how did I get here this time?"

"Haha! You have a lot of questions, Alaric, but, sadly, you don't get to spend much time here today. So I will make it quick for you. After the war with the Fect, the Cult of Wizards had suspicion that they would return one day because we never managed to capture Caden. The Cult of Wizards figured it was best that, in the meantime, we continued improving our knowledge of the cosmic language so that we can hand down this knowledge to future wizards. So far, the only ones that were successful at doing that that I know of is me. Otherwise, I would have already encountered my fellow brothers here at least once."

I grew sad hearing this, then said, "Then that must mean my grandfather, Remo, is dead."

Abir stroked his wrinkled chin a few times with his right hand and said, "Perhaps not. Remo the wizard actually had a special task assigned to him that I wonder if he has fulfilled yet."

"What was that task?" I asked.

Abir hesitated but then said, "That, Alaric, you will need to find out for yourself. For now, you will need this!" He held out the magnificent golden pointing stick toward me. As my hand wrapped around its handle, I immediately felt life pouring into me again. As my energy began to rise, my hands began to fade, then my legs, then my chest. Abir told me, "Believe in yourself, wizard. You possess more power than you allow yourself to believe." I woke up to a turtle bumping its head against mine. When I looked over, I saw Kogi was still passed out, and so was Honovi. I thought I had been dreaming until I looked to my right and saw a golden pointing stick levitating above the sand, just out of reach.

Chapter 11

"And you're sure they were warlocks?" asked President Nilla.

"Absolutely sure, Madam President. There were five, to be exact," Lata said.

"Did any escape? I don't want to hear about any warlocks rampaging through the countryside. We have enough problems as it is."

"None, Madam President. I took care of it."

"What did they want?"

Without hesitation or emotion, Lata said, "The silver orb, Madam President."

The president, now pouring a glass of brandy for herself, asked, "And what of Alaric the wizard?"

Lata responded with, "Still no word."

The president's hands trembled as she raised the glass to her mouth. "Will we be able to hold off until they arrive?"

Lata looked the president directly in the eye and said, "Yes."

Zow, who now looked like a panda as part of her rare species' daily transformations, walked up to the president and told her, "Take a seat." She began to give her a brain massage, and seconds later, she was asleep.

Lata looked at Zow and said, "Thanks. I was afraid she was going to have a heart attack."

Zow said, "It was the least I could do for now." The secret service took off their black shades, looked at one another, then looked at how well the president was sleeping, shrugged their shoulders, and continued to stand quietly.

Lata was concerned, now more than ever, wondering, *What's taking him so long? They should have been back by now.*

Lata said, "Since they've left, three cities have been nuked, leaving one more before the capital."

Zow told Lata, "I'm getting word that at the main gate to the north, the Second wishes to speak to you directly face-to-face."

"What does he want?" Lata asked with a frown.

"Captain Raider asked the Second, and he would not say anything else." Lata thought about it for a few good minutes and decided she would go down to speak with the Second. Zow told Lata, "Make sure to be careful."

Lata arrived at the north gate of the capital and shook Captain Raider's hand, telling him, "I'd like to congratulate you on the job you've been doing in defending the capital thus far."

Captain Raider told Lata, "Just doing my job."

Lata said, "Please, open the inner gate, but leave the outer defense gate closed. Whatever the Second has to say, he can say it through the outer gate, and if he tries anything, immediately close the inner gate, preferably on him, if you can." Captain Raider snorted, and a few of the soldiers standing around choked on their laughter.

Lata walked through the main gate and waited for the Second to present himself. After a few minutes, a mist appeared, and out of it came the Second. Lata told the second, "State your business!" The Second grabbed the outer gate, and his hand lit on fire. He cursed and slapped it on his knee, patting out the flames. Lata gave him a particularly ugly smile. "You like what I did to the place?"

The Second snarled at Lata, "Why do you people have to be so difficult? All my master wants is the silver orb and you're all free to go."

Lata told the Second, "Because we know it is not that simple. Actually, bowing down is not what we do, nor is it something the green wizard does."

The Second, in disbelief, took several steps back from the gate and, with a flutter in his voice, screamed, "The green wizard is back?"

One of the Sharm came out from the mist and said, "Message for you, my lord. Lumusi the Warlock has been slain...by a wizard in green." Upon hearing that news, a fire grew in Lata. She knew they had a chance if the green wizard could arrive on time.

The Second told the Sharm, "Report back to the First and tell them that I have a problem here that I need help fixing…NOW!"

"It would appear that you guys do know what fear is," Lata said with a grin.

The Second gave an evil stare directly at Lata and said, "You better hope that the green wizard arrives in time, because I will burn this city and watch your corpse char in its ruins!" The Second disappeared, and Lata walked away with her head high.

Motivated by the information she learned, she returned to Zow and informed her, "Brace for war. The main attack should be coming anytime now. Let all of the generals know what the plan is while I go and speak to Vanas and the others."

Lata walked into Vanas's room. She had just finished talking with Varun and Catalan. Lata broke down the details of everything she knew up until now. Vanas was the first to stand up, still bandaged up underneath her red robes. She was about 80 percent recovered, but she still shook and winced at times. Vanas was motivated by the news of the green wizard's return as she grabbed her ribs with a hardy look on her face. Varun asked, "What does Lata want us to do in the meantime?"

Lata told Catalan, "Use your exoskeleton suit to support Captain Raider and the rest of the ground forces. Varun, I want you with the infantry until then, and make sure you have enough explosives ready if they do take the city. We'll make sure they never claim it for themselves."

Vanas looked at Lata and asked, "What about her?" pointing a finger toward President Nilla, who was sound asleep from Zow's brain massage.

Lata said, "Protect the president, and be the last line of defense."

Vanas told Lata, "Are you sure that you are going to be able to handle both the Second and the First?" Vanas was concerned, because what if Alaric and the others didn't arrive on time, or the green wizard? Vanas begged Lata to let her stand with her on the battlefield to support her and level out the playing field.

Lata said, "For your own good, you will be our last level of defense."

Vanas told the other two, "Leave us. There are a few things I want to speak with Lata about, alone."

Vanas looked out the window and said, "Now that the green wizard is back, I can finally pass the burden on."

Vanas turned around and told Lata, "The time has come for me to transfer all of my powers...to you."

"No. It's not time yet."

"At this point, I will only get in the way, and, with my power bestowed onto you, you will get a significant boost. Tell Alaric when you see him that I am happy with the outcome of things. I am more than pleased with his progress, and he will soon grow beyond anything I could ever teach him. And maybe one day, we might meet again...beyond this world. Let the Cult of Wizards know that I fulfilled my duty, as did the remaining mages at the temple." Vanas grabbed a glass of water and took a bite of an apple. She smiled, chuckling at how she loved eating apples. Vanas told Lata, "Make sure the final wizard finishes off Caden, and make sure that Honovi gets proper training. That girl has the potential to start a new generation of wizards with your guidance."

Lata, tearing up from both eyes, told Vanas, "I will make sure Honovi does her part."

"I know you will... It is time."

Lata stomped her brown staff on the floor and pleaded one last time, "I am not ready to let you go!" Vanas struggled to her feet and confidently limped toward Lata, radiating a red aura. Vanas wrapped her arms around Lata and squeezed hard. As the two tightly embraced one another, Lata closed her eyes. Vanas still could hardly stand, so Lata was holding her weight up. Her heart skipped a beat as that weight slowly faded away, and the pressure against her body slowly dissipated. As Lata slowly began to open her eyes, a feeling of stickiness ran through her body as she winced with pain for a few seconds. Lata opened her eyes fully, and she stood alone in the room with her arms in front of her, curled around the air. Vanas was gone. Lata could feel Vanas's presence within her, and she smirked when she saw Vanas's special air tubes on the counter. Tears welled in her eyes, but she knew her friend was finally free.

As Lata took time to soak it all in, a few minutes later, the door opened, and Zow, now all green resembling an avocado that had been cut down the middle and opened up to expose the seed inside, said, "The fighting has started."

Lata summoned her brown pointing stick and said, "I'm on my way."

The First appeared, bearing the gold mark on his purple forehead, with magnificent armor made of gold, next to the Second who was missing an eye, bearing the gold mark, and had one mechanical foot. All the Sharm soldiers around them bowed their heads and got on one knee. The First told the Second, "Walk with me. You and everyone around will refer to me as my Fect name Matvey, and you will also use your Fect name proudly in battle, Timur." Matvey started quietly as his voice tone rose, "Caden is now in control, and do you know what that means? We have a bloodthirsty psychopath that is becoming impatient."

Timur was stuttering with his words from his damaged throat and vocal cords. "Did Caden really kill the Successor this time, or did he only manage to suppress him like last time?"

"The Successor is finished this time. It could be bad for the Fect, because, technically, Caden is a wizard who betrayed his own kind. We cannot be sure that this was all a grand plan by the wizards."

Timur, having difficulty speaking, asked, "What should we do?"

Matvey spoke silently, "Caden, without the power of the Successor, is not immortal. Once we get through with finishing off the last wizards, we will leave to go take care of him. Once we kill him and lay claim as the new successors of the Fect, we will determine the best course of action from there to eliminate the green wizard once and for all and finally finish the wizards once and for all. How many brigades do you currently have with you?"

Timur responded, shuddering, "As of right now, there are about eight brigades present, rounding out to about forty thousand Sharm."

Matvey told Timur, "Stop! This is where I am going to show you all of the toys I brought along for the invasion of their capital." Matvey summoned a few Sharm soldiers, demanding that they bring him a few captured civilians since he has grown hungry in their travels.

Matvey pointed to the right to tell Timur, "Over there! Look as our giant titans approached the city." The titans were grotesque abominations composed entirely of dead bodies from Devansh that had been killed by the Fect. They had giant black rods placed throughout their enormous body and various electronics grafted into the flesh. A large device was grafted into the chest with bundles of cables feeding into it. It was the brain of the beast, sending signals to force the amalgamation of corpses to move on command. One of the titans threw a punch at the city, and its entire fist was vaporized. Matvey was surprised at how good of a shield Lata had set up. One of the Sharm brought back three captured civilians, and Matvey was now smiling as he placed his hand on one of their foreheads and absorbed all their life energy. Their skin shriveled and grayed, cracked like desert sand, and crumbled to dust. Matvey placed a hand on each of the other two civilians and took his time enjoying the meal. When he was done, he held his pointing stick firm in his hands.

Timur stuttered and asked, "How did you manage to get a pointing stick?"

Matvey told Timur, "Caden had the dark god graciously bestow one upon me." Matvey told the Sharm to bring three more prisoners for Timur to consume. Matvey looked on as airplanes went by dropping bombs on the shield, and still, nothing was happening. Matvey placed the head of his pointing stick on Timur's chest and yelled out the word "Activate!" A black aura consumed Timur's entire body. Timur had been swallowed by the darkness and slowly was bestowed the powers of a warlock.

"A gift to you from the dark god," Matvey said with a grin.

Timur looked at his hands and arms, feeling the power flowing within. "What now?" he asked.

"Follow me."

As Matvey made his way to the eastern wall with his pointing stick, he conjured up a giant black ball of energy, and he sent it in the direction of the wall. Upon impact, a big chunk of the shield gave way, including part of the wall that came down crumbling. Matvey yelled out, "Forward," pointing his pointing stick in the direction of the newly formed gap. The Sharm soldiers made their way in, indiscriminately firing at everything in sight as bullets made their way beyond the gap. Matvey began using dark magic on several Sharm soldiers, turning them into super soldiers capable of withstanding more damage and delivering it to the enemy. Sharm soldiers began advancing as the gap widened from every ounce of fire they were delivering that included rockets, mortars, blasts of dark magical energy, and the titans, who hulked toward the wall, ready to stomp it into dust. Within the first five minutes of the breach, bodies had piled up on top of one another. Purple blood was splattered all over the bodies, including the building's walls from the heavy fire and deadly land mines of the city's defenders.

The wounded defenders began screaming and hollering for help as red blood made its way down the roads. The defending soldiers made their stand as they were strategically positioned and had every bit of firepower you could think of with them. What they were not anticipating were titans making their way into the capital, tearing formations apart, striking down buildings like play sets, and devouring soldiers. The titans were making such a bloody spectacle that the defenders began to leave their positions, cold chills running up their spines as they tried to get out of the titans' way. They either ended up a meal or riddled with the Sharm's bullets. Matvey, in a state of bliss, told Timur, "Everything is going according to plan."

Timur asked, "What are you up to?"

"Let me show you." He looked up into the sky. Timur did not see anything at first, but then he saw two space towers heading their way.

Timur asked, "How could this be?"

Matvey told him, "At the end of the war with the wizards, I sent a signal out, and I received an answer. Say hello to our reinforcements. It may have taken a while, but nonetheless, they arrived at a good time." One of the space towers landed nearby and began firing on the capital. The other space tower was traveling away from the capital. Matvey was ecstatic! Timur, struggling to speak, finally stuttered enough to ask where the other space tower was going.

Matvey said, "It's time for you to manage things here and end all this. Meanwhile I am going to use the second space tower's reinforcements to raid Caden's base and end him. Remember, you may have the power of the warlocks, but you are not at your full potential. Do not hesitate to feed as I have shown you. Their life energy will show you to true power." Timur shook his head as Matvey disappeared.

The Fect that came out of the space tower were wearing full futuristic battle armor with firearms at hand and a sword attached to their backs with an armored helmet. Commander Yarah had his Sharm soldiers locate who was in charge of the current attack. After some time, Timur appeared before Commander Yarah. Commander Yarah touched the gold mark on his forehead, bowed before Timur, and said with a stern tone, "We are ready to fight at your command. What is the status of the battle, and what are our orders for the city once we wipe out its defenders?"

Timur briefed Commander Yarah on the situation, and he added, "I insist that you take Joao with you. She's been studying all forms of magic. She is eager to practice." Joao learned much from the tapes and reports sent after the first war, and she was given the title master necromancer by the one dark god. Timur told Joao, "Follow the troops. There is a wizard named Lata that needs to be removed before the green wizard arrives." Joao's purple face bore the gold mark on her forehead, but she was also covered in piercings, one for every life she has ever taken. Joao had one purple eye to show herself she was still a Fect at heart and one black eye for her loyalty to the dark wizards and their one dark god. To be amongst Joao's presence required a damn strong personality. Joao demanded Timur to describe to her the wizard named Lata in more detail. Timur stuttering briefly as he told Joao that Lata was the only one here at the capital wearing brown robes, a brown hat, and wielding a brown pointing stick. Joao's excitement grew as she looked in her pockets to see which piercing she was going to add to her face next. Timur informed Commander Yarah, "Do whatever it takes to lay waste to the city." The commander did not waste time as he rolled out his hover tanks, firing beams of energy into the heart of the city. Along with the bombings by the air force, the city's once beautiful facade and modern architecture was being leveled into ruin and dust.

Varun had just finished laying waste to about a hundred Sharm soldiers when Joao passed by with Timur. Varun carefully followed from behind. Varun watched as Joao raised both her hands in the air. Dark magic emanated from her body to all the dead Sharm soldiers before her, bringing them back to life as they looked at each other with empty eyes. Varun got on the radio quickly and reported back to the command center, "There is some kind of thing bringing Sharm back from the dead on the battlefield."

Lata overheard and said out loud to herself, "How in the world do they have a necromancer on their side? They haven't existed since the Cult of Wizards was first formed. Lata told Zow, "You will be in charge of things on the battlefield. Sorry to add to your list of chores, but make sure President Nilla not only remains calm but that she remains safe."

Zow told Lata, "The president is safe with me. Take care of yourself." Lata was already concerned because she could not do anything to raise the shields that she had put over the city, and she was still wondering where Alaric was.

Catalan had been busy supporting the ground forces when the Fect air force struck. The battalion that Catalan was leading took heavy losses in the bombing. She had always felt more of her passion had always been fighting in the air, so she led the remainder of her forces to the capital's air force base. Catalan came to a complete halt, raising her right fist in the air to give her soldiers the command to do the same. Catalan took a second to make sure she was hidden as she saw Timur consuming the living by turning them into dark fruit and the necromancer raising both hands in the air, revitalizing the enemy fallen soldiers. Catalan called it into the headquarters and was informed, "Lata is on her way to deal with that problem." Catalan continued forward. Once trouble was out of sight, she finally made it to a hangar. She got inside one of the military jets as she commanded everyone else to do the same as they were about to join the fight in the air. Catalan and her battalion of soldiers quickly began providing much-needed backup and even fired a few missiles at the titans. The titans started throwing giant stones into the air at Catalan.

Catalan got on the radio and asked, "Who's in charge?"

General Orange responded, "I am."

Catalan asked, "What's going to be done about those titans?"

General Orange said, "Watch!" The city's offensive laser cannons aimed themselves at the titans, and, with multiple thundering bangs, they were sliced up by the tremendous power of the beams. The titans' body parts began falling onto the streets, houses, and cars. The titans had been reduced to a pile of flesh, but not after having dealt some damage to the city.

Zow and the entire command center witnessed as missiles made their way toward the space tower, including several other selected areas of the city from the navy's battleships that were twenty-four miles off the coast. The space tower took some good hits, including the Sharm ground forces and remaining titans. President Nilla had awoken, and Zow kept having to make sure the president stood relaxed as she had to breathe into a brown bag, since she was panicking from everything that was going on. Zow finally slapped President Nilla straight across the face as the secret service quivered at what they just witnessed. Zow told the president, "Put in the codes to release the sentinels onto the battlefield." The president put in the code 130924.

A platoon of Sharm were taking cover among the ruins of a city square when the ground beneath them began to shake. A roar erupted underneath them, and they had lost focus on the defenders, who were just as concerned at what was going on. The concrete split, and the ground began to sink into a ramp. The Sharm jumped off the cracks and clambered on top of one another to the edge, but some fell in. Screams filled the air as mechanical soldiers, the sentinels, marched out of the darkness, ripping the Sharm to pieces and unholstering their laser rifles. The defenders cheered on as the Sharm ran into the alleys with powerful lasers blasting them in the back. The sentinels emerged from underground bunkers from all over the city, taking the Sharm by surprise. The sentinel machines were the most sophisticated combat technology Devansh's scientists could create. They each cost hundreds of thousands of dollars to make, but their firepower was unmatched. They were about six feet tall, with the standard design of two arms, two legs, a body, and a head. They were nicknamed the Angels of Death with their angelic chrome-lined exteriors that were soon splattered with purple blood. Their brains were connected to the military satellites above the planet, allowing them live feeds of satellite imagery and new information. Combined with their rapid calculating computers and adaptive artificial intelligence, they were unmatched by most living beings, save for a group of wizards.

Zow said, "You had a sophisticated army of sentinels built for annihilation stagnant this whole time and didn't think to use them earlier? You can see how crazy things are getting out there!"

President Nilla said, "You're right. I need to get my act together and make some stuff happen. I am the president of Devansh after all." The president ran off, out of sight, out of mind. Zow decided it was best for now to focus back on what was happening on the battlefield.

"Lata the wizard" were the words Timur spoke when they finally came face-to-face about four miles from the capital headquarters.

Joao told Lata, "It's a shame that I am only going to be able to put my fist through your mouth once."

Lata told the necromancer, "This does not have to lead to any more violence."

Timur told Lata, "We are way past that. If anything, I have come to see wizards as an abomination to this planet. Once we are done destroying you, the Fect will make sure to wipe away any reference to your kind. You will be forgotten in history when we're finished."

Lata said, "It does not matter what you think. You are going to die, now that the green wizard is back." That hit a soft spot for Timur as he summoned a pointing stick that Matvey gave him from what was recovered on the Island of Wizards. Matvey had informed Timur it had belonged to Lumusi, recovered by Fect soldiers sent by Caden to investigate Lumusi's failure.

With his pointing stick, Timur hurtled a car at Lata. Joao brought down a wave of fireballs from the sky on Lata. Lata put a brown shield around herself as she made her way to Timur, sending brown blasts of energy waves toward him. Lata fired her staff and brought down a skyscraper on Timur. As Timur was blocking the falling debris, Lata touched her legs and said, "Super speed." Lata became a phantom to the eye, and she overtook Timur before he could make out her face. She leaped toward him and placed her hand on his head, whispering, "Death." Timur's eyes went white, and he keeled over, his lifeless body slamming to the ground. Lata turned and ran toward Joao but stomped her heels into the ground when she saw she wasn't there. Joao stood by Timur's corpse and raised both her hands in the air. She powered herself up, eventually creating a black tornado around her. When a black aura consumed her, she pointed both her hands at Timur's body, sending a wave of black energy at him. He croaked out a scream as he shot straight up on his knees. He wheezed and growled and snatched the pointing stick off the ground.

Lata shook her head and said, "It looks like I am going to have to take out the necromancer first."

Timur told Lata, "You will be doing no such thing. Caden wanted me to personally let you know when the time came that he has a few surprises for you wizards." Timur's face lit with confidence as he told Lata, "Caden wanted me to reveal one thing, to let you savor the fact that the one dark god recruited him."

Lata looked on, telling Timur, "Caden will soon get his!"

Timur brushed Lata off. "The Fect are the pinnacle of evolution. This time around, the Fect will emerge victorious over you wizards." Timur struggled to his feet, but he felt renewed with energy. "Death has no meaning to us. Unfortunate for you that there will be nobody to bring you back when I'm finished tearing out your spine."

Timur told Lata, "This is the end," as he pointed his staff at Lata and shot a black blast of energy her way. She could not contest it as she raised a shield in front of her. It was so powerful that it was pushing her backward. Timur gathered as much dark energy around him as he could and formed a charged rotating ball above him that he sent hurtling toward Lata. She was struggling to hold back this much dark energy fired at her, but she stood firm, mustered her energy, and, with her brown pointing stick, she managed to redirect it all outward. When the dark energy finally hit the outskirts of the capital, it went off like an atomic blast. Lata was surprised to see how much of a punch that much amalgamation of dark energy packed.

Zow was concerned with the blast that had just gone off and went to go look for the president. Zow found the president running toward her with a briefcase. Zow asked, "What is in the briefcase?"

President Nilla responded, "Well, we had been working on it for a while, but it's a weapon that we have orbiting the planet. It can gather energy from the sun and fire it down to a single selected, targeted location to completely obliterate everything in sight. We call it Project Sol."

Zow looked at President Nilla with a smile. "This is awesome. While we are on that topic, are there any other weapons we have that we can use on the battlefield? Anything else you have hiding in a closet or something?"

The president shook her head and quietly said, "No. Not at this time."

Zow received a call from Varun stating, "It looks like Lata is in trouble."

"What is her position?"

"In Blondon. I would take my troops to support her, but one, it looks like some heavy wizard business, which we would just be getting in her way, and two, we need to go support Captain Raider as they are getting pushed back in the south."

Zow got another call from Catalan reporting, "It looks like Lata needs some support in the Blondon region."

Zow asked, "Is there any way you can support her by air?"

Catalan responded, "I don't think I will be of any help. From what I have been seeing, there is some heavy magic being thrown around down there. Catalan reported that the entire region has been flattened out."

"Thank you, I will see what I can do." Zow told one of the soldiers, "Get Lata on the screen." Zow was surprised to see the level of devastation that had taken place, let alone the damage Lata was taking from a two-on-one assault. Zow got in contact with the navy and told the admiral, "Fire a wave of missiles to the exact target coordinates that I've transmitted to you." Lata noticed multiple missiles making their way toward them. Lata did a triple snap to momentarily enhance her offensive and defensive magical powers and then raised her staff to shoot a brown beam of energy at Timur. She then pointed at Joao, shooting a continuous barrage of wind bullets, holding them both in place. Lata knew they were all going to get hurt. Since she could not waste precious seconds, she was not able to put a full shield around her. Zow and everyone at the headquarters looked on as these missiles impacted the Blondon region, and the screen went black for a few minutes. When the screens finally returned, all that could be seen was debris, and everyone at the command center started yelling in concern and fear.

One voice rose above the rest, "How the hell are we supposed to win if we bomb our own city?"

As things began to clear out, Zow saw Timur on the monitors. He had taken heavy damage as a giant opening in his back revealed a purple spinal cord. When Joao got up, she was missing her entire left arm, but there was no sign of Lata. Zow was worried that they had killed Lata until her hand reached out of the rubble and she pushed herself out of the dust, coughing and covered in her own blood. Lata could not stand as her left leg was seeping out, and Lata's right leg was broken. Timur crawled out of the rubble and screamed in agony as he lifted himself up, using his pointing stick as a crutch. Blood seeped out of his wounds as he reached into a pouch on his belt, pulling out a dark fruit, one he had saved from earlier in the battle. The juice ran down his chin as he greedily bit into it. He winced and groaned, and his entire body began to twitch. Lata watched in horror as his back began to pull together, closing the wound. Once the pain began to subside, Timur's laugh bellowed through the streets, praising victory, as if he had already won the battle.

"Praise the dark gods!" he shouted. His bellowing laugh of joy quickly silenced with a croak, and Timur stood with his eyes opened wide, holding his pointing stick out and shaking.

Joao asked, "What's wrong?" The street before them was clouded in fog. Timur screamed at the intense green glow that emanated from the dust cloud. He immediately lost it and fired everything he had into the dust cloud. Lata turned around and did not see anything.

Timur went into a blind rage, blasting everything and screaming, "Face me, coward! Face me!" Joao turned her focus to Lata.

Joao told Lata, "Don't worry. I'm going to make your death clean and quick," as she pulled out a dagger from underneath her robes. Joao had gotten close enough to Lata where she thrusted the dagger toward her face. Joao winced and closed her eyes, blinded by a blue light. When she opened them, her arm was locked into place, and her dagger was stopped by a single index finger.

Lata laughed and said, "You always have a way of making me wait, wizard."

I smiled and said, "We had to stop at Aziza's Temple for a change of clothes. We even brought extra company—all five mages." Joao's hand wouldn't budge, so she heaved a kick toward my crotch. I annihilated her with an energy blast that I fired from my gold pointing stick, ripping her into millions of pieces.

Lata looked at me, "So you managed to talk to Abir, huh?"

I smiled. "Yeah. Crazy old guy."

Lata said, "Well, it's good you are here, because so is the green wizard."

I got pumped up. "Finally, I can introduce myself. Where is the green wizard?"

Lata said, "Fighting Timur."

I told Kogi and the other mages, "Spread out and help wherever you could." I asked Honovi, who was sporting her orange robes, to take Lata to the headquarters while I assisted on the battlefield.

Honovi told me, "Why can't I ever join you on the battlefield?"

I told her, "How does next time sound?"

Honovi thought about it and said, "Fine. But if you don't, you owe me."

I decided it was time to lend some support to the capital's forces. I raised my staff in the air until it rose above the city. I pointed at the gold pointing stick and whispered, "Do your thing." From the head of the staff, gold lightning fired off and arced toward the enemy forces all around the battlefield. I watched in awe as the arcs of golden lightning jumped between bodies, zapping the Sharm soldiers and bouncing through their ranks like a storm. I felt it was time to finally meet the green wizard, as I was confident that I had done my part. I made my way over to the guy Lata called Timur and asked, "Could you point me in the direction of the green wizard?" Timur looked at me like I was insane. I said, "What?"

Timur said, "Behind you," as he shot a blast directed at me. I turned around, excited to finally meet the green wizard. I looked, but there was nobody there. Timur pointed again and said, "Look, damn you! Right there in the sixteen-story skyscraper." I went running into the building that was called the Monduck Building according to the name on the wall. Timur began blasting the building as I ran up the stairs.

Commander Yarah pulled out a pair of binoculars and looked toward Timur's last reported position, wondering where he had gone. He focused on the building whose windows were being blown out with bolts of black energy. "What in the hell is going on down there?" the commander snapped.

One of the officers said, "It's because of the green wizard. The one we were warned about."

Commander Yarah asked, "Where is this damn green wizard now?"

One of the officers said, "In an area called Blondon, fighting with Timur."

"And where is Joao?"

None of the officers wanted to respond until one said, "Dead, sir."

The commander lost it. He ordered, "Fire everything we have on board the space tower at the green wizard. Now!"

"But, sir... Timur..."

"I don't care! Fire everything!"

When I exited the Monduck building, it came crashing down, sending debris everywhere. Timur yelled out, "Over there!" But when I would make my way over, the green wizard was gone.

I told Timur, "This green wizard is one fast person."

I suddenly heard something coming as Timur yelled out, "Those idiots!" We noticed laser fire and missiles were on course for where we were standing. Zow was looking at the screen silently, along with

140

everyone else in the headquarters' command room. As the missiles came down, the room began to shake violently, and the screens all went black. Zow bit her lip so hard that a little trickle of blood began to seep out.

She wondered, *How in the hell is he going to survive that? No one in this world could.* At that moment, Honovi entered the room with Lata as Zow greeted them. Zow watched as Honovi helped Lata be placed on a chair. Once she spotted the blood dripping from her leg, Zow immediately yelled out for a medic. Zow asked Lata, "Was the green wizard always so reckless?"

Lata blushed, saying, "That wizard is one of a kind."

Zow got close to Lata and whispered, "Does he know?"

Lata asked, "Does he know what? That you like him?" Lata blushed even more. "I'm not sure. That wizard can be such a loose cannon that it is hard to say."

Zow asked Lata, "How can you even like him? He seems a bit off his rocker, don't you think?" Lata sighed a bit. Zow shook her head and told Lata, "You are crazy. That wizard looks like an adrenaline junkie." The screen came back on, and Timur came into view, panting and bleeding. The green wizard looked like he was sitting in midair. Zow looked at Lata and said, "He's nuts!"

Lata laughed, "Yeah, he is."

Reports began coming in from what was left of the commanders, or their seconds, that the Fect were in retreat. Zow ordered Kogi, "Go and support Captain Raider and Varun." Zow sent the other four mages to retrieve the dead, then support the wounded and provide food and supplies to the soldiers. Zow asked Lata, "So what is he doing now?"

Lata looked at the screen. "It would appear that he was looking for something. Are you sure he was not hit on the head too hard?"

Lata said, "Let him enjoy himself. I'm happy he's back. I had feared he would never return. And yet here he is, doing his thing, as if nothing had ever happened."

I told Timur, "I'm beginning to get impatient. I was really hoping to finally shake the green wizard's hand." Timur's jaw dropped as he was pointing in my direction. I decided it was time to stop playing games and get serious. I summoned the gold staff and pointed it at Timur, whose eyes looked like they were going to pop out of their sockets. Timur began yelling out as he made a run for it. I sent a gold blast of energy his way that consumed his entire body. I was standing there, a bit saddened that I could not meet the green wizard. As I made my way to the headquarters, I saw a reflection of a green hat from the broken windows of one of the skyscrapers. I went chasing after the green hat thinking, *Man, this green wizard is superfast.*

Chapter 12

Commander Yarah ordered another all-out strike on the green wizard. Missiles went flying, and lasers ripped through the city. At the end of it, the commander asked for an update. One of the soldiers said, "The scanners say that the green wizard is on top of the space tower." The green wizard raised his staff and shot down an enormous green blast of energy into the tower. Zow and the rest of the command center shouted in glee as the space tower radiated from within with light before cracking all across its facade and blasting apart in thousands of bits.

Zow said, "I will admit that the green wizard is pretty impressive." The cheers and hollering began to be quickly drowned out by an ear-piercing alarm.

The lights dimmed red, and one of the officers in the room shouted, "Red alert!" as all the screens displayed a radar tracking system showing that two nuclear warheads had been fired from the Land of the Gods. They were heading to the capital. One of the screens showed the green wizard powering up and raising his staff in the air, sending a giant blast of green energy in the direction of the incoming nukes, creating a massive explosion that lit up the entire sky green. Everyone in the room shielded their eyes from the blinding green flash. As they noticed the light subside, they looked back toward the screen and watched the cloud of dust bellowing into the sky. Lata very faintly noticed a small green dot moving closer. Lata ordered one of the soldiers to zoom in at the green wizard. The screen filled with the image of a tall man in flowing green robes walking toward the cloud of dust.

Zow asked, "Where is the green wizard going?"

Lata shook her head, saying, "It was only a matter of time."

"What are you talking about?"

"The green wizard must have finally decided it was time! He is going toward the Land of the Gods. We're going to want to finish up things here before we can go and support the green wizard. I'm going to take Honovi with me to grab something to eat and rely on you to finish things up on the battlefield."

Zow, now Lata's height, bearing an all-red skin tone and the face that resembled a dolphin, told Lata, "I got this." Lata retreated in her wheelchair.

As she neared the door, Honovi tugged at her robe's collar and asked, "I want to talk with you about a few things." Zow got on the radio and started sending orders to every brigade. On one of the screens, she caught a glimpse of the Sharm soldiers being run out of the capital.

Caden was staring into Matvey's face as he drove his staff through her heart.

"Who knew that traitor's blood flows the smoothest?" he said, relishing in the stains across his staff.

In Caden's rage, he gutted everyone, separating their organs from their bodies. Everyone that once stood on the Fect council was now on the floor in a perfect ring around a pile of organs. His dark eyes bored holes into Matvey's, and he whispered, "How could you?"

In Matvey's last words, she told Caden, "It is not betrayal to attack the betrayer. You killed the Successor. You are not one of us." Caden let Matvey's body drop, lifeless, to the floor and looked around at all the carnage he had unleashed in the council room. Caden felt so betrayed. His lust for blood was still unfulfilled, so he ordered everyone outside. He knelt before the Successor's corpse, now a shriveled husk, and he grabbed the head with both hands. He stared into blank eyes and sighed deeply before pushing his palms together and watching the head split like a melon. He wiped his hands off on another body's white robes before leaving the room.

A space tower sat motionless in the courtyard, and thousands of Fect poured out like an angered beehive. Every Fect that could find themselves outside had lined up in formation. Caden climbed on an elevated platform and raised his voice so that it boomed across the yard.

"The Fect…have become something of family to me. Where there were those who cast me aside, there was the Fect to greet me with open arms. I felt that I had meant something to you, and to your cause. I found your cause just. I lent you my support, my knowledge…, my life. I felt as one of you. Betrayal by family…is the harshest of all." For a brief moment, it looked as though Caden fought back a tear, though whether it was from true emotion or from the specks of blood splattered across his face, none of the Fect in the front row could be sure.

"But I know in my heart that not all children deserve punishment, for not all of you shared in the bad habits of your siblings. I am a just father, and so I dispensed punishment where it had been earned. Your lords are dead, crumpled like discarded tissue upon my floor. I will still hold a special place in my heart for each and every one of you, but I know that I must do what every parent should do… educate their children. Today's failures are not your own but of mine. Don't abuse my love and generosity again." To push his point, Caden used his staff to open a portal into another dimension that began tearing away at the space tower until it was completely gone. Caden, still not satisfied, raised his staff to open yet another portal for him. Caden walked through, and a few seconds later when he walked out, he was wearing black wizard robes. Caden unleashed hell on all the Fect so that they could see for themselves the true monster that he was. He went around separating Fect's bodies as the psycho danced in their blood. Caden unleashed bursts of energy that ripped bodies apart from within. The darkness that began emanating from Caden was like none other. He reminded the Fect why the one dark god named him the black wizard of death. The remaining Fect dropped to their knees and begged for forgiveness. Caden said not another word as he turned around and stepped back inside his laboratory, leaving the carnage of bodies and the trembling survivors.

Caden asked one of the Fect scientists, "Have either of our last two nukes hit the capital?"

The Fect scientist said, "No, sir! The green wizard destroyed them."

Caden, still a bit annoyed, began to scream out, "Damn you! Damn you, green wizard!" Caden began to calm down, but the scientists had already begun shuffling out of the door, not wanting to become his next means of "self-care." Caden began saying to himself aloud, "Everything is going to be fine, because I'm going to kill the green wizard. And then there will be no one in my way from being able to conquer all of Devansh and the world." Caden gave a wide grin, remembering the look on Magni's face when he sapped the life out of him all those years ago, how he relished in it like an addict. The nerves across his body tingled just at the thought of it.

Lata rolled into the cafeteria with Honovi, and the two began just casually talking. Lata asked Honovi, "What do you think of Alaric?"

Honovi ate the rice she had just scooped off her plate with her spork and said, "He is a bit much at times."

Lata smiled. "Has he taught you anything?"

Honovi responded, "Not really. He just tells me stories of where he is from and of the wizards."

Lata cut a piece of her steak and dipped it in some steak sauce, telling Honovi, "I've been wanting to tell you for some time now."

Honovi stopped drinking her orange juice when she said, "What have you been wanting to tell me?"

Lata struggled putting the sentence together and finally let it out. "I am your mother."

Honovi knocked over her cup of juice and stood up from her seat, telling Lata, "You're lying!"

Lata told Honovi, "I'm telling you the truth."

Honovi asked Lata, "What made you think that when I was created in the laboratory?"

Lata told her, "Using my eggs."

Honovi yelled at Lata, "What the hell do you mean your eggs!"

Lata told Honovi, "Will you listen to me? When Caden had started hunting wizards after the first war, Caden showed up to my home one night. I thought he had come to kill me. Caden had snuck in and locked my staff away in the closet, and he pinned me down to my kitchen floor. Someone in a hazmat suit came in. He looked like a scientist now that I think about it. I assumed the worst that night, figuring they were going to butcher me or subject me to all kinds of experiments. Well, the scientist used a device to extract all of my eggs. When the scientist was done, Caden knocked me unconscious, and when I came to, they were both gone. I had to break open my favorite cabinet to find my staff." Lata tried to take a sip of water, but she didn't feel like she could keep it down. "One day afterwards, I was with Remo, Aziza, and Maska. We were looking for the secret entrance to Caden's laboratory. We had wandered deeper into the Land of the Gods than we had wanted to that day. After a few days of riding on horseback, we decided to turn around. Well, right as we did, we bumped into a girl that looked exactly like you. She had not eaten in days. The girl was so terrified she did not want to speak. She grabbed my hand and had me follow her. She led us to a mass grave with dozens of bodies inside, all of the same girl. One was clutching an old tablet whose screen was scratched and turned tan with dirt, but I could still make out one word on it—Honovi. Worse yet, the girl, like you, looked a lot like I did when I was that age. I put two and two together. A few hours later, that girl died, and it broke my heart knowing this was going on. So when I first saw you at the dam, I immediately knew who you were."

Honovi began to cry and choke on her words. "You're right. I wasn't the only one. They all looked like me. As time went on, something would happen, they would get sick and die. They would find out they had irregular organs or that our bodies couldn't handle Caden's DNA, and their bodies rejected it. The most horrific thing I remember was when Caden would get into one of his moods. Caden would transform into some demon-looking thing and torture who- ever he wanted until he got bored. Just like that—bored, as if we didn't matter to him. I was eventually the lone survivor, and Caden welcomed me with open arms. He began to tell me how I had a higher purpose in this life and how my parents could not understand that, as to why he forcefully took me from them." Honovi's hand began to twitch repeatedly as her face went blank like she was stuck in thought. Honovi snapped out of it and summoned the orange pointing stick, blasting Lata in the chest. Honovi took the silver orb from Lata's brown staff and ran off.

Lata lay on the ground and didn't move, blood seeping from her wounds as she began to scream in pain from having landed on her broken leg. Her mind began to wander, *When did it get to this point? Were the wizards responsible? Should we have killed them while we had the chance? Should we have killed him when we had the chance?* Lata recalled when Remo the wizard had tracked down Caden and engaged him in battle. Remo had managed to disarm Caden, and for whatever reason, he could not strike him down. Caden later became the black wizard of death when he cut off a piece of his spirit to offer it as a sacrifice to the one dark god. Caden had found a temple in the north of Devansh that was built by the first dark wizards. The dark wizards understood the cosmic language differently than wizards did. They felt that in order to get connected to it all, you had to continuously offer parts of your spirit until nothing remained. That would then allow the dark power of the one dark god to fully enter your body. The one dark god was really a representation of all that was evil in the universe, the embodiment of rage, cosmic destruction, and even cosmic cannibalism. When Caden entered the temple, it was as if his destiny had found him. A few wizards had arrived to stop Caden, but on that day, they met the black wizard of death.

Lata had a vision as she grew colder, as she began to feel her life slowly slipping away. She saw the green wizard being defeated and Caden taking over the world as the black wizards rose to power. She saw Alaric, the last of the Cult of Wizards, on the ground with lifeless eyes and a golden staff stuck through his chest. Lata could not let this come to pass. As she tried to lift her body up, Lata yelled out for help. Lata yelled out to Alaric, "Everything is riding on you!" Several soldiers burst into the room and ran to Lata. She struggled to push the words out of her mouth, but she told them, "Put the base on high alert, and tell Zow to send a team to find Honovi. She does not know what she is doing."

Zow received the information from one of the soldiers and was so angry, yelling out, "These damn wizards are like children." Zow got in contact with Kogi and informed him, "Gather all the mages and track down Honovi. If she's not in the base, then she's likely going to the Land of the Gods."

Kogi asked, "And what about Alaric?"

Zow sighed and told Kogi, "He was last seen chasing after the green wizard."

Alaska looked confused and asked, "What is all that about?"

Zow said, "Look, I do not know. The green wizard is quite the character and a package I don't feel like opening up right now."

Kogi informed Zow, "I'll let you know when we find her."

Zow had decided it was time she got some coffee in her system. She walked down to the cafeteria to grab some, poured in her caramel creamer and sugar, and began to wonder how many lives had been lost today. Zow had never imagined she would keep being put in a position of command. She felt useless, because every victory they achieved, Alaric had come swooping in right at the end. Zow scratched her head in frustration, and frustration turned into anxiety. Zow kept trying to tell herself, *You'll be no good to anyone if you keep acting like this.*

Zow got a call from Varun letting her know, "Things are cleared up on this end." Catalan and all others in charge also started reporting on their final status. The fight was over.

Zow pressed the button on her receiver and said, "Congratulations to you all! Without you, Devansh would have been lost. I'm going to dispatch Division 0, a division of advanced robots to set up security around the capital. They will help civilians in need, gather the dead, help the wounded, and so on."

Zow had taken a walk around the capital with President Nilla, who went around gathering as many PR pictures and opportunities as possible. The president shook as many hands as possible and gave every speech of encouragement and enlightenment as she possibly could for one day. President Nilla looked over at Zow and said, "I would not have been able to handle everything I had without you."

Zow told the president in a frank tone, "Look, you better help these people out."

"Did I ever tell you how I made it to become president?" The president asked with an inquisitive look.

Zow looked at her, annoyed, and said, "No! What does that have to do with this?"

The president smiled and said in a warm voice and with a smile fit for the media, "Because of a wizard. Maska the wizard and I shared the same vision—democracy for all, a place where everyone in Devansh was free. Before I came to power, Devansh was in complete political disarray. One moment, we had a monarchy, and the next a socialist government. It was just a political playground. The other headache was all the gangs and organized crime that had gained strong roots over years of political unrest, including the old families with prestige. Maska was not only a powerful wizard with her abilities but with her words. Maska and I set up tons of organizations for the kids who were homeless, and we made sure there were programs in place for the ones who aged out of the system. She worked with me to create vocational programs for them and opportunities to work. We just took over Devansh's issues by storm. After I was elected, I'd say three years into my first term, she told me she had to deal with some wizard stuff aside from looking for a new location for her temple for young wizards. Well, a few years later, I got word she was killed by a black wizard of death, and my heart fell. I was deeply hurt by the loss of my friend and the opportunity to not be able to do more with her in helping Devansh and this world." Zow took out a napkin from her pocket and wiped the president's face. President Nilla said, "Thank you. The point of that story was so you know that I will do everything I can for these people."

Early the next day, President Nilla went to see Lata to see how she was doing. Lata told the president, "Make sure to never have children. They can be hurtful."

President Nilla asked Lata, "What type of danger is Devansh in?"

"There is no telling what will happen if Caden gets his hands on the silver orb."

The president sat on Lata's bed and said, "When I laid eyes on Honovi, I saw a very confused teenager. Maybe she just needed her parents to reach out to her and help her understand."

Lata turned her head as a tear ran down her face, telling the president, "You may be right."

The president laid her hand on Lata's shoulder and said, "I am relying on you, Lata, to ensure victory for Devansh and this planet."

Lata shook her head in her pillow and said, "I don't know if I can commit to that."

"I'm not taking no for an answer!"

Lata sat up in her bed, winced at the sudden pain, and said, "There is no guarantee that the wizards can win this time. We're not the answer to all of your problems."

President Nilla looked at Lata one last time and said, "I'm confident that you, Lata, can bring the wizards back together like in the days of Abir."

Caden had just walked through the dark portal and arrived at the temple of the black wizards. A nasty storm was raging on as thunder struck in all directions as Caden made his way in. Caden walked through the darkness and approached the statues of the one dark god. Caden raised his black staff, rammed it into his body, and cut out the last sliver of his spirit that remained. When he removed his staff from his body, a white light shined. Caden placed the last piece of his spirit onto an altar. Whispers emanated from the walls as the light was consumed by the darkness around it.

"Pleased I am with your performance, and of your offering."

Caden got to one knee and bowed his head. The voices rang out and slowly combined into a single comprehensible voice, "You will bring the beacon."

Caden asked, "And what of the green wizard?" The one dark god was quiet, and for a minute, there was nothing but silence and darkness. Then Caden felt a cold radiance protrude his body, and Caden felt as though his soul was replaced by something darker, like dark matter in the vacuum of space. Then two disciples came forward from the darkness.

The voice boomed, "Two servants will accompany you. The girl comes with the beacon. Retrieve it." Caden's mind filled with a vision of a girl panting and running from a city in the distance. He knew exactly where she was, and he set off.

*****

I had been chasing the green wizard down for a few days now until hunger and exhaustion finally kicked in. It was nighttime, and it looked like it was going to rain. I had no idea where I was. I saw a green blast go off in the distance, and I made my way over. As I got closer, I saw a giant hole in the ground that looked as though a bomb had gone off here. I saw a brighter green flash go off further ahead, and by the time I got there, a giant hole had been made into the mountains. I walked through the hole and eventually came to a cliff on the side, where I was pushed off. I quickly turned around and grabbed the ledge as my entire body hung from the edge of the cliff. As I looked up, I saw a green wizard looking down at me. The green wizard bellowed over the edge, "Why have you been following me?"

I said, "Because I wanted to introduce myself as Alaric the wizard and to find out a few things from you."

The green wizard said to me, "I am just passing by. So far, you just happen to be everywhere I am at. So I decided to lend a hand. I'm just looking for a way to get home. I have no actual plans to help this planet or you, Alaric the wizard."

I asked the green wizard, "And what of my grandfather, Remo the wizard?" I could tell the green wizard did not want to keep talking with me, but I had caught some of his attention.

The wizard asked me, "And what of him?"

"I simply want to know if he is still alive."

The green wizard pulled out his pipe, loaded some tobacco, and told me, "No." My head rolled down to my chest as tears ran down my eyes.

I snapped, "How did he pass away?"

The wizard kept puffing until he told me, "Remo the wizard passed away in his attempts to try and obtain my powers."

I told the green wizard, "I'm not completely, 100 percent sure what you meant…" As my arms had gone numb from hanging on the cliff, I spotted a root to help hold my weight.

The green wizard scratched his long white beard and asked me, "How far does my beard reach down?"

I looked at him, a little confused but said, "To the floor."

The green wizard said, "Perfect. It has taken me lifetimes for my beard to reach that point, and now I am ready to go home."

I looked at the green wizard and yelled out, "You can't go yet. We need your help!"

The green wizard told me, "You are not listening to me! Your grandfather impressed me one day when I learned he was one of the only amongst the Cult of Wizards who was adept enough to keep up with me. In fact, he was about as annoying as you were, but I was more patient back then. But he eventually grew on me, and I allowed him on my adventures. We even became friends. Your grandfather had managed to convince me that he would take my place in order for me to finally go home. When I transferred my powers to your grandfather, what was supposed to be something celebratory for the both of us became a disaster. Your grandfather, for whatever reason, could not handle the power within him, and he died. I fell to my knees crying. Not only had I lost a friend but I was also trapped in your world, unable to find peace. So, no, I will not help you."

I looked at the big-nosed wizard and said, "I can make sure you finally find the peace you have been craving for so long."

The green wizard poked a bushy eyebrow at me. "How can you be so sure?"

"Because all my life I have had to be a fighter. I never had much while others had to look over me since my father would not show me anything. I got beaten up by others, and I kept going because I have always felt a fire inside me so powerful that it has always wanted to come out. I know I can do great things for the world. I have just never had the power to be able to show myself or others what I can really do until I became a wizard. I am sick and tired of being looked down upon or being talked down to. I am willing to go the distance, even now. I am all in on helping you out, even if it costs me my life."

I could tell the green wizard was probing me, thinking about looking to see if there was any evil within me.

My arms were becoming like jelly, and I wasn't sure I could hold on much longer. The green wizard stroked his beard and finally said, "It is important that you know, Alaric the wizard, that I fought with Caden not too long ago. I bruised more than just his ego, you know, but I noticed that I have become substantially weaker than I was a thousand years ago. I have lived as the green wizard for about four thousand years now, and my energy just isn't what it used to be. Hell, I'm even getting a little belly going here these days, and I'll tell you, there aren't many exercise programs out there for people my age. Look, Alaric, if you become the green wizard, you are at your prime right now, and your power would be immense. I need to know, and I need to hear it from you that you would do whatever it takes to be a protector of peace and symbol of hope for everyone. I know you fear showing the world your true self, Alaric, but right now, what this world needs is the power that you have in your heart—the one that kept yourself going when you were a child. I need you to use the power that told you to go the distance for your peers, family, and others. Right now, I see a mighty beast within you, Alaric. I command it to rise to the surface now!"

The green wizard yelled, "You have been granted the opportunity to take my place."

I said, "Awesome! When do we start?"

The green wizard took another hit from his pipe and said, "Right now." The green wizard raised his hands in the air with his staff. Everything around me went green, and I couldn't tell from where, but a green blast of energy hit me square in the face. I could hear the green wizard's voice begin to fade away as he said, "Thank you for finally allowing me to go home and find peace." When I opened my eyes, I was standing on the ground, breathing a little heavily, wondering when I came down from the edge of the cliff. I looked up and saw how far of a drop it was. I began to check my entire body until I looked down and saw my reflection in a little pool of water as the sun began to rise. I saw a green glow and a pointed green hat and a set of flowing green robes. I looked at my robes and hat and felt that green suited me a lot better.

I took a knee and said, "Thank you for trusting me."

I could hear a faint voice saying, "I lied. Right before your grandfather passed away, he told me to seek you out. Your grandfather told me that you, Alaric, would be more than capable of sending me home, and that you have the heart of gold. I followed you around for years. I agree with your grandfather. You are worthy of the power of the green wizard. Farewell."

Chapter 13

Honovi had been crying in a forest, hidden within the trees. Light was barely visible in the thick canopy and great trunks. Honovi felt in her heart that she had done something terrible by hurting her own mother, but at the same time, she knew what a lunatic Caden was. She tried convincing herself that she had good reasons, but somehow, it wasn't enough. Honovi was so confused as she tucked in her head with both arms, wishing someone would make sense of things for her. Honovi threw her pointing stick to the ground, and she fell to her knees crying, wishing she could take back her actions. She did not want to be the reason for the end of the world. That was just too much for her to bear. Honovi screamed at the top of her lungs in frustration, cursing Caden for giving her life in a laboratory, and cursing the world for keeping her in it. Honovi wanted the pain to go away. She did what had to be done out of fear. She did not know if her mother would protect her the way parents should. Honovi thought she would abandon her when things got tough. If Caden came demanding for her, she wondered whether she would fight for her or not. Honovi wanted a second chance, but she did not know how to make things right. As she went to grab her pointing stick, she heard Caden's voice from behind, and her spine froze.

Honovi wiped the tears off her face as Caden grabbed her and said, "Young girls shouldn't be in the forest all alone...especially in these...dangerous times. What are you doing?"

Honovi noticed the other two black wizards and said, "Getting ready to call you."

Caden, not buying it, told Honovi, "Please, dear child, don't make me punish you for lying to me. I don't have the materials to make another one of you." Honovi couldn't find the words, and as

Caden motioned to slap her, an immeasurable green blast went off in the distance, making its way into outer space. Immediately, Caden murmured in disgust, "The green wizard." Caden told the other black wizards, "Go on ahead and deal with the green wizard while I finish things up here." The two black wizards left, and Caden slapped Honovi to the ground, telling her, "I hate that you make me do this, but I must punish all of my children equally. No favorites."

Honovi began to shake as she told Caden, "But you told me I was important! You said you wouldn't kill me because I was the one destined to enter the silver orb."

Caden gave a maniacal smile, telling Honovi, "I just told you those things so that you could feel better about yourself. What I learned from my experiments is worth far more than your life as it stands."

Honovi began to cry. "You're just awful."

Caden told her, "It's a shame that I will never get to see your full potential, because your time ends here." Caden raised his pointing stick to strike Honovi down when Kogi stopped the blow of the pointing stick with his elbow.

All five mages snatched a hold of each limb, holding Caden tightly in place. Kogi told Caden, "How dare you speak to Honovi as if she was nothing! Regardless of who you may think you are, you have no right speaking to a teenager like that."

Caden could care less as he said, "It's funny how mages these days think they can speak up to a black wizard." Caden powered up and emitted a black energy blast that threw all the mages into the ground and the trees. Caden shouted, "A lowly being such as you shouldn't even possess a tongue. I'll have to fix that."

Kogi looked at Caden. "For someone claiming to be the wizard of death, you sure are dumb and blind." Caden had not noticed Kogi's fingers twitching at all directions into the trees, but as he blatantly pointed his finger at him, the forest burst to life, and the trees threw themselves at Caden with branches as daggers and trunks as hammers. Kali grabbed Honovi, and before they took two steps, a blast ripped a hole through the largest tree's trunk. Behind it, a bolt of energy zipped through the hole like an arrow and pierced through Kali's chest, dropping him dead. Honovi screamed in horror as Caden then emerged from the darkness with the burning eyes and frown of a serial killer. Honovi knew that look all too well, and she bolted into the forest, running faster than she thought imaginable.

Hardrock had managed to touch Caden's right shoulder and yelled out the "touch of death," but nothing happened. Caden looked at Hardrock and told him, "Let me show you how it's done." He pointed his pointing stick and blasted a hole through Hardrock's chest, dropping his lifeless body to the ground like a discarded toy.

Kogi grabbed Honovi and told her, "No matter what, you are to stand behind me at all times!"

Caden stepped over Hardrock's corpse and slowly approached Kogi, saying, "Your efforts here are fruitless."

Kogi told Caden, "Our efforts here will be remembered forever…" Caden pushed the head of his pointing stick in Lugii's direction and released a blast of dark energy. Lugii managed to point and deflect the stream of energy while Mayoko snapped his fingers six times, slashing Caden across his face and chest six times with swipes of energy.

Caden yelled, "Mages should not possess such power. You are inferior beings!"

Mayoko smiled, telling Caden, "Sounds like you still have a lot to learn about the cosmic language."

Caden responded, "And what would you know about the cosmic language? I am raw power that has no equal!" He aimed his pointing stick at him, firing another stream of dark energy. Lugii deflected the blast, and Mayoko snapped his fingers twelve times. Blood started to seep from Caden's wounds, but the smell, like a starved wolf, emboldened him. Caden shouted, "Enough games, children!" as he opened a portal and jumped in. They stood in awe as another portal ripped apart the trees nearby, and out came Caden in his devastating demonic form, expelling the broken shards of wood strewn around in the direction of the mages. Mayoko snapped his fingers, but Caden did not show any pain or marks. Mayoko wasn't sure if he had blocked his attacks or if he was now immune. Mayoko didn't get long to think about it as Caden lifted his pointing stick toward him and shot a bolt of energy through his skull, dropping him dead.

Lugii and Kogi shoved Honovi behind them and readied their spells. Caden began to lift his pointing stick but stopped and turned his head at the boom of two supermassive explosions. In that moment, two colossal green blasts went off that could be seen like massive beams lighting up the entire region. Caden wrote off the two disciples he brought along. They were surely dead. "Useless," he whispered. "Strange, I do not recall the green wizard having such power." Caden snapped his fingers, and Honovi's orange pointing stick flung off the ground and into his hand. Shoving the pointing stick under his arm, he snapped again, and the silver orb flew from Honovi's pack. He caught it like a softball. With his pointing stick in his other hand, he blasted the ground at his feet with a thick fog, and he ran in the other direction. Kogi and Lugii choked on the fog as they snapped and flung their hands in front of them, whisking the fog away from them.

"Honovi, are you okay?" Kogi asked.

Honovi pointed into the fading fog and choked out the word "look." A green glow permeated the fog, and a sharp wind flung it away. As the figure inside approached, the glow subsided, and their eyes widened at the sight of a familiar face.

*****

When we got back to the capital, I made my way to see Lata with Honovi, Lugii, and Kogi. Upon arriving, President Nilla gave each of us a hug and asked to speak with Kogi and Lugii about a few things. I continued walking. Zow stepped in my way with a cup of coffee in her hand. Zow, now all blue and bold with white eyes and lips, was about as tall as me at six feet tall. She said, "I would shake your hand, but right now, anything I touch is left with some slime. Just part of another one of my transformations." I looked at the coffee cup in her hand, which was slick with a white slime.

I said, "Of all the people that I have come across, you are by far the most interesting." Zow looked at me with dissatisfaction. I told Zow, "You must excuse me, I need to go speak with Lata."

"Lata is in the botanical garden."

I said, "Thank you," and made my way past her.

Zow said after me, "Last thing. I am keeping Honovi with me for a bit."

I looked at Zow with suspicion and then I asked Honovi, "Is that okay with you?"

She said, "Of course. I am grown."

I said, "Okay, whatever you want."

When I finally reached the botanical garden at the other end of the building from where headquarters was stationed, I was ready for a meal. I opened the door into the botanical garden and was amazed at the collection of plants. I forget at times how many beautiful things exist in this life that I need to find more time to just enjoy being in the moment. I made my way through the garden, taking time to soak it all in, until I came across Lata sitting on one of the benches looking out into the horizon. The view was spectacular with mountains, rivers, and wildlife. Lata looked around and smiled. "I knew you would get the job done."

"Why do you say that?" I expected her to be upset considering we just lost the orb.

"Because you are now the green wizard."

I told Lata that Honovi had rejoined us, and she smiled, saying, "That is good to hear." Lata said, "I knew you would be back. You always come back." I hugged Lata, and the two of us stood there for a bit, soaking in the moment. I wanted to know how she could be so calm knowing we had lost the orb.

I was thinking, *First time she mentions it, she gives me a lecture about how dangerous it is. Now she hasn't even brought it up once!*

Honovi came out of nowhere to join the hug and told her mother, "I'm so sorry for what I did."

Lata let go of the group hug and started tearing up, telling Honovi, "I'm never going to let you out of my sight again. I'll watch over you and care for you like I should have. I'll always make sure you know that you're loved, no matter what."

Honovi smiled and said, "This is what I have always wanted to hear." Honovi kept apologizing and saying over and over how she was scared until the tears stopped. All three of us spent the rest of the day together, eating, talking, laughing, and I finally got to get to know Honovi a bit. Honovi actually had a morbid sense of humor, but she knew how to make people laugh. Honovi also had an amazing smile, and for the first time, I saw a little twinkle in her eyes. This was all still new for me, but I felt that I had found my peace.

Later that night, Lata pulled me aside one last time. She told me, "There was something else I have been wanting to tell you." Lata took me to the highest balcony in the facility and told me, "I have decided that it is time for you to know why your grandfather built a temple for Aziza—as in why he felt it was that important. Aziza wanted to help any way he could. Aziza did not want Caden to be the end of the Cult of Wizards. So Aziza went traveling all around Devansh, suspicious that the enemy may be lurking in the shadows. I did not see him for years until, one day, Remo brought him back wounded and said it was done. Aziza mentioned how he used his connection to the cosmic language to lead him to the valley, where he encountered a metaphysical entity. Aziza told of how the metaphysical entity, without a pointing stick, just raised its hand, and the valley sank even more. Then the entity created a natural vibrant body of water that flowed down from the edge to a single spot, stating that 'if any dark wizard were to ever consume the water, they would abruptly meet their end.' Aziza thanked the metaphysical being and made his way back to us to share the info, and that was when he was attacked by the Sharm. Aziza, desperate to survive, did everything he could. He even sent a signal into the air, letting any allies know of his location. Well, eventually, Remo found him barely alive. As you know, Alaric, he wound up passing away from his wounds. The loss of his best friend led Remo to build Aziza a temple and seek out the green wizard so that he could strike a deal so he could finish the job himself."

I told Lata, "This power cost my grandfather Remo his life."

"Don't look at it like that. It was a risk your grandfather would take all over again to protect the people he loved, as well as this planet. Look, Alaric, you now have the power of the golden staff, the power of the green wizard, and your wizard family. You have everything to lose now, and I need you to understand that as of right now. Caden is dangerous, but so are you. I tell you this because I want you to defeat Caden in the Valley of the Wizards. You will have the upper hand there. One, he does not know it even exists. Secondly, it would keep anyone else out of danger from the battle. One last thing, Alaric, the advantage is still on our side." Lata pulled out the silver orb from inside her brown robes.

In astonishment, I blurted out, "When and how did you get that?"

Lata told me, "I made a decoy in case I needed to throw Caden a bone, so to speak. Apparently, he never bothered to look."

I shouted, "Yes! Finally, a nice little break."

A few days later, President Nilla had everyone present for an emergency meeting. The president started with, "Thank you, everyone, for your services in protecting the final lock and the capital. There is one more thing I need from each and every one of you, and that is to gather your strength because we now fight for all of Devansh. We have the enemy, the Fect, right where we want them, and from our gathered intelligence, we have the exact location of where they are gathering—Caden's laboratory in the Land of the Gods. Now we want to ensure we destroy Caden's laboratory, and according to our scouts, Caden already did us the favor of destroying the other space tower. There is division amongst the Fect. They do not want to be led by Caden, and some have already shown resistance toward him. But as we are aware, he is a black wizard, and he won't be dethroned that easily. Even so, we have the one thing that he fears most—the green wizard." Everyone stood up and cheered out loudly. The president continued, "Once we get in and plant the explosives in the lab, I will have our troops fall back. From there our plan is to use Project Sol to annihilate whatever remains of the Fect forces."

A single local elder named Pancho stood up and asked, "What about our families? Haven't we given enough? I've lost both my sons, my daughter, and some of my grandchildren to this damned war!" Pancho's voice echoed as he said, "My wife and I only have our grandchild left, Elizabeth, who will be turning eighteen in two days. Are we expected to offer her up to be slaughtered too?"

President Nilla paused for a moment and then said, "Make it known, for those families that have lost more than one parent or child, Devansh thanks you for your contribution, and those families will not receive further draft notices. Also, those families who have lost all but one child, like Pancho here, will be awarded a monthly payment. Children who have been orphaned as a result of the war will be cared for by the state, and family or friends who will take them into their homes will receive the same monthly stipend." President Nilla told one of the sentinel robots, "Make sure Pancho arrives safely back to his home, and keep a watch over his family until I say otherwise."

President Nilla now opened her broadcast to all of Devansh, telling every civilian from every city, "The final moment of the war with the Fect is upon us. Remember that the strength of our people comes in unity, as it has always done in the face of adversity. Does anyone remember why our flag is on a field of green? Recall the story of your ancestors, who came to this land from the West with nothing but the furs on their backs. When they settled in the oasis of the world, their neighbors grew jealous of their newfound prosperity, and they came seeking to steal what they had sown. In a time of uncertainty and fear, a single man stood above the crowd and waved an ax wrapped in a green cloak, and he shouted, 'Follow my beacon! Fight with me, for your homes, for your families, and for your people!' And the people followed him." President Nilla tore the green sash from her waist and held it high in the air. "I call upon you, citizens of Devansh! The enemy has come to steal what you have sown. Follow my beacon! Fight with me, for your homes, for your families, and for your people!" The crowd erupted in a roar. Anything that they had that was green was proudly waved in the air. Across the country, as the president's image waved on giant screens, green flags propped out of windows and on rooftops and in the streets. The roar thundered throughout the land, and as the president smiled at the reception, she gave a deep bow.

President Nilla had Zow, Lata, and I follow her to the presidential lounge. Once inside, I was blown away. It had everything you can think of to relax: a personal chef, Jacuzzi, movie room, training room, shower area, six rooms sized for a monarch. The president came out with a few drinks and said, "I wanted to thank you again. Join me in a toast!"

I raised my glass, and we all yelled out, "To Devansh!"

That night, the president let us sleep in the presidential lounge, including Honovi, who fell asleep early. I found myself staring out into the darkness as the rain hit the glass and the wind brushed the trees against it. Lata stood behind me and said, "You're scared, aren't you?"

I told her, "I'm not sure how to answer that question."

Lata reminded me, "A little fear is good. It keeps us cautious. Follow me. I have a surprise for you." I followed her to the living room where Kogi and Lugii were standing next to a mannequin wearing green wizard robes, a green hat, and green boots. Lata looked at me and said, "All three of us contributed now that Mayoko is gone." The room went silent for a bit. Then Lata said, "You will enjoy the upgrade of the material from its casual comfort to its flexibility for combat."

I told Lata and the others, "What is wrong with the green robes I am wearing?"

All three of them laughed at me and said, "Those robes are pretty outdated, and they don't completely fit you, Alaric!"

Kogi told me, "It would appear that the previous green wizard had a smaller head. He also seemed to have a bit of a belly. The robes look bulky on you, and the green is worn and faded."

Lugii told me, "Also, those green boots look way too tight and uncomfortable. These boots have a special gel inside of them that conforms to your foot and cushions it better than any natural material you could use. They're also durable enough to stand up to any weather or terrain, but they're not too heavy. The material is specially made to be waterproof, fire-resistant, and it adjusts to the outside temperature. You'll be cool as a snowman in the desert, and you'll feel like a bear in the snow." The more the three spoke of the uniform, the more I was buying in since my current green robes always did itch, and they didn't feel like they were designed for my frame. I put on my new robes and immediately felt the difference. I hugged all three of them, and a smile came out as I looked in the mirror and saw a completely different wizard.

I even asked the mirror, "Who is that guy?"

Lata said, "That guy is the one who is going to save the world." Those words echoed to my core and ignited the fire within me. My green robes began to glow as Lata came up to me and told me, "You know what has to be done and what is on the line?"

"Yes."

"Good. Kogi and Lugii are coming with you to the Valley of the Wizards."

"There is no need for that."

"Really? Do you know how to get to the Valley of the Wizards?"

I looked at Lata for a second, scratched my head, and said, "No."

"That is one of the reasons why I have them going with you."

"And what are the other reasons?"

"Two, so I can keep an eye on you through them. And three, none of your damn business." She smiled as wide as she could and added, "Because I can do what I want."

Chapter 14

A week had passed, and preparations were ready. I had everything that I needed for the journey, and the capital was ready to move its forces into the Land of the Gods. I had spent the week with Lata and Honovi helping as many civilians as we could around the city, mostly with healing. Many still needed help with restoring water and electricity, but the president had promised that the engineer corps would take care of it. A few days ago, while we were out, Honovi found a beautiful tanzanite stone. Her mother, Lata, helped put it together into a pendant, and they gave it to me as a gift. I put it around my neck, and it's a good reminder that I have something to finally come home to. Honovi told me, "Not only is it my gift to you but it's to remind you to never forget where you started. You were once the blue wizard. Now you are the green wizard. Hold onto what you have gotten, and never let it go." I hugged her as hard as I could.

I was out late one night rebuilding the walls of the capital with my golden staff when Zow stopped by to have a word with me. Zow called out to me, "Green wizard!" When I turned around, I saw Zow was the size of an elephant with muscles the size of a car engine. Zow had been walking her pet Tiger, Ada, as it shifted in colors, looking at the stars, but then she felt it important to come talk with me.

I asked, "What do you want?"

Zow said, "Is that how you speak to your elders, wizard?"

I apologized, telling her, "You wear four thousand fairly well."

I was a bit annoyed at the time and did not want to talk, but Zow has a way of commanding your attention. She raised her voice and said, "Green wizard, I have something you need to hear."

As the tiger looked like she was confronting me as well, I said, "You have my undivided attention."

Zow said, "Perfect. As you know, Lata and I are close, and we keep nothing from one another."

I said, "Okay?"

Zow followed with, "Lata has told me of two separate visions she has had involving you, wizard. In her first vision, she saw you out in the field having fun with a young teenager, showing her how to control things with her fingers. The second vision involves you in a bloody heap in the Valley of Wizards. That's why Lugii and Kogi are coming with you." Zow got close up in my face and said, "I have my own form of connection with the cosmic language, and after four thousand years of life, my feeling is that if you let Lata come with you too, the results will be disastrous."

I asked Zow, "What should I do?"

Zow, already looking conflicted, said, "I'm not sure, because I feel that I have said too much just by sharing these two visions with you."

I told Zow, "Thank you," and I went back to fixing the wall.

After a couple minutes, my mind began to wander, and I couldn't stand it. I threw down my tools, looked up to the stars, and screamed at the sky, or anyone who would listen to me, "What must I do?" I took a seat on a stump, putting my hands over my head.

Through my fingers, I saw a bright light approaching me, getting brighter until I heard a familiar voice, "You still have not learned how to calm down and just breathe, have you, Brownie?" I took my hands off my face and saw my grandfather, Remo the wizard.

I asked him, "How is this even possible?"

He said, "Through the cosmic language. Have you learned nothing, Brownie? I am simply what us wizards call a cosmic projection. You are still learning, but one day, when you have a greater understanding of things, you will be able to talk with the rest of the wizards."

I began to sob. "I spent so long trying to find you, dreaming of what you'd say when I found you. I'm sorry we didn't have that time when you were around. I'm sorry I wasn't there to help you. I'm sorry I took the power you spent your life trying to earn." I dropped my hand back into my hands.

My grandfather raised my head and said, "You do not have to apologize for that, Brownie. If anything, it gave me just enough power to save you from your father right before you made your way into Devansh. After that, a few minutes later, my body couldn't handle the power of the green wizard, and it destroyed me, but I want you to keep in mind, Brownie, that at that point, I had lived a full lifetime. Honestly, I had been ready to go for quite some time, more so after your grandmother had passed and I was left alone for several years."

I wanted to know, so I asked my grandfather, "Why did you never take the time to train me or even try to stop my father?"

My grandfather took a second and said, "Because, as you know, your father's bloodline was that of a warlock. When he got with your mother, he did not know she had wizard's blood in her, so he felt that, somehow, I had lied to him or tricked him. He aimed all the blame at me. Well, your father already had a disgust for wizards, and he tried many times to kill me. He only stood against me face-to-face once, but each time he attacked me, I disarmed him with ease, but I could never bring myself to kill him."

I asked, "Why?"

Remo smiled. "Because at the end of the day, I did not want you to grow up without a father, and I knew at that time I could not just take you away from him, so I mainly spent my time watching over and protecting you. Look, Brownie, I need to tell you something before I go. Caden is actually your uncle." I looked at my grandfather in shock. He raised a hand to shush me before I said anything. "Before I met your grandmother, I was with another woman that I met here in Devansh a very long time ago, and not too long after, Caden was born. I helped raise Caden for the longest time. I felt like I had found my place in the world. I had a family. I had built myself a home. I was at peace. I was content enough that I was blinded by the monster that Caden was growing to be. While he was a naturally gifted wizard, he began to show some disturbing signs. It started with killing insects. Then it led to birds. He would torture them until he got bored, and he would eventually grab onto the wings and tear them off. Caden would then pull the legs off, making sure the bird was alive until the very end. To finish it, he'd twist the bird's head off and squish it between his fingers.

"When he got older, he started abusing other animals. As he neared adulthood, he became curious. I don't know the full story, but one day, he met a young lady out in the woods, crying her eyes out. She had brought a knife with her, and she was making the choice to end her life. Caden told me afterward that she asked him to help her. I realized after the fact that he didn't do it to help a poor woman out of her misery. He was curious. He wanted to know what it felt like. What he did to her... I won't even describe it to you. I used my powers to try and keep his mind right, but I only had so much of an impact. In fact, I think I made him worse. I managed to keep him stable during the day, but as the hours went by, he became more and more erratic, and then he'd have a meltdown. One night, he blew up, and it changed my life forever. In my ignorance, I couldn't bring in anyone else to help, not after he murdered his mother. I delved deep into his mind and forced in some barriers, blocked portions of his brain that fed into his violent emotions. He became a little dull, but it worked, for a time. I tried to bring him into the Cult of Wizards so that I could keep an eye on him better. I also thought that if he ever broke free, the wizards wouldn't let him go far.

"Magni the wizard, the second-ranking wizard in our hierarchy, saw right through the ruse. When they refused Caden's entry, he was so angry that he broke the locks I put in place, and all that evil in his mind had slowly pooled into a dark pit. He was obsessed with death. He grew a malicious hatred of wizards, but he had a particular disgust of Magni, and he hunted him down and killed him after the war. Shortly after, I found out from the green wizard that my son had become a black wizard, and he had gone as far as to name himself the black wizard of death. It broke my heart, and it was too little too late that I realized that there were a thousand things I should have done long ago. I never felt capable of killing my own son, no matter how much I tell myself that I should have. The Cult of Wizards has faced much evil throughout time, and had fought many wars, but your uncle, single-handedly, has become the greatest threat we have ever faced. Our order has nearly gone extinct because of him."

My grandfather gave a sigh and told me, "As you are one of the last of the wizards, it will be your duty to ensure the success of the next generation and to ensure that the sacrifices of the wizards of old are not in vain. With your guidance, Honovi will help create a new Cult of Wizards, one that fits with the times much better than the ancients did. Listen to me now, Alaric. No matter what, do not hesitate to strike down your uncle, for he is a great deceiver and has forfeited his humanity. You must fulfill your new duty as the green wizard to not only protect our way of life but to protect the people of this world, and Honovi." My grandfather placed his hand on my cheek and smiled as his arm slowly began to fade. "I'm truly sorry I must leave you this way. Know this, you will never truly be alone—never again." My grandfather vanished, and I stood, staring up at the stars, telling myself it was time to bring an end to all of this so that we could all move on.

I woke up at three in the morning, ate some breakfast, got ready, and made my way out. Before I left, I peeked into the darkness of Lata and Honovi's room. They were curled up together in the warm bed. I whispered, "Sleep well," and started on my journey. I managed to sneak out without stirring the sleeping mages. I didn't need them to find the Valley of the Wizards. My pointing stick showed me the way. It was cold and rainy, and the wind felt like ice was chipping away at my bones. I wrapped myself tighter in my robe, and after a few minutes, it started to work its magic. The cold faded away, and I felt like I was being hugged by a bear. I wandered my way down muddy roads and passed herds of cows. After a time, I snuggled under the cover of a peach tree to nap. I don't know why it made me think of my siblings. When I awoke, a single green caterpillar was walking up my sleeve that I jokingly said, "Well, look at my cool new friend."

My gold staff, for the first time, told me, "And I thought I was your friend, but you choose to talk to caterpillars instead of me!"

My eyes got big as the voice roared in my head. "I, uh, sorry. To be honest, I didn't know you could talk."

"You have hardly tried," said the pointing stick. "All wizards talk to their pointing sticks. Well, ALMOST all," it added.

"Okay, okay, I'm sorry."

"Did you ever wonder where I even came from, or who made me?"

I scratched my chin for a moment. "To be honest, I didn't really think about it until now. Where are you from?"

Even though the pointing stick didn't have a face, the jolt of energy I felt made me imagine it smiling back at me. "Well, thank you for asking! Your grandfather, Remo, found a beautiful tree on Duster Island he called a Blue Tree. Creative, I know, but the wood was actually blue. The Blue Trees are indigenous to the island, and through the cosmic language, he asked the tree for permission to take a piece of it. And out of that piece, he made me!"

"Why did he go to the island?" I asked.

"He loved that island because of the big and juicy shrimp that you could catch off the coast. You know, I'm still upset that he decided to leave me in the middle of the forest. I had to ask a black bear to take me to the temple. You ever try giving directions to a bear? They sent me along to, uh, what's her name… VANAS! She was supposed to know where Remo was so she can give me back to him. I was going to scold him so good…, but I can't anymore. I felt it when he passed."

"You can feel things?" I interrupted.

"*You can feel things?*" the pointing face repeated, sarcastic and mockingly, in the voice of a five-year-old. "Of course I can feel things! I may not be a person, but I have feelings too! Everything has feelings! Your new caterpillar friends do, the tree I was cut from does, how about you ask the grass how it feels having you sitting on top of it and crushing it!"

I jumped to my feet, startled, and a roaring laugh boomed through my head. "Kidding! Kidding!" the pointing stick said. "Anyways, I ended up not going to Vanas. They asked the black bear to take me there, and when I felt Remo had left this world, I asked the bear to take me to the coast instead. I went through so much with that man, all the battles, all the trials, all the mischievous pranks and terrible deeds. I felt like I didn't have any purpose. I asked the bear to hand me over to a whale, and the whale brought me home, back to the island. I thought I'd feel at home, but the island was gone,

171

scorched. All of its beauty was gone, including the tree I was cut from. The whale dropped me on the beach, and I just wanted to roll myself into the ocean and float on the surface until I became so waterlogged that I'd finally sink to the depths and be gone forever. But then Vanas grabbed me and told me that my duty wasn't yet fulfilled. Honestly, I didn't know how she got there so fast, but a pointing stick will take what a pointing stick can get. And then she gave me to you, and with your strength, I was able to finally transform into what every staff dreams of becoming—a golden staff. There's only one other staff in wizard history that has ever had that honor—Abir's staff."

"Wait," I said, scratching my head. "You're the blue staff I originally had?"

"That's right. And to think this whole time, you didn't even say hello or ask me how my day was. But I'll give you this—your adventures have been about as much fun as the ones I had with Remo."

I snatched the pointing stick and said "Well, then let's finish this one."

When I arrived at the Valley of the Wizards, nothing about it looked embracing. The mountains were corroded, the cracks within them gushed out blood. The river that ran down into the valley was pitch-black; a dense darkness loomed over the valley. Life that ventured into the valley was obliterated as I witnessed a flock of birds make their way through only to be vaporized by a black flame. Something about this place was off, as if I was walking right into a trap. I brightened my golden staff as my surroundings got darker. I then felt like the darkness was wrapping around my neck and choking me. I began to crawl on my knees until I came across a giant stone statue of a dark wizard. I asked my staff, "What the heck is that doing here?" The staff did not have an answer for me, and both of us were equally lost. The air got harder and harder to breathe as my thoughts became erratic. I felt like my energy was being drained from me. I punched my hand into the dirt several times and attempted to draw in natural energy, but all that poured in was more of the darkness. I raised my pointing stick to power myself until I got on my feet again.

I kept walking until I heard a voice say, "Over here!" I was using most of my energy to just keep walking in a straight line. It felt like

I had vertigo. When I arrived at the voice's location, a hooded figure stood there, waiting for me. "Ahh, we meet again. It's been too long, green wizard."

I said, "Who are you?"

The black wizard levitated closer to me and said, "Gilsavel, the one dark god. And you, green wizard, have been set up, deceived, and lied to for the very purpose of luring you into my domain." I stood quietly as Gilsavel educated me. He hovered around me in a circle, as if he was playing with his food before he took the big bite. Caden steadily came out of the darkness, indulged at the idea that the green wizard could be deceived. Steps could be heard approaching as servants to the one dark god revealed themselves, all pointing in my direction. I continued listening to the dark god as my heart started to beat faster and faster. "How do you think Caden found all of the wizards? Do you think he was really that good of a hunter?" I shook my head, not wanting to hear the answer. I couldn't see his face through the hood, but I could see a nasty, grimy grin. "There is only one who has survived thus far. Lugii has been a faithful servant through these many years."

I screamed, "Liar!" so loud that my voice grew hoarse.

Gilsavel cackled in glee. "So focused on war and politics, so desperate for young men and women to come and die for the good of all. So desperate to force their beliefs and bolster their strength, the wizards stopped asking questions. Nobody asked where Lugii had come from, what his purpose was, or what his ambitions were. The Cult of Wizards was just happy to have bodies to replace those they had lost. Nobody thought to put the puzzle pieces together. Whenever he was allowed in plans and meetings, someone would die. Such a spinner of tales, that one is. The one dark god revered at telling me how Lugii used old dark magic on Lata and Zow to sway me in coming here. The one dark god raised his old boney fingers to the air, telling me, "Lugii has ensured victory!" I could not make sense of any of this. My mind was blank. My heart felt as though a knife was jabbed through it. The one dark god spoke louder in piercing words as he told me, "Lugii will use your father's pointing stick to bring an end to the capital and everything you love. The one dark god, now mocking me, told me, "You were all too focused on the war and everything going on that you forgot about your father's pointing stick that was left on the battlefield."

My pointing stick sensed my mindlessness and urged me, "Snap out of it!" I ignored it.

I was wrestling within myself internally now, and as I looked at my robes, they were turning from green to black as anger, fear, hate, disgust, sadness, and so much more was running wild in my head. *Don't fight your feelings. They're natural after all. You're human, but I can make you so much more, give you so much more.* It was no use. Half my robes had turned black. I could not resist the evil thoughts in my head from the harsh upbringing I had experienced. I couldn't let go, and I was ready to drop my staff and give myself up. But then I heard a whisper in the air. Its voice faded and then came back, a little louder this time. Then the whisper became a harsh bang, followed by a cosmic slap, demanding to know what I was doing.

I stuttered, "I-I-I don't know. I-I'm l-l-lost and conf-u-u-used. Everything h-u-urts."

The whispering voice told me, "Are you so vain and foolish that you'd forget your oath so easily? You accepted a responsibility when you became the green wizard. That responsibility wasn't just to the mortal people. You have a responsibility to the cosmic language…to me. I will not allow you to betray me, or yourself. I see you can use some assistance."

The whispering voice approached me in a blinding light, and the entity of the cosmic language placed its hand of light on my chest. I felt my heart radiate with power as my robes returned to a vibrant green.

"How did y—?"

"Your mother may have brought you into this world, and your father may have put you there, but ultimately, I am your creator. You are energy, as is everything around you, and I am the architect of energy. For me, it's a simple matter to repair you and to give you life, like anything else. Now end this." The entity of the cosmic language dissipated, and I finally came to my senses again.

"Most impressive," Gilsavel moaned. "But where she is the bringer of energy, I am the master of emotion. You cannot deny your deepest feelings."

"Shut up!" I screamed. "I understand now that my weakness only comes from me. I am my own worst enemy. I feel pain because I let myself dwell on it. The only thing that can harm me is me." I raised my golden staff and pointed its gleaming head at Gilsavel. "The Cult of Wizards will never go extinct because we all exist through the cosmic language. We are never truly alone, in life nor death." With the boom of my voice, I began to see matter fizzle into existence in the corner of my eye. Several figures faded into clarity, and I was soon flanked by the wizard of old. Abir stood beside me with his golden staff. Remo shuffled to my side and raised his along with Magni and all the other ancient wizards. In unison, we unleashed a volley of bolts. The entire area lit up like a rainbow. Gilsavel had taken a tremendous amount of damage as he fell next to Caden, reaching out for help. Caden ripped the skin off his face and shoved it down Gilsavel's mouth as he yelled out in mad fury, proclaiming himself to be the embodiment of death as he put his pointing stick through Gilsavel's skull.

Caden raised his pointing stick in the air and consumed all the servants around him into his body. The entire area we were in went pitch-black as Caden released dark-purple energy from his entire body, sending toes and hands in every direction that stood a wizard. You could hear Caden yelling at the very top of his lungs how much he hated the wizards. Myself and all the wizards formed a barrier, holding back the rushing void. I asked my grandfather, "He just consumed a god. How can we stop him now?"

My grandfather thought hard and eventually said, "I have no idea." Caden's jaw dropped to the floor as more purple energy began firing out of his mouth toward me. Caden lost it when he realized he could not kill any of the wizards I had summoned. The lunatic went over the edge as he began tearing more flesh off his body. Caden looked at me and, with a piercing, sadistic gaze, told me he was going to rip the flesh off my face.

Caden yelled at the top of his lungs. His voice echoed across the valley. "I am the true dark god!" Caden ran in my direction as each wizard in the area began blasting him with their pointing sticks, but he would not go down. I ran toward Caden as a full rainbow color of energy was trying to hold him back. I powered up my pointing stick until it began to glow gold and rammed it into the side of his neck. I looked on as half my pointing stick was inside Caden's body as he tried pulling it. I summoned every ounce of green energy I had within me and pointed both my fingers at him, yelling out, "Bang, bang," as a spiral of green energy consumed Caden until his darkness faded away from existence.

The light came out for the first time in an area that had been filled with darkness, and sure enough, I saw a few statues of wizards that fit more of the scene of what I was initially expecting to walk into. I shook the hands of all the other wizards, and I told them, "Thank you for all your help." My pointing stick yelled at me as I was trying to take a five-minute break.

"We need to get back to the capital as quickly as possible!" The pointing stick made it clear that with Lugii being a dark wizard and Lata still recovering, they were going to need all the help they could get.

I stroked my beard a few times and asked the pointing stick if it could teleport us back to the capital. "What are you, slow? You can walk. Besides, you used up a lot of my power on Caden." I threw my green hat to the ground and started to feel a little wobbly. The staff told me, "You still don't realize how much power you just pumped out in summoning all those wizards, do you?" I did not have time to think about such things. I had to figure something out quickly. I took another step, this one heavier than the one before.

I asked the pointing stick, "Do you have any food?"

"What am I, a walking restaurant? Haven't I don't enough for you today?"

My stomach began to growl loudly as I told the pointing stick, "Nope."

"Oh yeah? To hell with you, then!" the pointing stick snapped before dropping from my hand and rolling away from me.

"Oh, come on, I was kidding! Come back!" I yelled. I slowly leaned down to grab a rock to throw at the pointing stick when the tanzanite stone around my neck began to glow brighter and brighter, completely consuming me.

Chapter 15

A few soldiers at the capital had just gotten done eating lunch and returning to work within the weapons department when they spotted someone breathing heavily by the table of confiscated items. One of the soldiers pointed her gun at the individual and shouted, "Turn around slowly!" The individual grabbed his face, and pieces of flesh came off.

One of the other soldiers yelled out, "That is Lugii!" As Lugii began to yell out, he grabbed the black pointing stick on the table and began to be consumed by a dark flame as his black robes revealed themselves. Lugii raised the pointing stick, and black flames went in every direction, incinerating everything in the flames' path. Lata was a few miles outside the capital walls with Honovi, enjoying each other's company by a small lake, when a giant explosion went off that echoed across the land. Lata, still recovering in her wheelchair, had a really bad feeling about this.

Lata told Honovi, "Stay close by and have your pointing stick ready."

Honovi said, "Don't worry, I'll protect you, Mom."

Lata smiled and said, "Don't you forget who the grand wizard is."

President Nilla had just walked into the command center, demanding answers, when she saw the mayhem she had just walked into. The president surveyed the entire room of mangled, twisted bodies and told Lugii, "What is wrong with you! Who do you think you are?" Lugii had just pulled out his pointing stick from the mouth of a dead soldier when he delightedly looked at the president.

Lugii advanced on the president as his eyes turned black, telling her, "I'm going to enjoy burning you from the inside out." Lugii

raised his staff when Zow made herself into the room, quickly pulling the fire alarm as Ada jumped on Lugii, tearing into his arm as the
president and Zow quickly made their way out. Lugii, aggravated,
blasted Ada with his pointing stick, sending pieces of the tiger in
every direction. Lugii continued to make his way throughout the
headquarters, laying waste to the entire facility and all that stood in
his way until he came face to face with Kogi. The dark wizard was
delighted. At last, the final mage in existence. Koji shook his head
as he made another bun on his head. Lugii pointed at Kogi and told
him, "If you simply bow before your new master, I will not only
spare your life but I will show you how to wield this power yourself."

Kogi took a few seconds to think the offer through until he
tightened his blindfold and told Lugii "There is only one true master,
and that title belongs to the cosmic language." Enraged, Lugii raised
the pointing stick. He was completely enveloped in a black aura.
Black lighting repeatedly struck all around him. Kogi was forced to
take several steps back as Lugii unleashed a wave of energy from the
pointing stick. The blast was so great the walls began to crumble, and
the sky became visible through new holes in the ceiling. The building
started to collapse, and their lungs choked on dust that filled the void
between them. Neither could see anything in the cloud.

As the dust from the rubble cleared, Lugii emerged from the
dust. Darkness radiated around him as he laughed at Kogi slowly
making his way out of the rubble. Lugii used the pointing stick
to raise all the bricks near Kogi into the air and began rapidly firing them toward Kogi as he could only point at so many before he
started getting hit by multiple bricks. Lugii was enjoying himself so
much that instead of quickly killing Kogi, he began having fun with
him, slowly tearing Kogi apart. The dark wizard pointed his index
finger at Kogi to freeze him in place. Lugii began hitting Kogi across
his chest using the pointing stick like a crowbar. Lugii forced Kogi's
face open as blood went everywhere. Lugii tore off Kogi's red robes
and said, "What a joke you mages really are." He shot a black blast of
energy at him, sending his body through the rubble.

Lugii did not take one step until he heard the president's voice
through the telecom. "Take one more step, and I'll press this button,

and Project Sol will turn this building into a crater. Even you can't survive getting shot by the sun!" Lugii looked up to the sky and began radiating, pouring his power through the pointing stick, sending an enormous black burst of energy into outer space and blowing up the satellite that Project Sol operated off of. Lugii, annoyed at these little tactics, raised his staff and began forming black balls of energy over the capital, and he began throwing them into the streets below. Immediately, the cries of pain and death carried through the city and echoed over its walls. The president, now inside the remains of a bathroom with Zow, screeched into a radio, "Have all forces, including Division Double Zero, hunt down Lugii. Use every possible means to kill him! Now!"

Lata continued to slowly make her way toward the capital's walls with Honovi when Varun, Catalan, and Captain Raider ran up to them. They all looked at Lata with determination in their faces. "Lata was briefed on all the details by Varun, who had hacked into the capital's security system some time ago. What does the grand wizard have in mind to stop this madness?" he asked.

"There might not be anything we can do at this point."

Varun, not satisfied with that answer, told Lata, "You shouldn't let that handicap stop you. We can do anything." Lata looked at Honovi, whose face was wet with tears.

"Honovi, what's wrong?"

"You promised me you were done fighting!" Honovi said in her angry teenager voice.

Lata wiped the tears off her daughter's face and said, "I am the grand wizard. It is my duty to protect this world."

Honovi dropped to her knees and told her mother, "I am scared because I do not want to lose you."

Lata used both her arms to raise her daughter up and told Honovi, "One last time."

Honovi still wasn't completely buying it. She said, "Promise me right now you will return!"

Lata put on her brown wizard hat and looked at Honovi directly into her eyes." I promise I will return to you."

Lata looked at everyone present and told them to each lend her a little bit of the cosmic power within them. Varun and everyone looked at each other and said, "Whatever it takes." Lata told each of them to reach out their hands. Catalan, Varun, and Honovi all reached out their hands toward Lata.

Captain Raider looked confused and said, "But I'm no wizard. How can I help?"

Lata motioned him forward and said, "You don't need to be. All living beings have the cosmic power within them." Captain Raider's hand joined the others', and, immediately, a stream of light started pouring out of their hands into Lata's body. The light around Lata's body became so bright that Lata began to rise off her wheelchair as everyone fell to the ground after giving as much cosmic power as they possibly could.

As the light dimmed down, everyone gasped, "Wow!" At the same time, Lata's brown robes were radiating brightly.

Varun, in amazement, said out loud, "She even looks younger."

Catalan said, "Her pointing stick has even changed. It looks like someone polished it."

Captain Raider looked at everyone with a loss of words as his mouth hung wide open. Honovi screamed out, "Now that's my mom!" as Lata teleported away.

Lugii had just annihilated Division Double Zero when the pointing stick had just sniffed out the location of the president. Lugii took one step forward when, suddenly, his body felt the force of a typhoon. Lugii slowly turned around, seeing an immense flash of brown light make its way toward him. Each brown flash Lugii witnessed was followed with sonic booms so mighty that Lugii never had time to react to the brown wizard standing behind him. Lugii calmly turned around and was face-to-face with Lata, just a few feet away. As the black flames began to burn darker and deeper into Lugii's flesh, he let Lata know, "I'm delighted you were finally able to join me." It was as if the bigger his smile, the hotter the flames burned.

Lata pointed her finger at Lugii and told him, "This ends today!"

Lugii pointed at Lata and said "And that is where you're wrong. You do not know the power that I have been blessed with by the one dark god."

Lata slowly began to walk toward Lugii, telling him, "It is not going to matter either way."

Lugii closed the distance and snapped, "You're doomed to fail!" They each swung their pointing sticks and met one another's blows, the sticks vibrating from the collision. Lugii kicked Lata backward and formed a black ball of energy before him that he hit with his pointing stick like a baseball, sending it flying toward Lata. As it grew closer, it grew in size. Lata hit it back at Lugii. With a surprised look on his face, the black ball of energy continued to grow. Lata teleported behind Lugii, grabbed him by the back of the head, and forcefully rammed his face into the behemoth ball of dark energy. The explosion was violent, and Lata quickly put up a barrier over the remaining half of the headquarters building, shielding the president from the blast.

As the dust settled, Lugii's voice could be heard yelling out, "Liberation!" Excitement ran down Lugii's face that did not sit well with Lata. Lugii's body was wrecked from the explosion as he kept yelling out the word "liberation!" Lugii's flesh had now been completely consumed by the dark flames. Lugii yelled into the sky, "Liberation!" once more as magical black balls with thick heavy chains appeared around each of his legs, each arm, and one that was chained around his neck. Lata looked on, wondering what the heck was going on as Lugii kept yelling out the word "liberation." Lugii stopped yelling as things went dead silent. Nothing could be heard until a dark shadow appeared before Lugii, bearing a black key. The dark shadow began unlocking all of Lugii's shackles until the last one across his neck fell to the ground, and the dark shadow disappeared. The entire capital was covered in darkness as Lugii's body began to quickly repair itself. Lata began to sense something terrible was about to happen, so she began shooting brown blasts of energy repeatedly at Lugii until she stopped to witness a Lugii that had accomplished what in the Cult of Wizards was called cosmic cannibalism.

Lugii, no longer able to hold himself back, clapped, telling Lata, "You ARE worthy of the title grand wizard." Lugii shook his head at Lata, telling her, "You do not understand the gift I was given to ensure the end of the wizards, including that damn green wizard." Lata, gripping her pointing stick tight, asked Lugii to enlighten her. Lugii was more than willing to oblige. "It is simple. I sacrificed part of my body using the black flames to activate old dark wizard magic that unlocks the shackles we all carry with us upon creation. Once those shackles are released, we consume the natural cosmic power within us that bears the light. As we turn that natural cosmic power to darkness, we are reborn with a greater affinity of all-around magical power steered from the darkness of the cosmic language itself. Essentially, I am the opposite of the green wizard, only I am vastly more powerful than him."

Lata, tired of hearing all the talk, sent a brown blast of energy at Lugii that fizzled out before it reached his body. Lugii looked at Lata and asked her, "How hardheaded are you? Prepare for your demise." Lata fully powered up and was completely covered in her brown aura as the two began to exchange blows with their pointing sticks, creating shockwaves that vibrated down the street. Lugii eventually landed a blow on Lata's thigh, which he followed with a large blast of dark energy. The blast momentarily dropped Lata to her knees as she spit out a bit of blood. Lugii sent another blast of dark energy at her, which, with all her might, she deflected with her pointing stick. Lugii used his speed to snatch Lata's brown pointing stick out of her hand. He took time to admire its marvel. As he stared at it, light began to fizzle at its end. He pushed his face closer to the end and squinted. Brown bolts of lightning shot out of the pointing stick, lighting up Lugii's face until he dropped the pointing stick. Lata summoned her pointing stick as she was running toward a screaming Lugii, who was clutching his face in his hands and screaming. Lata raised her pointing stick to the sky as she jumped in the air, powered up her pointing stick, and ferociously threw it at Lugii's body. It streaked through the air like a mighty brown lightning bolt. The explosion was violent enough to blow Lata backward with such a force that the wind was knocked out of her before she even hit the ground.

President Nilla could no longer watch from the bathroom what was happening to Lata. The president adjusted her pants and told Zow she is not going to let Lata die alone. The president made her way out to where Lata was, and she yelled out Lugii's name. Lugii took his focus off Lata as she attempted to regain her breath. President Nilla was now pointing her finger at Lugii, telling him that if he does not stop this madness, things are not going to end well for him. Lugii burst out laughing as he continued making his way toward the president. Lugii asked the president, "Who are you expecting to come save you? The green wizard is dead, Lata has already displayed her best, and yet you think things aren't going to end well for me!"

President Nilla looked up to Lugii and told him, "I may not be a wizard, but I am the light of Devansh."

Lugii, unhappy with her answer, asked the president, "And what happens when I extinguish that light?"

President Nilla smiled and said, "Then a new light will be born."

"I don't believe in fantasy talk."

"What a shame it must be to have so much power only for you to still lose."

Lugii stood face-to-face with the president and kicked her to the ground. Lugii aimed his pointing stick at her and sent a black blast of energy at her. President Nilla saw her life flash before her eyes. She closed her eyes and embraced the end. Right as the blast was about to hit the president, Zow leaped in front of her, dropping dead. President Nilla screamed out in anger and in grief. She pulled Zow's body into her arms and asked, "Why? Why, when it was my time?"

Lugii chuckled and said, "Don't you worry. I am going to grant you the death you desire." Lugii had gotten so fixated on the president that he had forgotten about Lata. The brown wizard whistled at Lugii, who turned around.

"These are for you," she said as she sent dozens of brown energy spears into Lugii's body. As the tips penetrated his back, the spears exploded. Screaming, Lugii's broken body lunged toward Lata, pointing with his left hand as he fired off blasts of black fire with his pointing stick in the right. Lata was matching Lugii blow for blow until Lugii decided to play dirty and sent multiple blasts toward the president. Lata did not have time to deflect them all, so she teleported in the path of the blasts and took them head on.

Lugii was drooling in anticipation at the result. The president was alive, but Lata lay on the ground in a bloody heap, breathing but unable to lift her left arm. President Nilla crawled over the Lata and yelled, "What were you thinking? You're worth far more to these people than I am. Where's the green wizard?"

Lata took a deep breath and said, "That's a good question."

The president jumped to her feet and stomped angrily to Lugii. She screamed at him, "You really are a waste of space!"

Lata yelled out to President Nilla, telling her, "Stop!"

The president said "Shut up! No one is taking this moment away from me." The president came face-to-face with Lugii and slapped him across the face, calling him a bully.

"See you in hell," he responded as he raised the pointing stick and brought it down to smash her head in.

Lata yelled out to the president, "Get out of the way, you suicidal idiot!" Excited to finally have her moment, the president closed her eyes and awaited death until she noticed nothing happened. President Nilla slowly opened her eyes and began to make out the green wizard standing before her, holding Lugii's hand back.

"About damn time you showed up, show-off," President Nilla said. I headbutted Lugii, and he stumbled backward, black blood running down his face.

President Nilla lifted up Lata and asked, "Why does it look like the green wizard is not at full power?"

Lata told the president, "Because he isn't at full power. If anything, he looks like he is using all his might just to keep up with Lugii." President Nilla noticed Kogi's fingers pointing at her in the rubble, asking for help. The president began digging Kogi out of the rubble.

Once Kogi's face appeared in the dust, he groaned, "Lata..." Lata crawled over to him with her one good hand, and Kogi reached out his hand, passing along to Lata all the remaining cosmic power within him. Lata groaned and began moving her left arm up and down, good as new. Kogi smiled, relieved he was able to make a difference before his eyes shut and he fainted. Lata told the president to take Kogi's body with her and get to safety as she walked away to assist the green wizard.

President Nilla yelled out, "What more can I do?"

Honovi, Varun, Catalan, and Captain Raider rang out in unison behind her, "You can start by helping out the people of the capital." Honovi left the group and started to walk toward Lata.

"I'm coming to fight with you and the green wizard," she said, her head held high.

Varun and the entire group were against it, and the president spoke out loud, "You're too precious to risk!" Honovi did not want to listen. She was too caught up in her emotions. She did not want to lose her mother. Honovi pulled out her orange pointing stick, ready for whoever tried to get in her way. When Varun tried to stop Honovi, she immediately pointed at him and froze him in place. Catalan had tried to grab Honovi from behind, but she snapped her fingers, disappearing and reappearing a good distance behind Catalan, giving her the window to freeze her in place as well. Captain Raider did not even try, because he knew he had no chance against a wizard, so he told Honovi, "If you go, make sure you're going for all the right reasons. Win us the victory!" The president begged Honovi to at least help her take Kogi's and Zow's bodies to safety. Honovi groaned but nodded.

Lata and I stood side by side as we raised our pointing sticks, and, together, we fired a ferocious energy blast at Lugii that he struggled to deflect. This gave me time to run up on Lugii and beat him with my golden pointing stick like a club. I hit him so hard I could hear his ribs cracking. Lugii returned the favor and shot multiple black energy blasts at me, with the final one being too much for me to stop. As it struck me, it dragged me six feet under the ground as it exploded. While Lugii had been paying attention to me, Lata kicked the pointing stick out of Lugii's hand, and, with her left hand, she punched him in the face. With her right hand, she shoved her brown pointing stick right into his face, blasting him point-blank. Lugii yelled out in pain as Lata took a step backward to see she had wiped out half his face. Lugii pushed out his hand and summoned his pointing stick to him. As it flew into the air, I grabbed it in midair. The moment I grabbed the black pointing stick, my muscles froze, and bolts of electricity flowed through my body. I couldn't move, and the pain was unbearable. Lugii snickered. "The darkness of the staff won't allow just any wizard to wield it, you fool."

Suddenly, I felt released, and the pointing stick stopped electrocuting me. I dropped the stick, and my arms hung at my sides, limp.

"Are you okay?" Lata yelled.

"Ye-yeah. I'm fi-ine," I lied.

"How did you manage to get here so fast?" Lata asked.

"Turns out that the tanzanite stone Honovi gave me contained some cosmic power that allowed me to teleport. Nifty, huh? I wonder who helped her with that." I tried to laugh, but my chest ached and felt heavy. I could barely breathe. Lugii, tired of hearing all the chitchat, grabbed me from off the ground and hurtled me directly at Lata as he fired off multiple blasts from his fingers. I had never been hit so hard in my life, and I had just been electrocuted. By the time I even felt the explosion, I was in a daze. Lata stood up in front of me as Lugii approached one stomp at a time.

President Nilla was looking for some sort of microphone to reach out to everyone when Varun brought her a wireless one he created from scratch. President Nilla smiled and flicked on the switch.

"People of Devansh. The final hour is upon us! Everyone evacuate to a shelter immediately! The wizards shall protect you!" As she shouted into the microphone, Honovi mustered all of her energy and mimicked her mother's movements, projecting a large shield over the ruins of the capital. She struggled, and the shield grew in stages. She had much to learn about her power, but she improvised as best she could.

"When the day is over, we shall rebuild a new city, one so grand and full of light that it will be seen from outer space, miles above our planet!" Captain Raider clapped his hands. "Great speech, Madam President!"

"Yeah, inspiring, but...what now?" Catalan asked the group.

The president sighed. "That's a good question. We need to WIN the day first. I need you to support anyone you come across. Get the people to safety! We need to give our friends the space to end this." Everyone stormed out of the ravaged conference room except Captain Raider.

The president raised an eyebrow. "Are you deaf, Captain? I gave you an order!"

"Madam President, all my life, I have been a soldier, taking orders. But today, I feel I should make my own decisions. Seeing as you have no staff, and the secret service is practically disbanded, I have made the decision to stand by your side. It is my obligation to protect you."

President Nilla chuckled, and her eyes beamed with light. "Well, thank you…, Major."

"Major, Madam President?"

"I'll need someone with a little more authority to help me keep this ship running." Raider clapped his heels together, stiffened his spine, and almost hit himself in the forehead with an enthusiastic salute.

Lugii had Lata by the hair with his left hand and me by the neck with his right. Lugii had begun to drain our power, but he continued to squeeze my throat hard. He didn't care whether he drained me first or I suffocated. Either way, he enjoyed watching me suffer. I started to feel as though something was tearing out my internal organs. As we slowly faded out of consciousness, Lugii cackled.

"The dark god Gilsavel would surely reward me for such an accomplishment!" Lugii oozed ego and flattery, and his lips became loose. Lugii could not hold it back; you could see the glee in his face.

"You know, it was I who gave up the location of the temple. Admittedly, I lead to unforeseen injuries, but it was well worth it! It was even I who caused the death of one of the greatest wizards of all! Maska could not bear to let Caden escape. Any information, whether it was true or not, she ate up like candy. I wish I could have watched her die… I was a wizard once too… A blast to the head by the Sharm put me down. The wizards abandoned me…, left me to rot in a pit of dead. Gilsavel offered me life…, vengeance…, power.

Admit it. If you were shot in the head and left to bleed to death in a put of corpses, it would sound like a good deal too. And MY OH MY, what a good deal it was. LOOK AT ME NOW! Oh, how I wanted to slaughter them all…, wring their necks…, tear out their hearts…, but I had to bide my time and allow my powers to grow. I was a purveyor of goods… I could get them anything they wanted. I gave them things to soothe the pains of war. Many of them were fond of drink, and some had more…exotic tastes. As the war dragged on, minds began to wander, lips loosened, and I had good ears. They would tell me their strife, and I would put dark thoughts into their minds. All it took was little suggestions. Wizards really are weak-willed. Some flung themselves off the balconies, unable to bear the pain any longer. Each dead wizard only grew my power. Remo long suspected there was dark magic at play, but he was too blind to see it. Nobody suspects the cook after all. His favorite dish was mushroom stew, only he, or any of the other wizards, knew there was always…a little extra added in."

I tried to struggle and break his grip, but he only clenched harder. I could feel his fingers digging into my arteries and bones, and I could only imagine he was tearing out small strands of Lata's hair at this point.

"You really are a piece of work, you know that?" I snapped.

"Why thank you! Since there hasn't been anyone left to feed for a long time, that's the first compliment I've gotten in…ages. You know, I would have had Aziza too…if it wasn't for that stupid staff. I spent many nights filling Aziza's ears with his failures. If only that staff didn't rip him from my grasp, I would have seen him launching himself off the balcony too."

I had begun to feel the light fade in my mind as I felt my body go limp. I had done all I could, and in the end, it was beginning to look like I was going to come up short. My life began to flash before my eyes when I could hear a voice followed by a flash, and next thing I knew, I was on the ground trying to get my mind right. I could hear a voice that sounded familiar yet very distant, as if muffled. My sight began to become clear when I realized Honovi was exchanging blows with Lugii. I looked over and saw Lata passed out on the ground. I crawled my way over to her and placed my fingers on her neck, over the artery. Her pulse was low, so I mustered what little cosmic energy I had left and transferred it to her. Lata groaned deeply and slowly sat up, rubbing her eyes.

"What in the world is happening?" she asked. I pointed, and she gasped when she saw Honovi and Lugii fighting. She sprang to her feet and pulled hard on the back of my collar.

"What the hell are you doing sitting down? We have to help her!" Lata grabbed her pointing stick, and I could see the determination and focus of a parent to protect and rescue her child. I could see a renewed energy arising within her as she blasted Lugii in the chest, and she did not stop until she sent him hurtling into outer space. Lata hugged her daughter as I tried getting up. I just could not move. Honovi began to run over to me when a sonic boom erupted overhead. A shock wave blew dust in my face, and I could barely hear Lata scream. I shielded my eyes and squinted. Time slowed down as I saw Lata's eyes close and her body fall to the ground, and Lugii stood behind her, clutching a bloodied staff. Something within me cracked. I felt a dormant power rise straight to the surface. My green aura was so herculean that my surroundings began to warp. I stared into Lugii's eyes with such violent anger. Before Lugii could blink, I had placed both my hands on his chest.

"You took her from me, you bastard! I'm going to kill you! You HEAR ME!" I dug my fingers into his chest like claws and screamed, "ADIOS!" at the top of my lungs. The spell welled into my hands, and I poured every ounce of hate and anger I had. I hated him. I hated him. I hated him. I wanted him to die, die, die! The energy burnt into his flesh and grew into a ball inside his chest. He gurgled on his screams, and his skin began to fall off his bones into ash. The dark flames roared and consumed what was left. I grabbed Lata's bloody robes and screamed at the top of my lungs. My voice died, and my throat felt hoarse, but I kept screaming in silence. I tried with every ounce of power I had to try to bring her back, but in the end, her eyes remained shut. I could not stop myself from crying. The pain ran so deep. I could feel a darkness violently rising in me until Honovi hugged me with such heavy tears that they began to soak the back of my robes.

"Alaric, please calm down!" she sobbed. "I need you!" The tighter I held Honovi, the more I felt a warmth course through my body, bringing a sense of calm and focus to me.

She cried her eyes out and wailed, "If only we were stronger… Why couldn't we have been stronger?"

I dug my face into her shoulder and whispered in her ear, "This will never happen to anyone again… I will show you… I promise."

A few days later, I was reading the local newspaper on the tablet. As I was eating my scrambled eggs and toast, I saw that Raider had been promoted to major, officially. The paper went on to talk about all of the major's heroic efforts throughout his life. I was happy for him, but I was trying to get an idea on what to do next. I figured I'd take Honovi to Aziza's temple and raise her there. After a couple more nights, I told the president that if she ever needed me, she knew where to find me. President Nilla handed me a cell phone so that, in her words, she can "bug me" all she wanted. I got one more look at the capital as Honovi, Kogi, Varun, Catalan, and I made our way to the temple. It took us a few days to get there because everyone wanted to stop every five minutes to take pictures. I wanted to just teleport all of us there, but they told me that would be taking the fun out of it. When we finally arrived, I felt like I was in bliss just by feeling the breeze hit my face. We made our way in and saw all the animals doing what they do best: eating.

I made sure to enhance the glory of the temple by pumping more of my magical powers into the environment, really bringing the forest, the animals, the quality of the water and air to its full potential. Each day, I walked the vastness of the temple, checking on the health of the trees, the quality of the soil, and the insects, and I helped feed some baby elephants. I immediately began to train Honovi with the help of Kogi, who really became an amazing friend. Honovi was such a quick learner. It was amazing to see how strong of a connection she had not only to the cosmic language but to her own natural abilities. Varun made sure to add a few technological upgrades inside the temple, making sure we had a few robots that could maintain cleaning and to do the cooking and washing. Varun brought to my attention one day that he felt it was time for him to go. Varun looked at me and said, "You have become a great wizard. Enjoy what you have now with Honovi. You have more than earned it." The very next day, Catalan mentioned how it was time for her to go as well. She was ready to go back to being mayor and seeing how she could improve Varmington. I thanked Catalan for everything she had done and told her she was welcome anytime. I made sure Kogi loaded up a backpack of fresh fruits and veggies for Catalan's journey back home. I sat down on a giant turtle shell as I watched Honovi practicing with her orange staff, and an idea came to me to build a statue of Lata, the brown wizard. The idea made me smile, and it also brought a tear to my eye. Then, suddenly, there was a crack, and one of the rocks in the Dojo was split in two. Honovi's staff glowed a brilliant orange, and she had her hand over her mouth, stifling a gasp. I burst out in laughter and clapped.

"Someday you'll be an even greater wizard than me!" I laughed. Honovi started giggling, and my heart felt warm. It had been a long time since I felt this way. Ever since I was dragged out of the snow, which felt so long ago now, I felt that something was missing. The joy that I felt, the warmth, the laughter, and Honovi's big smile told me that I had finally found what I was looking for: peace.

Inside the temple, I had placed a picture of Remo in a stoic pose. His eyes looked downward, and he watched over something very precious. Below his gaze sat the silver orb atop a marble pedestal. It shined brilliantly like a mirror. Beside it, shackled by magical chains, was Lumusi's black pointing stick. Its black wood was dull and dead. Not even a hum stirred within its heart. The mirror shine began to pulse, and, from within, a dark hand reached out, its fingertips lying gently on the surface inside the orb. The orb cracked and split down the middle, and a dark figure cloaked in shadow stepped out and breathed in the fresh air deeply.

"Aah," the figure groaned as it spotted the pointing stick. As the shadowy fingers wrapped around the shaft, the dark and dead wood pulsed with energy, and a low hum grew within like a beating heart. The figure's shadow began to fade.

"Tell me everything," he demanded. His mind was filled with images. He saw a bloodied woman in a brown robe lying dead in a pile of ash. Standing over her was a man whose robes and pointed hat glowed a brilliant green. Blood stained his hands. The shadows fell from the man's body, and he screamed in rage.

"My baby girl...my sweet granddaughter... You killed her... you killed her...you...killed...her...GREEN WIZARD!" He gripped the pointing stick hard and snapped his fingers, disappearing from the room beneath the temple. All that was left behind was an echo of his scream traveling down the corridor.

He stepped out before the statues of the Valley of the Wizards. The purple and orange hue of twilight crawled across the valley floor.

"Where?" the man growled. The pointing stick raised itself in his hand, tugging his arm forward. He began to walk. With several steps, the stick suddenly dropped, tugging his arm down. He stood before a pile of ash and bones, with half a skull eyeing him with a partial grin. He knelt down and picked up the skull. A voice growled in his mind.

"You? It was you inside the orb? Oh, how delicious!" the voice cackled. "You are the next dark wizard?!"

"Shut up, Caden!" the man growled.

"No respect for the dead, huh?"

He ignored Caden's remark. "I want you to tell me where the Temple of the Dark Wizards is located."

"What do you care? There's nothing there," Caden said.

"That's because you don't know where to look. WHERE IS IT?"

"Amuse a dead man for a moment, Row. What's hidden there?"

"You'll find out soon enough, Caden. You're coming with me." Twilight turned to dusk. Row stuffed Caden's skull into his bag and walked past the statues toward the valley's exit. Behind him, shadows stirred and followed close behind. Row's sobs hummed through the silence, and his tears dripped into the dry sand.

Thank you for reading (or listening, for the audiobook users)! If you can, please leave a review on Amazon and Barnes & Noble. I read your reviews and look at your feedback so that I can keep improving my work. It also helps introduce others to my books. If you enjoyed this book, check out my other works as well: *Twenty-Three and Blue Neptune.* Keep a lookout for my next book.

About the Editor

Alexander "Alex" Rada was born and raised in Las Vegas, Nevada. He's always had many interests and has taken different paths—from the culinary arts to computer science to his current work in children's mental health. There was always one thing that continued to draw him in and take his interest: writing stories.

Alex adores books and history, and he's always been drawn to fantasy. Someday, he wants to combine all his interests into his singular passion for writing and to tell stories with characters brought to life with the real behaviors and experiences that others can come to relate to. While stories are usually driven by plots and events, it is the people within them that build those plots and are those we tend to remember most. Alex takes his inspiration from those around him and of those before him.

When he's not working on something, he's usually in the kitchen, figuring out some concoction, or he's watching reruns of *Star Trek*.

About the Author

Joel Riojas is an army veteran living in Las Vegas, Nevada, who was originally born and raised in Chicago, Illinois. Joel grew up on the south side, in a community called the Back of the Yards, on Forty-Seventh and Wolcott. Joel Riojas has written other books such as *Twenty-Three*, which many have viewed as a creative adventure with twists and turns. Others viewed it as a great story that gives you time to escape and enjoy a nice read.

Joel really enjoys writing, taking someone on a journey, and inspiring them in hopes of leaving them excited to read more. Joel Riojas draws his inspiration from his family, life experiences, and his array of friends.

Joel Riojas lived in Alaska, Anchorage, for six years, and traveling throughout the state was an awe-inspiring experience that drove Joel to explore different ways to express his creativity.

Printed in the USA
CPSIA information can be obtained
at www.ICGtesting.com
LVHW071615240923
759037LV00003B/353